MARINE RAIDERS

A NOVEL OF WORLD WAR II

Paul Nickerson

HERITAGE BOOKS
2009

HERITAGE BOOKS

AN IMPRINT OF HERITAGE BOOKS, INC.

Books, CDs, and more—Worldwide

For our listing of thousands of titles see our website
at
www.HeritageBooks.com

Published 2009 by
HERITAGE BOOKS, INC.
Publishing Division
100 Railroad Ave. #104
Westminster, Maryland 21157

International Standard Book Numbers
Paperbound: 978-0-7884-4923-9
Clothbound: 978-0-7884-8176-5

Dedication

This World War 2 book is dedicated to the greatest generation of Americans. To the men who fought in this horrible conflict and the women who supported them.

Also to my Father's cousin, Junior, who gave his life at just eighteen years old for God, country and the continued freedom of his family. He fell in battle like so many others, fighting an evil enemy that sought to enslave the free world.

Found on a rock on a Pacific Island battlefield by a combat Marine:

The battle's over, the enemy gone.
My time on earth is done.
When I get to heaven and the roll is taken
I will finally say,
One more Marine reporting, Sir.
I've done my time in hell.

* * * * *

They say the streets in heaven are paved with gold and guarded by U.S. Marines.

Table of Contents

Acknowledgements

I would like to acknowledge the U.S. Marine Raider Association Web Site for the research availability they provided for this effort.

I would also like to acknowledge the U.S. Naval Archives (World War Two Pacific Theater) for their research help.

I truly appreciate the consideration and support of Leslie Wolfinger, Publishing Division Director of Heritage Books, Inc.

I wish to thank my faithful editor/secretary, Ruth Nickerson. Her continued support throughout the development of this book is recognized with thanks.

Introduction

This story is based on historical fact. Because this is a novel of fighting men in World War 2 and not a documentary, some of the places and events are fictitious. Places such as Guadalcanal, Tulagi, Gavutu, Tanambogo, Makin, Bougainville are Pacific Islands where actual combat did occur.

Marine Raiders helped to secure all of these islands and many more. Some of the most brutal combat in Marine Corps and U.S. Navy history occurred in this area (Solomon Islands). Other places were created to emphasize the tactics, training and ability of the Raiders.

The Marine Raiders were the first Special Forces unit in the U.S. Naval Service. The first of any special American units to see combat against the Japanese in the Pacific. This novel will take you from the beginning stages of the war against imperial Japanese forces to the Raiders last action in the war.

The Raider that portrays the main character in this book and the Marines in his squad are typical of Marine Raiders and their actions. The combat and training scenarios were described to the author by an ex-Raider and other World War 2 combat Marines. Other scenarios were suffered by all World War 2 servicemen and described as such.

The hell of jungle combat and the men who fought in that hell are the basis for this story.

The Raiders were disbanded after the Bougainville campaign. The Fourth and newly formed Sixth Marine Divisions needed men badly. So the disbanded Raiders were used for replacements for these units. Ex-Raiders saw fierce and deadly combat on islands such as Iwo Jima, Saipan, Guam and

Okinawa. Raider tactics are still being used today by Navy S.E.A.L. and Marine Force Recon, and Scout Sniper Units.

"Gung ho" (work together) was their battle cry, "never give up," their creed. They proved it many times in jungle hell.

Chapter One

TOULABONG

The Gato class submarine Tigerfish cruised through the blue green waters of the South Pacific. She was venting; taking on air and charging batteries. It was April 1943, midwatch 0300 hours. A dark night, no moon, overcast with a slight squall and a following sea. Just the way the Captain liked it. A Jap ship could be within five hundred yards of them and never see them.

A faint red glow could be seen from the forward and after torpedo room hatches. This bothered the Captain but at least the red night lamps would not hinder the crew if they found themselves in a surface fight at night. Their night vision would not be affected by the reds but would be by standard lighting.

The Captain called the ExO through the bridge comm tube. He uttered the word, "batteries."

Lieut. Peter Dixon, the Executive Officer, responded from the control room.

"Batteries one hundred percent, air negative CO_2."

"OK, Pete. Take her down."

"Aye, Skipper."

Lt. Dixon gave the order through the boat's intercom.

"Prepare to dive. Close all water-tight hatches."

The Captain watched as the forward and aft torpedo room hatches were secured, then the gun deck hatch. The conning tower hatch would be secured by him as he re-entered the boat. He felt the boat settle as high pressure air blew from the pressure hull tanks causing sea water to boil and cascade through the pressure hulls, vents and scuppers.

"All lookouts below," was his final order on deck.

Lt. Commander Hesscox watched as his first officer walked the crew through the standard dive procedure.

"Flood safety, flood negative, rig bow planes, give me a ten degree down angle on the planes. Coxwain, level off at one hundred

feet and stay in the thermocline.
"Aye, Sir."
"Good job, Pete."
"Thank you, Sir."
"Pretty soon you'll be ready for your own boat."
If I live that long, Pete thought to himself.

* * * * *

Hesscox was nervous this trip. They were heading for
Blackard Straits and the Island of Toulabong in the Russell Islands
and Solomon Island Chain. The same area where that Kennedy kid
and his crew disappeared. That really bothered him. Hesscox had met
the young Lieut. at a party back at Pearl during a refit. Nice, polite,
smart kid.

God knows what he is doing here in hell, the Commander
thought. *With his old man's pull he could be home in a week. Oh,
well, he probably wants to get into politics some day and everybody
loves a hero.*

He hated the thought of what the Japs would do to him if they
took him prisoner. They usually killed PT crews and pilots on the
spot. Submariners, tincan Sailors and Marines were spared for work
parties. When the work was completed likely as not they faced
execution. The Bushido Code did not allow for prisoners.

* * * * *

Sgt. Rawlins cleaned his weapons for the fourth time since
leaving Pearl. He checked the recoil springs, feed ramp and bore of
his Thompson submachine gun. He gave the same service to his pair
of 45 caliber 1911 Colt semi-auto pistols. The long patrol on the
Canal where the Sgt. had served under Colonel "Red" Mike Edson of
the First Raider Battalion, had taught him well. The jungle was a
worse enemy than the Japanese. With constant rain and humidity
weapons rusted and malfunctioned constantly. Disease was a major
problem. Malaria, beriberi, dengue fever to name a few. And the
snakes. Vipers and Crates that would kill you in two minutes with

one strike. Crocodiles that would make you disappear if you were in their territory. They grew fat ad lazy feeding on Japanese corpses.

Atabrine and gun oil became the Guadalcanal survival kit. The venereal disease safety kit became very useful. The jell was useful for treating burns and jungle rot. The condom made a perfect muzzle cover for the M1 rifle. And every Sailor and Marine was issued a kit.

Rawlins hated submarines. He felt helpless inside this steel coffin. Having no control over one's destiny was a terrible feeling. One bomb from a Kawanishi float plane or a depth charge from a Jap destroyer could kill and bury every man on board this half sunken boat. The Sgt. listened to his men in the forward torpedo room as they played cards, talked about women and boasted about all the Japs they would kill in typical Marine Corps fashion. Finally one of the bolder of the group had to try him!

"Hey, Sarge."

"What?"

"How many Japs you get on the Canal?"

"Don't remember."

"I heard it was over twenty. How come you're forever cleaning that Thompson. It looks like a mirror now."

"Jammed once during a banzai charge. Had to fight with pistol and knife. If I'd cleaned the Tommy it wouldn't a happened."

The young Marine looked from the Thompson to the sergeant, uttered the word, "Shit," sat down next to his gear, pulled out the trigger assembly, mainspring and bolt body of his M1 rifle. No Jap was going to get him because his weapon was dirty.

"Sarge. Where are we going?"

"Search and destroy."

"Where?"

"Don't know. You'll get the dope when I do."

"Hey, Sarge."

"Yeah."

"What's the best place to stick a Jap with a Ka-Bar? Chest or neck?"

"Neck."

"How come?"

"A chest hit won't always stop a man. He'll keep fightin.' A stick in the neck under the ear or jaw will stop him every time for good. If you get yourself in a bayonet or knife fight remember the inside of the arms or legs with all their arteries are good targets and watch out for those hooks on the base of Jap bayonets. They can grab the muzzle of your rifle and rip it out of your hands leaving you in a very bad position. Never turn your back in a close fight or you'll die very quickly. Make no mistake. The Jap is a tough son of a bitch. His main goal in life is to die for the emperor and kill you in the process. They don't surrender and they fight to the death. Always keep a round of ammo in your dungaree pocket for yourself if you're overrun. The Jap doesn't believe in the Geneva Convention. Better to go quick than to be tortured and starved to death."

This brought looks of consternation and self doubt. The torpedo room grew very quiet as the young Marines considered their own mortality. Rawlins almost laughed at the so-called Jap killers of the South Pacific area. He had given them something to think about besides idle bullshit. Then it hit him like it always had on the Canal before a fight.

By this time tomorrow half of these boys might be dead.

The Sergeant's mind drifted back to another place, another time, another world. Nineteen thirty six, Buffalo, NY. The smoky pool halls, coffee shops and movie houses on Hertel Avenue were his home. A teenager had a tough time finding work in that depression ridden city. Young Rawlins got lucky and hired on at the Buffalo Pool Room. Old man Costanza knew the family and gave the kid a break. Costanza knew Rawlin's father was all shot up and couldn't work. He was so full of German steel that any more surgery could cripple or even kill him. Young Rawlins didn't mind helping out. It gave him a feeling of self worth that was very gratifying. To this day he sent home half his pay to the old folks.

Being a teenager working in a pool room became quite boring. His father had been a Marine during the Great War and had been awarded the Navy Cross for single handedly destroying two German machine gun emplacements with hand grenades and a German P08 Luger Parabellum pistol. During the Belleau Wood battle he was severely wounded by artillery. Now he spends most of his time in therapy at the VA Hospital on Genesee Street.

Down the street from the pool room was the Armed Forces Recruiting Station. The young man would have lunch with the Marine Gunnery Sergeant at Santora's Cafe. They would talk of his father's exploits during the war with the Hun and the Gunnys in South America. Finally, the big question would be brought up.

"When you gonna come aboard our lash up and stop bein' a kid? Or did yer old man tell you you ain't allowed?"

"I do what I want no matter what he says and I ain't no kid."

"Oh, sorry. I thought you were still a civilian type too good to be a Marine like me and yer old man."

"I'll join when I'm ready and not until."

* * * * *

PARRIS ISLAND RECRUIT TRAINING CENTER, 0300 hours.

"Get off the bus you maggots. Move, move, move. Last one off gets his ass kicked. Line up dummies and stand at attention. My name is Sgt. MacIntire. I am your mother, your father, your drill instructor. If you screw up or get out of line I'm your worst nightmare. You will address me as "Sir" before and after each statement because you are worthless boots and I am as close to God as your miserable asses are likely to see. There are no dagos, kikes, niggers, limeys, krauts or wetbacks on Parris Island. You're all a bunch of civilian shitbirds."

And so it goes. Ten weeks of misery to be called a Marine.

* * * * *

The reverberation of the klaxon horn and PA system brought Sgt. Rawlins back to reality.

"Now hear this. This is the Exec. All officers and NCOs of the landing party report to the Officer's Ward Room on the double."

Rawlins stowed his gear and headed for officer country. Lt. Pruit, Second Platoon Leader and Gunnery Sergeant Parker saved Rawlins a seat by the water-tight door.

"Morning, Lieut., Gunney."

"Morning, Rawlins. Have a seat."

Real Navy coffee was served and the briefing began.

"Toulabong, gentlemen, is your target."

Commander Hesscox stated the facts.

"The Nips have an observation post on that island and are fast becoming a real pain in the ass. Every Allied ship or plane that cruises the slot gets reported to Truk or Rebaul and are intercepted by Jap air and sea forces. Fleet wants the place destroyed. All equipment and no prisoners. Is that clear?"

A unified "Yes, Sir," was given to the Commander.

"Pete, hang that Jap chart on the bulkhead, please?"

"Aye, Skipper."

"Compliments of the Marines at Tulagi. They thought we could use it. All right, men, this is how it's going to happen. Sgt. Rawlins and his squad will infiltrate by rubber boat through Red Beach on the north shore and kill and/or destroy anything he finds that may be useful to the enemy. Lieut. Pruit will lead first squad across Green Beach and set up a blocking force on the south side to eliminate any Japs that escape Sgt. Rawlins. Gunny Parker will land with third squad and hold in reserve and protect the Lieut's flanks. Infiltration will be 0300 and pickup will be 0500. If anyone doesn't make the pickup a secondary will occur at 2100 hours if the area's not too hot to surface the boat. Any questions? All right, gentlemen, good luck and dismissed. Lieut. Pruit and Sgt. Rawlins stand fast."

The room cleared and the Captain gave Rawlins a manila envelope containing a small Minox camera and a roll of infrared film.

"You know how to operate that thing?" the Lieut. asked the Sgt.

"The Sgt. Is OSS, Lieut." advised the Captain.

This brought a look of shock and amazement.

"I thought you were just a mud Marine Raider. It's not even in your file."

"Need to know, Lieut. Always need to know."

"That's where the knife came from."

"Knife, Lieut.?"

"Yes, Sgt. That long, thin double edge dagger you're so fond of. The Sykes-Fairbairn Commando Fighting Knife."

"Yes, Sir. I trained with it in England when I was there with Colonel Carlson, learning from the British Commando."

"You were in England with Carlson?"

"Yes, Sir."

"Gentlemen. Please save the history for later. One week ago the New Zealand destroyer Kiwi forced a Jap I boat (submarine) to surface and they boarded it. The Japanese Naval Code J N 25 was captured. Your mission, Sgt., is to photograph any code books you find and any documents that look important. Leave them undisturbed. We want the Japs to think we missed them. Just get the photos and get the hell out. If you're captured, Rawlins, you know what's expected."

"Yes, Sir. I have my pill."

"Any questions?"

"No, Sir."

With that he wished them good luck, God bless, shook hands and left the wardroom. The Sgt. and Lieut. moved rearward to the after torpedo room and met with Gunny Parker.

"I'll take the fire team with the A630 cal., Gunny. You take the B.A.R. team. Sgt., you take all the Tommys you can find that the Navy will let you borrow. And remember fire discipline. We'll be facing each other and we don't need a friendly fire incident. We have twelve hours until jump off so get your men ready and get some sleep."

* * * * *

"Hey, Rawlins, who's the new kid?"

Chief of the boat Clark had to know. Senior Chief Petty Officer Clark had to know everything on or about his submarine or there would be hell to pay in the EM ranks.

"Lieut. Pruit. Annapolis class of forty one, Naval War College. Action on Tulagi and Gavutu. First rate junior officer. Lots of smarts."

"What happened to Rogers?"

"Our last op - when you were in sick bay - Jap sniper put a

7.7 between his bars on his steel pot."

"Just wouldn't listen, would he?"

"Afraid not. The Japs just love to see rank; and he had just put on his new Captain bars."

"You write the letter."

"Naw. The Gunny took care of it. Hell of a note. This keeps up we're gonna run out of officers. Damn shame. He was a nice kid. Especially for a Marine."

On this note Rawlins left the senior chief and began to prepare his men for action.

"Listen up. Our target is a Jap held island called Toulabong. Fleet says they're using it for an OP. We're gonna knock it out and take no prisoners. Fleet wants it destroyed and sanitized. Is that understood?"

"But, Sarge, we might find my mother-in-law. We can't sanitize her can we?"

This brought a round of laughs and broke the tension which you could cut with a knife.

"Joker, if we find your mother-in-law I'll have her decorated for putting up with you; and leave you there with a bunch of dead Japs."

This brought more laughs.

* * * * *

Corp. Holland Hays from Pittsburg, PA, alias Joker, had a big mouth and was aggravating but was good in a fight. The Sgt. could rely on him no matter what. They had been together since the first Matanikau River battle on the Canal. The Joker claimed his Viking ancestors had bestowed upon him their almost insane ability in combat that was world renown.

"Now remember. We have to be as quiet as possible. If the Japs catch us in the open in those rubber boats we're as good as dead. Tape your dog tags together. Wear your soft cover. No steel pot. Keep your canteens full till you hear different. Wear a pair of socks over top your boondockers. Bootblack on face and hands. Any sentries will be eliminated quietly. The old hands will take care of this.

"Vito."

"Yes, Sarge."

"You got your safe stuff?"

"Right here, Sarge."

"Good, When we land you're on me."

"Aye, Sarge."

"Riflemen. Carry a 180 round basic load; two M2 frags with three second fuses; two canteens and just your 782 gear. No ruck or rations."

"No rations, Sarge?"

"This is gonna be a short party and ration cartons are noisy. If we get held over we'll eat Jap food like we did on the Canal. And besides their rations are better than ours. Three round bursts or semi auto. That way you won't run dry."

"Sarge. Why can't we have more ammo?"

"Ever try to swim with lead weights strapped to your body? What if you wind up in the water?"

"Aye, Sarge."

"We disembark at 0300, pick up will be 0500 on the other side of the island. Secondary will be twelve hours later if anybody gets lost. If the Japs break and run for the other side of the island don't chase 'um, let 'um go. The Lieut. and the Gunny have A6 and BAR teams in a blocking position. Let them take care of it. You new men listen to the old hands and you'll be fine. Now gear up and get some sleep and remember, 'gung ho.'"

This brought a resounding "gung ho" from the Raiders about to go into combat, some for the first time. This was a Raider battle cry, meaning, "work together."

* * * * *

"Now hear this. This is the Captain. All Marine personnel report to the E.M. Mess. That is all."

"Steak and eggs. The condemned man's last breakfast." joked the Raiders as they ate their pre-invasion meal which was Navy and Marine Corps tradition. In the Control Room the Exec. reported to the Captain:

"Four hundred yards from target at one hundred feet, Skipper."

"Thanks, Pete. Give the order for battle surface. I'll be right up."

"Now hear this. This is the Exec. Prepare for battle surface. I repeat, battle surface. This is no drill."

The Sailors donned life jackets and broke out weapons and ammo and finally their steel pots. Just under the conning tower hatch the Captain gave the order:

"Battle surface decks awash."

"Aye, Captain," replied Senior Chief of the Boat Clark.

"Blow main ballast. Give me a ten degree up bubble."

The submarine lurched toward the surface.

"Lock and load on deck and remember no noise, no talking, hand signals only. Hold her fast when the tower breaks."

"Aye, Senior Chief."

"Switch lighting to red."

"Aye, Lieut."

There was a whooshing of compressed air escaping the conning tower hatch when the Skipper cracked the main water-tight hatch cover. He ascended the conning tower ladder, opened the hatch cover and stepped out on deck. The deck hands and gun crews looked like iridescent phantoms in their light blue shirts against the dark background of the island and sea. The Raiders, with their green and brown camo and black faces, looked like prehistoric lizards standing at attention on deck, waiting to board their rubber rafts.

Final orders. Torpedo Man's Mate Second Class Meyers cracked the forward hatch and was deluged in a stream of sea water. The hatch combing held back the rest of the sea like the dikes of Holland. That is until the Nazis blew them up and flooded the countryside to keep out the British and Americans.

"There you go, Sarge."

"Thanks, Meyers. All right people, listen up. You new people stick with the old hands and do what they do. If you get separated stay put and we'll find you. No sense running around like an idiot, making yourself sniper bait. Leave your 782 gear loose and don't sling your rifle. Strap your Ka-Bar to your leg just above your boondocker. If you have a second knife leave it where it is on your gear. If you find yourself in the water drop your rifle and gear and swim for the island. I know you've been told to never give up your weapon but it will drag you down and you may have a long way to swim. Besides you will still have your Ka-Bar so kill a Jap and take his rifle."

The combat vets looked strange to the new men with their edged weapons of every description from butcher knives to Burmese and Indian kukris to Japanese ceremonial daggers, a few Type 99 Nambu pistols and, much to their amazement, a Type 97 Nambu light machine gun 7.7 caliber Woodpecker. The Marines named it that because of the peculiar noise it made when firing. Vito had the barrel cut down to twenty inches, bypod and bayonet lug removed, bolt body, carrier and sear springs lightened for a higher rate of fire. Compliments of the Navy Comsubpac Machine Repair Division back at Pearl. Price - one Jap Katana (sword), one Nambu pistol, two bottles sake (rice wine). The shortpecker, as the Raiders called it, proved to be a deadly weapon in the jungle. For breaking up banzai attacks and suppression fire on bunkers it worked quite well.

* * * * *

"Hey, Ken."

"Yeah, Chief."

"If you get the chance, get me a Jap sword and maybe a battle flag. The kind they write their names on. I can get two cases of Johnny Walker for that stuff. I'll split with you."

"OK, Chief."

At this time they shook hands.

"Be careful, you old jarhead. Yer gettin' too old to get killed."

"Take care, Chief. I'll see you in the morning."

So with stern, determined looks on their faces, the Raiders climbed the ladder and stood on deck, loaded their weapons, boarded their rafts and headed for Red Beach. Rawlins could barely make out the white strip of sand that was Red Beach. The submarine gurgled and popped as compressed air was replaced by sea water, causing the sub to disappear beneath the waves. The sub would have to place the blocking force in position, which would take another hour. They did not dare attack until then or the whole operation would be in jeopardy. Rawlins could smell the bougainvillea flowers and jungle rot and the beach was now clearly visible. They were getting close. No Jap fire yet. Good sign.

Funny thing. That smell reminded him of the New Orleans funeral. He had lived there for a while with Susan in her Navy Captain father's house. He and the Captain, being amphibious warfare specialists, were assigned to the Higgins Boat Works for research and development of landing craft for the Navy, Army and Marines.

Fifty yards to go. Why did he have to think of her now. Too much depended on his ability as a professional. If he blew this mission he might as well tuck in his tie and go home to Buffalo. His career in the Corps would be over. She always showed up at the worst time. He wondered if her slob Navy officer boyfriend was still around. The son of a bitch had cost him his wife and his stripes. If Father Captain hadn't liked him he would still be in the brig.

The wind dropped off and it started to rain.

Good, the Sgt. thought. *It'll cover any noise they might make. Rotten son of a bitch of a swabby.*

Ten feet from the beach Rawlins jumped into the water and dragged his boat ashore. Raiders jumped out and headed for the tree line. They talked in quiet, almost indistinguishable tones.

"Joker, I want a recon of the radio site. Ramirez, pick two men and go with Joker. Remember, no contact. If you have to eliminate someone do it quiet. Vito, get ready with the Nambu in case they come back with a tail."

"OK, Sarge."

The recon team drifted into the jungle but not before fixing bayonets on their M1 rifles. Almost to the edge of the clearing, a Japanese soldier stood up in front of them, drunk as a Sailor on a two day liberty. Bottle of sake in hand, the Jap started to mumble something. Ramirez drove his bayonet through the Jap's chest, twisted it, pulled it out and buried it in the Jap's throat. The son of Nippon was dead when he hit the ground, having never made a sound. The team moved to the clearing, laying down near the edge in the ground cover. The Joker was watching intently. Soon he turned around, pointed at both eyes and with two fingers made a walking motion. Then he held up two fingers. Two sentries. On the way back they grabbed the dead Jap and carried him to the squad's position. Now they had to break silence or risk being shot by their own men.

"Ramirez and Joker comin' in."

"How far."

"Two hundred yards. Layout - one platoon size barracks, two storage huts, one office with radio equipment, two roving sentries."

"All right, Joker, you're on me. We take out one sentry and the office."

"Right, Sarge."

"Vito. You're with us."

"OK, Sarge."

"Ramirez, you and the rest of the squad take the other sentry and barracks and don't fire till I frag the office. Any questions? OK. Let's do it."

The Raiders slid through the jungle like predators on the hunt. They reached the clearing without incident. The Sergeant and his two comrades crept into the clearing, staying in the shadows. Vito grabbed the Sgt.'s arm and revealed the sentry's position. They hid by a storage shack. The Jap should pass by. Rawlins gave Vito his Thompson and pulled out his commando knife. When the Jap rounded the corner, the Sgt. grabbed him by the face, closing off his mouth and nose, shutting off his air. The Jap began to thrash instinctively, knowing whatever had hold of him from behind was not friendly. Rawlins drove the long blade of the commando knife under his right ear, through his neck, severing the carotid artery. The Jap grunted, kicked once and joined the land of the rising sun.

Another Jap was in the shadows of a group of trees less than ten yards away, not seen before. He was the Captain of the Guard. While making his rounds he noticed a guard scuffling with an intruder. He ducked into the trees to watch, figuring there was more than one invader. He was not going to put himself in jeopardy for one lowly compound guard. He would just shoot the invader when he was ready. Just as the dead Jap slid to the ground Vito Russo from

Chicago saw movement to his left in the small group of trees. *Jap,* he thought. And in one deft motion pulled and threw his commando blade at the self important Captain who died without even knowing it as the steel penetrated his right eye and lodged in his brain. Vito from Chicago was good with a knife. He had had lots of practice before the war, being one of big Al Capone's strong arms. The Sgt. heard the stories but never asked Vito about it. Vito was also the best safe cracker in the South Pacific.

Lieut. Pruit's men were in position, utilizing any cover they could find and the fire teams were getting their weapons ready. The Browning 1919 L1A6 with shoulder stock was modified with a drilled out bolt body and lighter sear springs for a higher rate of fire. The rpm rose from 550rpm to 750rpm. It fired the U.S. thirty caliber of 1906 round, better known even today as the thirty oh six. This round was also used in the M1 Garand, 1903 Springfield M.103 and M-1903-A3, Remington Enfield rifle, Browning 1918 B.A.R. - Browning automatic rifle. Also the Browning 1919 L1A1 water cooled medium machine gun. This round with its 150 grain bullet, traveling at 2900 feet per second, was devastating from point blank to twelve hundred yards. The machine gunner oiled the feed tray, laid in a link belt of two hundred rounds, cranked the charging handle twice and was ready for action. The B.A.R. team was also ready with twenty round magazines and grenades laid out in easy reach.

When Pruit's men came ashore they ran right into a Jap patrol. Two of the Japs were bayoneted. The other two were clubbed with rifle butts. Lucky. No noise.

Rawlins pulled an M2 frag from his gear and told his cohorts it was time to start the party. He pulled the safety pin, let the safety lever fly free and tossed the hot grenade into the radio shack and hit the deck. A mila-second after the detonation Rawlins kicked in the door and gave the occupants a burst from his Thompson. An officer shot at him with what looked like a German Luger. The Sgt. stitched him up the middle with full metal patch 230 grain 45 cal. slugs at a velocity of 830 f.p.s. He was knocked back against the wall and fell dead on the floor.

Ramirez rose from the jungle behind the barracks like a giant anaconda on the prowl. The Jap sentry, only four feet away, never

saw him. The Indian kukri nearly decapitated the sentry with one
swipe. Corp. Ramirez positioned the squad to cover both doors. His
only order to his mates was:

"Kill 'um all when you hear the frag."

He readied a grenade and threw it into the thatched building
when he heard the Sgt.'s grenade detonate. The Corp. hit the deck and
rolled behind a palm tree. At the detonation he was up pouring fire
into the jungle house and the stunned Japanese. His 1928A1
Thompson sub machine gun grew hot as he burned a twenty round
magazine into the house. Japs were pouring out of the windows and
doors like evil martinets escaping hell.

Pfc. Taylor launched trip flares for visibility. This made the
enemy look like spectres dancing to and fro in the strange light. The
new men were firing wildly; not taking their time. The Japanese were
beginning to form up and fight back.

The Sgt. and Vito were in the office working the safe when
two Jap Soldiers burst through the door and surprised them. The
strange looking Marines looked like the jungle demons they had
heard stories about. Rawlins spun around and cut down the Japs with
a short burst from his Thompson.

"Good thing you got that chopper, Sarge."

"Yeah. Comes in handy sometimes."

"Back in Chicago one like that saved my ass more than once.
By the way, if you remove the X block from behind the reciprocating
bolt your rpm will increase and you'll get fewer jams."

"Already done, Vito."

* * * * *

Joker was watching from the supply hut as a Jap officer
waved his katana over his head and tried to rally his men. Just as he
took a bead on the Captain the back of his head blew out and the dead
officer crumpled to the ground. Joker lowered his Thompson and
thought:

*Must be Eyes, the platoon sniper, or, as he preferred, Scout,
sharpshooter. He must be in the tree line picking out officers.*

With his 1903 Springfield rifle and Weaver K-4 telescopic site, George Fisher, alias Eyes, could eliminate a target out to 1000 yards consistently. Fisher was from Idaho where being good with a rifle meant you would have enough to eat. Idaho was very pissed off at the Japanese for bombing Pearl Harbor and the Bataan Death March and meant to do something about it. George had asked the Marine recruiter if he could guarantee he would fight the Japs. The recruiter assured the young cowboy that out of six million Japs there would surely be a few left for him to fight with.

* * * * *

Vito held the stethoscope against the safe door over the tumblers and listened as he spun the dial back and forth. Finally it popped open.

"Hey, Sarge, we're in."

"Well done, Vito."

Sgt. Rawlins began taking photos, one at a time, with the little Minox OSS infrared camera.

"Vito, put this stuff back like you found it. We want the Japs to think we missed it."

"OK, Sarge."

* * * * *

The Jap lieutenant spotted Ramirez and decided to take him in the traditional way according to Bushido. He would behead the invader and bring honor to the emperor and himself and family. Just as he was about to strike, Ramirez caught the blade reflecting flare light in his peripheral vision. In one motion the Corporal blocked the downward thrust of the long blade and smashed the Jap in the face with the butt of his Tommy gun. Ramirez gave the Jap lieutenant another butt stroke to make sure.

Dumb bastard. Bringin' a knife to a gunfight.

He picked up the katana and scabbard, slung them over his back and grabbed the dead officer's 8mm Nambu pistol and stuffed it inside his dungaree blouse.

I'll save these for the Senior Chief back on the boat.

* * * * *

The Joker spotted two Japs headed for the office. One with an Arisaka rifle, the other with a grenade. Three 45ACP rounds from the Joker's Tommy gun slammed into the Grenadier's chest just as he armed it by rapping it on his helmet. The Jap dropped the grenade as he died, killing his partner with the blast that had been meant for Vito and the Sgt.

"Shit, Sarge, that was close. Joker got him. His Tommy has the Cutts compensator. Makes a different noise."

* * * * *

Lieut. Pruit saw them coming through the trees; some walking, some running right into his area. He pulled the pin on an M2 frag and threw it as far as he could, safety handle discharging as it flew. As soon as it detonated the Raiders opened fire. A third of the Japs went down with the first volley. The remaining enemy troops rushed the line with bayonets fixed, as was their tradition. Amazingly, a good number of the Japanese soldiers made the line, bayonets flashing in the flare light.

"Up and at 'um, Raiders. Gung ho."

A fierce hand to hand fight broke out along the line. The L1A6 gunner stood up and fired his M.G. from the hip like a Tommy gun. Four Japs in his zone tumbled and fell almost at his feet. The B.A.R. man ran dry and without time to reload, pulled his .45 auto, thumbed back the hammer and shot a Jap in the face as he tried to bayonet him. Another came at him, slashing his right forearm, causing the gunner to drop his pistol. He drew the Ka-Bar from his leg sheath with his left hand, blocked another bayonet attack and stabbed the enemy where the shoulder and neck join, driving the blade deep into the Jap's chest from above. The attacker dropped his rifle, went limp, eyes rolling up in his head, fell to the ground dead. Shouts and curses could be heard up and down the line.

"Tenneco banzai American dog. Maline you die!"

"F--k you, Jap, we'll see who dies."

Lieut. Pruit shot a Jap three times with his M1 carbine. The Jap still got him with a bayonet before he went down. Gunny Parker came to the Lieut.'s rescue with his Browning A5 semi-auto 12 gauge shotgun, with shortened barrel and custom 8 shot magazine. This weapon was deadly in a close fight with its 00 buckshot load or slug load out to 75 yards. The Gunny stood over Pruit.

"You alive, Lieut.?"

"No, Gunny."

"Sorry, Lieut. I thought that bayonet killed you."

"Still here, Gunny."

"Semper fi, Lieut. Gung ho."

Two sons of Nippon rushed the two Raiders and the Gunny's A5 sounded like artillery. Boom, boom, boom. The two Japs looked like they had gone through a meat grinder. Dead as the Emperor's dreams.

"Hey, Lieut."

"Yeah, Gunny."

"How you feelin'?"

"OK."

"You know, Lieut., you really need a better weapon. That child's toy yer using won't stop a Nip if he's doped up."

"Yeah, Gunny."

"You all right, Lieut.? You sound funny."

"Took the morphine syrette in my aid kit. Feel kinda hot all over."

"It will pass, Lieut. Now lemme check yer wound. Puncture would, lower thoracic, blood loss nominal."

Parker dressed the wound and added sulfa powder.

"I didn't know you were a doc, Gunny."

"I'm your mother, too, Lieut. Remember?"

This made them both laugh.

Up and down the line it was much the same.

A Jap N.C.O. swung a sword at the A6 loader trying to decapitate him. The Marine's arm was split to the elbow blocking the strike. With his good arm he pulled his father's .38 cal Smith and Wesson military and police revolver and put three rounds of 158 grain full metal jacket bullets into the Jap, ending his life and saving his own. Later the young Marine wrote home telling his father about the incident; how the revolver had saved his life. He enclosed the Silver Star he had been awarded for staying in the fight although severely wounded. Private First Class Andrew Jones conducted himself above and beyond the call of duty in the highest tradition of the United States Marine Corps and the U.S. Naval Service. This made for one very proud father. He showed the letter to an editor friend and it really got his attention. Within a week the story of the young Marine Raider and his dad's pistol were in every syndicated newspaper in the country. <u>Dad's Gun Gets Jap in South Pacific Island Fight - Wins Marine Son Silver Star.</u> Army and Marine Corps riflemen are not issued handguns normally but are allowed to have them if privately procured. This letter began a new fad among parents with sons serving in the Pacific, Asian and ETO areas. Pistols, shotguns and even deer rifles began to show up at the front in the mail. Military staffers on Gen. George Marshall's team in Washington, DC were starting to grumble that this mass exodus of weapons was threatening the British lend lease program. If Winston Churchill got wind of this there would be trouble. President Roosevelt's answer to this was simple:

"Our boys first. I will not curb the enthusiasm of a united America giving her boys their best chance of survival in this terrible conflict. I will take care of Winston. After all, we are good friends. And I believe his fierce loyalty to God and country will help him understand our position in this matter. Am I understood, gentlemen?"

"Yes, Sir."

It's been said that the President's decision was due to the fact that his own son was a company commander in the Marine Raiders and distinguished himself in combat.

* * * * *

One Raider went berserk with hate after a group of Japs rushed him and his wounded friend during a first aid effort. One Jap shot him with a Nambu pistol, creasing his skull, knocking him down. The wounded Marine was bayoneted where he lay, unable to move.

"You dirty rotten bastards."

The Raider picked up his M1 rifle with fixed bayonet and charged the enemy soldiers. Unfortunately, the receiver was empty and the bolt was locked. He hit the first Jap with such force that the bayonet went right through him to the hilt. The Marine twisted the rifle, kicked the Jap hard in the gut and pulled the bayonet free. The Jap sank to his knees, gouts of blood pouring from his mouth, and fell over dead. He butt stroked the next Jap, driving the M1 skull crusher steel butt plate into the Jap's face, hitting him between the eyes, killing him. Now a Jap stabbled him in the back causing him to drop his rifle and fall to the ground. The wounded warrior grabbed his Ka-Bar, stabbed the Jap in the groin, dropping him, then cut his throat. Now he picked up an Arisaka rifle and shot two more sons of Nippon. Finally, the Marine was shot in the chest and knocked down and bayoneted in the throat as he tried to get up. Later, when their mates picked up the two dead Raiders, there were eight dead Japanese around their bodies.

* * * * *

Sgt. Rawlins and his squad were out of targets and his OSS mission was accomplished.

"Ramirez, form up the squad and police the Japs. Check 'um for papers and make sure they're dead. We don't need a Jap destroyer called on us."

Ramirez and Joker watched over the squad. They checked out the dead. The Japanese were noted for playing dead and striking when no one expected it. One Jap held a live grenade under his body. Although nearly dead he armed the grenade. When a Marine rolled the Jap over the grenade exploded, killing the Jap and wounding two Raiders.

Another young, inexperienced Marine grabbed a Jap officer who appeared to be very dead, began checking his pockets and the officer stabbed him with his ceremonial dagger. The one his father gave him on the fifth birthday, according to Bushido Samurai custom.

Warriors carry these daggers all their lives for protection against attackers or for ritual suicide called subbuku in case of defeat or failure. Neither is permitted in the laws of Bushido. And suicide or death in battle is the only way to maintain honor and go to heaven. The banzai charge, kamikaze aircraft or divine wind, and the kiten or cherry blossom one man submarine or more correctly, one man torpedo were all suicidal weapons and very effective at times. Kamikaze aircraft were responsible for the loss of over five thousand American Sailors and the U.S.S. Franklin aircraft carrier at the battle of Okinawa. The U.S.S. Indiana was sunk by a kiten the day after she delivered the atomic bomb to Tinean Island B29 Air Base next to Saipan Island in the Mariannas Chain.

Joker nearly sawed the Jap Lieut. in half with a burst from his Thompson, denying him the chance to die with honor.

Too bad, thought Joker. *How much of a chance did the guys at Pearl Harbor have.*

Outraged, he sprayed the surrounding Jap bodies with his Thompson until the magazine ran dry and the bolt locked open. To the dead Japs he said:

"Let's see you stick somebody now, you ugly little bastards."

That brought a laugh from the nearby Marines.

Ramirez found one crawling for the underbrush. He was so full of grenade fragments he couldn't stand. The Corp. put a boot in the middle of the Jap's back and he bagan to whimper and whine like a child.

What kind of warrior of Bushido was this?

Then he remembered Guadalcanal. He saw a lot of Japs do this. Even some that spoke English. Marines would let down their guard for a moment and try to take them prisoners only to be shot with a pistol, stabbed, or blown up with a grenade. The terror of San Antone had already decided he was going back to Texas with the same amount of holes in his body as he had left with. That meant no break for a Jap. Besides, orders are orders. The Sarge said no prisoners. With this thought Ramirez put his knee in the Jap's back, grabbed him by the hair amid Japanese curses, pulled out his Ka-Bar and drive it into the Jap's neck, severing the jugular and carotid arteries and the esophagus. The Jap gurgled once and died, blood running into the jungle floor. Ramirez checked his pockets. Nothing but a picture of a woman holding a baby.

Son of a bitch, he thought. *He's got a kid and an old lady.*

Shit. O well, he was dead anyway with all that shrapnel in him. I just helped him along a little.

* * * * *

"Johnson, gimme the handy talky."
"Aye, Sarge."
"Red Beach party calling Green Beach. Over."
"After a few seconds of static:
"Nock ta hey."
"Plain language, Joseph."
"OK, Sarge."
Joseph Flying Hawk, Navajo Code Talker, would confound any Japanese listening to the broadcast. Marine Code Talkers, mostly from the Navajo Bitter Water Clan, were radio operators trained by the Marines but using their own secret code. Code Talkers were scattered throughout the South Pacific area with various Marine units and Navy destroyers. These destroyers were capable of shallow water steaming and shore bombardment with their 5 inch 38 caliber Naval rifle batteries and depressed 40mm Hotchkiss anti-aircraft automatic cannon. They proved to be very effective weapons against Japanese bunkers and pillboxes, particularly so if a Navy or Marine fire coordination and observation team was included. The Navajo Code has never been broken to this day.
"This is the Gunny, Sarge. Go ahead."
"We're secure, Gunny, and ready to exfill. Over."
"Casualties?"
"Four wounded."
"Roger. Wait one. The Lieut. says to exfill in 1---5."
"Roger. Green Beach over and out. Joker. Tell the men to break out canteens and the smoking lamp is lit. And put out perimeter security. We don't need surprises. A few Japs may be between us and the Lieut.'s squad."
When Joker returned he brought Ramirez with him. The Sergeant lit a Lucky Strike and threw the pack at Ramirez, who did the same. The Joker didn't smoke.
"Ein cigareta Herr Hays?"

"Nein, Herr Feldweble. Nicht rauchen."

This made the three N.C.O.s laugh.

"I didn't know the Joker could talk Kraut."

"Sprecken die Deutsch to you pal. The Sarge has been teaching me in case we gotta go to Europe when we're done here."

He said,

"If I learn to talk Kraut, they will make me a secret agent. Then I can get lots of broads and stuff."

"You dumb bastard. You're too ugly to get broads no matter how secret you are."

"All right. Listen up. I want two columns, mutually supportive. Joker and Ramirez take No. two. Vito and I will take this one. Now look alive out there. Consider this a combat patrol. There's still gotta be Jap stragglers around. They will try to die for the Emperor and take you with them."

Half way to Green Beach it happened. Banzai attack. Dark forms screaming like jungle animals charged the columns. They were so close they were mixing in the ranks.

"Sarge. Look out."

Vito pushed the Sgt. so hard he hit the deck with a crash. Then he heard the shortpecker open up as Vito cut down two attackers who decided to kill the Sgt. since he was the leader of the column. The big 7.7mm slugs turned them into fertilizer when impacted from ten feet away. The Sgt. dropped two more with his Tommy gun, the big 45 slugs knocking the Japs down like bowling pins. Now he was empty. No time to reload. Should have done it back at the clearing.

Rawlins pulled his primary 45 pistol, thumbed back the hammer and shot a Jap just as he was thrusting a bayonet attached Arisaka Type 99 6.5mm rifle at him. Rawlins grabbed the rifle by the muzzle and bayonet handle and deflected it. With his right hand he held his 1911AL 45 cal. pistol and shot the Jap twice in the chest, which sent him off to the rising sun. At the same time the Sgt. ripped the Arisaka rifle from his dead hands, spun it around and thrust the bayonet into the Japs throat, just to make sure. Then he noticed something strange. The Arisaka rifle still wore it's bolt body dust cover, complete with the royal family Kersanthemum crest. Only a boot would leave that noisy rattling cover on his rifle. Must be new troops in the area. Like General Curibyoshi's Fifteenth Army from China. Like they did on the Canal. These troops could be some of the same. He would mention this in his after action report.

"How bad is the Lieut., Gunny?"

"Took a bayonet in the gut but I think he'll make it."

The wounded and dead were put aboard the rubber rafts and the Raiders paddled out to sea. The Red Beach party had a difficult time carrying their rafts across the island and fighting off Japanese attack, but they made it. The operation was reminiscent of Navy Seal training today.

"Green Beach to taxi. Ready for pickup."

"Roger, Beach party. Over and out."

The sub surfaced within twenty yards. The wounded and dead were taken below. Ten minutes later all hands were below. The Raiders were starting to loosen up and relax. As they removed their 782 gear and stowed their weapons they began to talk.

"Did you see the Jap that got the Lieut.? He took three or four hits and got the Lieut. before he went down. Gunny says we gotta get him a real weapon instead a that kid's rabbit gun. Gunny knows a guy at Pearl with shotguns. We're gonna chip in and fix him up right."

"Yeah. That's a real weapon. Too bad it only holds five rounds. Right, Eyes?"

"That's all the professional needs."

"Eyes. How many confirmed you got?"

"Forty seven from the Canal and Tulagi; two off the bridge of a Jap sub as it lay off Tulagi, 600 yards out, dumping supplies, and three tonight."

"Whatta you do if you get caught in a banzai?"

".45."

"How many mags?"

"Four and one ten round I had made back at Diego."

"No shit."

"No shit."

"Work OK?"

"Works OK. I got a little Remington .380 automatic in my

pants in case the .45 fails or runs dry or they try to take me prisoner."

* * * * *

The next day the submarine crew gave the dead Marines a proper burial at sea including a twenty one gun salute. Captain Hesscox did the honors.

"We are gathered here today to commit the bodies of our fallen shipmates who died in battle for their country to the deep. They will be resurrected in Christ when He returns and the sea gives up her dead. Attention on deck. Present arms."

The Sailors and Marines saluted and the Honor Guard aimed their rifles to high port, arms out to sea, and the seven Sailors and Marines fired three volleys of seven shots.

"Order arms."

The rifles and salutes were dropped to "at ease" as the remains slid into the sea.

"Burial detail dismissed. All off duty personnel report below deck. Gunnery Sgt. Parker, Sgt. Rawlins, Pharmacist Mate First Class Smith, report to the Ward Room on the double."

They were met by the Captain as they entered.

"Gentlemen. Please be seated."

Rawlins liked Captain Hesscox. He had real class and a man could talk to him, not like some he had known.

"Well, men, it looks like your mission was a great success. We intercepted a Jap radio message this morning saying a landing party from a destroyer found the Toulabong outpost completely destroyed with all but two of the garrison killed. The two said it was the lizard men. They crept our of the sea, fought like demons and went back into the sea and disappeared. That should scare hell out of every Jap in the neighborhood. Doc. How are the wounded?"

"The Lieut. is OK. The wound is stabalized and MMC2 Hernandaz gave blood for the transfusion."

"The motor mac is a good man; always helping out," said the Captain.

"How are the others?"

"I'm a little worried about the kid with the knife wound. I

think his liver is damaged and he's showing signs of infection. All I can do is give him sulfa drugs and morphine. He needs surgery at Pearl, Skipper."

"OK, Doc. Thanks and do what you can for that young man. You're dismissed."

"Aye, Sir."

"You Sgts. have done an outstanding job this mission and thank you for saving that fine young officer. He has a great future in the Naval service. By the way, I am recommending you both for decoration for above and beyond the call."

"Thank you, Sir."

"Rawlins. The camera please."

And the Mini Minox was handed over.

"Very good, Sgt. You men are dismissed."

All that was said in the corridor was,

"Semper phi, Gunny," and a sarcastic

"Gung ho," in return.

Chapter 2

THE BEGINNING

Early in World War II the Allies were not doing well. By 1942 all of Europe except England had fallen to the Nazis. In North Africa German General Erwin Rommel made the English look very inadequate by outflanking their fixed positions with mobile infantry and armour, overrunning their units and taking thousands of prisoners. It took a new British General (Montgomery) and the introduction of U.S. forces in the area (Operation Torch) to defeat Rommel. Also, there was a clandestine force operating in the area known as British Commandos. These units were made up of British M15, Intelligence Operatives, British Royal Marine Commandos, American OSS Operatives and U.S. Army Rangers. This force was led and trained by the British. They did an outstanding job of raiding Rommel's supply lines and eliminating strategic targets. The U.S. Marine Corps General, Holland Smith, took notice of their successes and decided there was room for such a unit in the Marine Corps.

At the same time but unrelated, Colonel Evans Carlson, a friend of President Roosevelt and the President's son, Captain James Roosevelt, after duty in China serving with the Chinese guerrillas, showed the President how effective a small, properly trained force could be against a larger one. After Carlson's recommendation to the President, Captain Roosevelt wrote to the Major General Commandant of the Marine Corps asking him to form a special unit similar to the British Commando. The British Prime Minister, Winston Churchill, when consulted, enthusiastically endorsed the plan and even offered training by the Commando, possible including combat, to any American Soldier or Marine. Both Carlson and Roosevelt accepted the Prime Ministers offer and sent some important N.C.O.'s such as Gunnery Sergeant Ken Rawlins, one of Carlson's top N.C.O.'s in China.

While men trained in England, General Smith was busy procuring landing craft for future operations. He commandeered three of the new APD high speed destroyer transports along with submarines. The APDs would carry the ten man rubber boats and launch them in shallow water strike zones and support them as necessary with Naval gunfire. General Smith's idea for the Raiders mission was a bit different from Carlson's and Roosevelt's. While their idea was covert commando raids, the General was thinking more along the lines of a reactionary force that could be used as a diversion to the main attack or an emeregency strike force in case a line unit found itself in trouble. Also to hook up with and/or relieve parachute regiments and glider borne air infantry regiments.

* * * * *

"All right then, you Yanks. Form a line, two ranks deep."

This having been done, the British NCO began his rhetoric.

"I am Color Sergeant Rothchild. I will be your instructor for the duration of your stay with the Royal Marine Commando. Officers, NCOs and EMs will be treated the same. Any sissies or cry babies will be returned to their units posthaste. There is no place for them here. It's been said that American Marines are tougher and fight harder than Royal Marines. We shall see. Now gentlemen, if you plan to engage the Jap or the Hun in close quarters and kill him without being killed, watch closely. I am your hand to hand combat specialist. Captain Simmons, you are the Yank Executive Officer. Am I right?"

"Yes, Color Sergeant."

"Well then, I'm the Jap that just killed your father and is raping your mother. I suggest you do something to stop him. After all, you are a U.S. Marine."

The Captain charged the Sergeant, grabbing him by the throat, only to have the Sergeant drop to one knee at the moment of contact. The Captain's momentum carried him over the Sergeant, breaking the hold and landing him on his back with the Sergeant on top of him.

"One dead U.S. Marine," shouted the amused Sergeant. "This story will be told at the local pub for years to come."

"Before we leave here, Color Sergeant, you're going to eat those words."

"We shall see, Captain. This is your main weapon. The Sykes-Fairbairn stiletto. It is capable of stabbing, slashing, and throwing at a human target with it's double edge balanced carbon steel blade. With proper training an enemy can be eliminated silently and instantly."

Standing to the Sergeant's left at twelve yards was a silhouette of a German soldier.

"Accuracy, men, is vitally important with any weapon."

With this statement the Color Sergeanat threw the commando knife, burying the blade in the German sentry's plywood forehead.

"Because of its steel construction and weighted handle the commando knife will penetrate the human skull. This will insure an instant kill."

* * * * *

The next three months consisted of training in judo and jujitsu, weapons training with the 9mm Sten submachine gun, the .303 Bren Squad automatic weapon and of course the venerable Lee Enfield SMLE No. l Mark 3 in. .303 caliber. This rifle was very popular with the troops because of its ten round magazine with cutoff, meaning it could be used as a single shot bolt action, maintaining its ten rounds in the magazine until rapid fire was needed. This was very useful for indirect fire support or sniping. German weapons were also explored. The Machinen Gevere MG38 and 42 in 7.92mm, the Smissere Machinen Pistole MP40 in 9mm; also the Carabinar 98K Mauser infantry rifle in 7.92mm; the P08 Parabellum Luger in 9mm and 7.65mm; also the Waffinfabrik Walther P38 pistol in 9mm Parabellum were studied. The 1911 Colt 45 Auto and the English .455 caliber Webly revolver were also used. The venerable Browning P35 high power was favored by English, Canadian and German forces. The Belgian high power built in Herstal, Belgium became Germany's infantry sidearm in 1941 after Belgium fell to the Nazis The Inglis high power, made under license in Canada in 1940 became the official sidearm of the Royal Marines and all special troops in Great Britain and all Commonwealth countries. It was popular because of its 14 round magazine of 9mm ammo, and the ease of field stripping and repair. The Webly revolver was retained for officers, pilots, service and support troops. The training became progressively harder, sleep was replaced by night maneuvers. Scaling walls and cliffs after hours of paddling in kayaks and rubber rafts became the routine. Swimming in ice cold sea water became a popular torture of the instructors. The more the Brits threw at the Marines the better they did. Finally, the end came. The final test would be an actual raid on the Nazi held Norwegian coastline. Gentlement of Royal Commando Squadron No. one, both American and British troops, were now regarded the same. Assembled in the Mess Hall, the new Commandoes were given their orders.

"Your training is over and you are all hereby given the title, 'His Majesties Royal Commando'."

There was an outburst of cheers and claps and much back slapping and shaking of hands.

"To celebrate your success we have a mission for you."

More cheers.

"For the Yanks this is strictly voluntary. Captain Simmons. Because of your family we feel and the Prime Minister concurs that you should remain in England until this jaunt is over."

The Captain addressed Colonel Wakefield in typical Raider fashion.

"Like hell I will, Colonel Wakefield, Sir. I earned the right to go on this mission like every other man present."

"But, Captain, the Senator. If anything were to happen ..."

"Colonel, Sir, my father knows war. Look what the Japanese have done to us. If I sit this mission out the Senator will think of me as a traitor and a coward. I would rather die in combat than go home in disgrace."

"Bloody good show, Captain. We knew you would be with us but we had to ask."

"Colonel Wakefield, Sir. After seeing what the Nazis have done to this beautiful country and the wonderful English people, I have a score to settle with them and if I get back to the States I'll make sure England gets all the help she needs."

This induced a rousing cheer from the Commando, both English and American.

"Your target, gentlemen: the heavy water factory near Rajivik, Norway. We don't know what 'heavy water' is, but we do know it's needed to produce Hitler's latest doomsday weapon. We have good intelligence from German defectors and Norwegian underground. If this weapon is completed the war will become far worse for the Allies than it has been. Success is critical and we're asking for an all-out effort here. You will be transported by the Royal Navy Corvette HMS Derby. You will board at Scappa Flow, the Derby will steam under cover of darkness and foul weather, if the Navy keeps its promise, to a fjord within ten miles of the target. Commando Frogmen will disembark first, abandoning their rubber boats one hundred yards or more from the beach depending on conditions. They will swim ashore and deal with any sentries or shore patrol. When clear the swimmers will signal the landing parties with electric torches. You will then move inland avoiding all contact if possible. A company of the First Parachute Regiment will be on the ground waiting to link up with you. Officers will be given coordinates for the link up. To give you an idea of target importance: The Shutze Staffal Panzer Lear Division has a regiment on loan to guard the complex, so be careful. Those blokes are Russian front vets and as mean as they come."

On the train ride to Scappa Flow Lt. Col. Jamison, Captain Simmons and Gunnery Sgt. Rawlins rode together.

"Nice speech, Captain. Your old man would be proud."

"Couldn't let the Limeys get the best of me twice. The first time was enough."

This produced laughs from the surrounding area.

"And besides, there is a certain Color Sergeant I have to even up with."

"Jolly good, Captain."

"I'd know that foghorn voice anywhere. That's him. Who let him on this train. He'll be calling cadence all the way to the target."

More laughs.

"On the other hand we might get to see Super Commando take on a few of those SS boys and give us a real show."

With this sarcasm the car grew quiet. Some men wrote letters, some played cards, some prayed and some just talked.

"How's your wife, Gunny?"

"Don't know, Sir. Haven't got any letters in a while."

"Having problems?"

"She doesn't understand why I gotta travel."

"Isn't her father a Navy Captain?"

"Yes, Sir, but it doesn't matter. She's not going to sit home while I'm off yachting with the Navy. And while I'm sunning myself on some exotic island she's not waiting around to see if I return. She's not going to be a sea widow to some misbegotten world traveler like her mother was."

"Fleet Marines and Sailors. They have suffered through this from time immemorial. I remember reading about a Polynesian Sailor two thousand years ago who mutinied and killed his Captain because he missed his wife so much. When he returned home he discovered his wife living with another man. So, in a jealous rage, he killed them both and was in such pain from grief that he killed himself."

"Sounds like he wasn't too bright, Sir."

"Intelligence has nothing to do with matters of the heart, Gunny. A jealous husband is the most dangerous creature in the world, especially if he's trained to kill. Remember that."

"Aye, Sir."

The Sgt. thought to himself, *that would be the day he would do brig time or lose his stripes over an unfaithful woman.*

As Color Sergeant Rothchild would say:

"We shall see, Gunnery Sgt. Rawlins. Every man has his breaking point and the near future may hold yours."

* * * * *

The cruise from Scappa Flow to the Norway fjord aboard H.M.S. Derby was uneventful save for a Kriegsmarine Dornier Maritime Patrol flying boat passing overhead in the heavy fog. The drone of its three Mercedes engines made indentification eay. It dropped no bombs and did not fire on the Derby with it's 20mm automatic cannons, and no radio transmissions were heard on German maritime frequencies. So it was decided by the ship's Captain that they had not been seen and the mission was still a go.

Corp. Fairbanks of the Commando and Petty Officer James of the Royal Navy's Special Boat Squadron, both qualified divers, would take the point. This meant they would disarm any mines they found and eliminate any sentries. The two men left the ship in their one man rubber rafts, wearing wet suits with combat kit underneath. Their weapons were Sten machine guns and Commando knives. Air tanks were left behind. They would get in the way on this shallow water operation. One man took the north side of the fjord; the other the south side. They reconned the shoreline as they silently paddled through ground fog and inky blackness. Corp. Fiarbanks spotted the unmistakable silhouette of a German Soldier with his broad rimmed, duck billed helmet and long Mauser Kar 98k rifle. The Corp. anchored the rubber boat in 15 feet of icy water, pulled his Colt Woodsman pistol with suppressor in 22 rim fire caliber from the wet suits inner pocket, inserted a full ten round magazine and cycled the bolt, loading the chamber. He then picked up his Sten gun and slung it across his back. Finally, the Corp. slid over the side into the frigid water where he knew he wouldn't survive long, and headed straight for the German.

Feldwebel Hans Wheeler was a good German Soldier. The weight of the Knight's Cross around his neck made him proud to be a Sergeant in the Shutz Panzer Lear Division. He was annoyed with the incompetent Private asleep in the guard house behind him but no matter. Soon he would be on his way home for a well deserved furlough. He would be a hero when the people saw the Knight's Cross adorning his dress black SS uniform. He would tell them about all the Poles in Warsaw and Bolsheviks in Vladivostok he had machine gunned for Deutschland and der Fuhrer. They would be so proud of him. He might even be promoted to Oberfeldwebel by Col. Von Piper.

Suddenly the Sergeant was pulled from his dreams of glory by the sight of a seal or sea otter looking for clams at low tide in front of him. In his black wet suit Corp. Fairbanks did not look human. He got to within twenty feet of the Nazi, stood up in four feet of water and shot the enemy Soldier three times in the chest with the .22 cal. pistol. The SS Trooper grabbed his chest, fell to his knees and pitched forward, dead. The Corp. pulled himself onto the lookout platform, crept up to the guard house and ran into the other German, half asleep, coming through the door. For a second the German stared at the Corp. with a horrified look on his face. He should have attacked the black alien from the sea but froze instead. Just before he died he called out for his Feldwebel, then received two 40 grain copper washed .22 cal. bullets in the head.

One less Waffin SS Grenadier to murder civilians and prisoners of war.

The Corp. disposed of the bodies in the fjord and moved on.

While working the shoreline Petty Officer James spotted two German sentries walking rounds near a guard shack on a platform by the water's edge. The shoreline where the SS Troopers patrolled was covered with large rocks. This would be an advantage. Petty Officer James remembered the Infiltration Specialist always stressed the use of cover above all else and these rocks were perfect. As the Petty Officer slid into the water to close the distance, Private Johann Stribel, SS Grenadier, sat on a large rock for a break.

"Nine Englisher soldaten das nockt."

The Nazi, thinking he was safe, lit a cigarette. Lying three feet behind him in the water was James, ready to strike. With his left hand he grabbed the Nazi's helmet lip, pulling his head back, then he put his right arm under his chin, across the German's throat and pulled back and to the left as violently as possible. The German's own weight broke his neck vertebrae, killing him instantly. Petty Officer James picked up the dead soldier's cigarette and finished smoking it so the other guard wouldn't get nervous. He could see him standing on the dock that extended from the platform out into the fjord. His burp gun was slung around his neck. James slid back into the black, freezing water and swam, mostly under water, to the dock. Only surfacing for air, he looked like a great amphibious swamp beast that people always talk about but never really see. He surfaced under the dock with the German right above him.

Carl Muller thought about how he was being wasted and it disgusted him. A combat vet of the Panzer Lear being used to guard fish for some ridiculous "win the war in one day" scheme. And besides the cowardly Englishers would never attack a regiment of the Panzer Lear Division.

James hit the sentry behind the knees with the steel collapsible buttstock of his Sten gun. When the German's back hit the deck, before he could react, the Petty Officer drove his Commando knife into the enemy's chest, cleaving his heart. Then he dragged the Nazi off the dock into the black water.

"Now you can feed the fish, instead of guarding them, with the compliments of His Majesty's Royal Navy."

* * * * *

Back in the States, Lt. Col. Merritt Edson, better known in the Corps as Red Mike Edson, an old China hand, was given command of the new APD battalion. This special unit of the Marine First Division, Fifth Regiment, would train and deploy with the Navy's new APD shallow draft destroyers. They would use ten man rubber rafts for landing the new ten man rifle squads at night. Their mission would be similar to the parachute regiments. Recon, search and destroy and small unit infiltration. The battalion trained at Quantico under Edson.

In January, just after Pearl Harbor was bombed, the Navy high command directed the Pacific Fleet to form a Commando type unit for use against the Japanese. In February 1942 the second separate battalion was formed and Lt. Col. Edson was transferred to train and oversee operations. A third of the APD battalion went with him to train the new battalion and lead them in combat. February 16 unit designation would be changed to First Marine Raider Battalion. Col. Carson's unit would be Second Marine Raider Battalion, with Major Roosevelt as Executive Officer.

Oceanside, California was the new home of Raider recruits. Recruiting was a tedious job but the Raiders needed men. Only the best and most experienced men were accepted.

"Why do you want to be a Raider?"

"I don't like Japs. They ain't human."

"You're accepted."

Next.

"Ever kill a man with a knife?"

"No, Sir."

"Think you could?"

"Ask my brother in the bottom on the Arizona."

"You're accepted."

And so it went. Many good men with many good reasons began the journey that day in sunny California to save the world from tyranny even if it meant giving up their own lives.

* * * * *

The training was tough. Twenty mile hikes with field gear, rifle and ruck. Hand to hand combat training during halts. Night problems with rubber rafts dropped from APDs a mile or more from shore with a target ten miles inland. The Raiders trained with all types of weapons like the men in England.

* * * * *

The First Raider Battalion's first major combat operation against the Japenese was Guadalcanal. Along with the First Marine Division under Gen. Vandergrift, the First Raider Battalion, better known as Edson's Raiders, slugged it out with the Japanese.

On August 7th, 1942, Edson's Raiders, under the command of Marine General Rupertis, attacked the island of Tulagi at the same time as the First Division Marines attacked Guadalcanal. Carlson's Second Raiders attacked Makin Island on August 17th.

Tulagi was secured on August 8th and Edson's Raiders moved to Guadalcanal. On this island, in addition to many combat patrols, they fought the Matanikau River battles alongside the First Division Marines, attacking and destroying the Tasimboko Supply Dump, the enemy's main supply and replacement depot, located near Henderson Field.

The First Raider's greatest moment came when the Japanese, trying to take Henderson Field, the island's air base, stormed a ridge line adjacent to the field. The Raiders took positions on the ridge and repulsed the enemy for two days and nights, taking terrible casualties. There were constant banzai charges by Japanese General

Kuribyoshi's 18th Division. Edson's one battalion of Raiders and one battalion of Paramarines, attached to the Raiders, held the line and saved Henderson Field and maybe the whole campaign.

* * * * *

Edson's Raiders shipped to Camp Bailey in New Caledonia in October. The spent a month in New Zealand for R & R and liberty. The Second Raider Battalion, better known as Carlson's Raiders, made famous by the Makin Island raid, shipped in December to Camp Gung Ho on Espiritu Santo for forward area training. The tired, depleted Second Raiders has a two week liberty in New Zealand in February 1943.

In September 1942 the Third Raiders were formed on Samoa from Marine units stationed there along with a small contingent of First and Second Raiders, used for leadership training under the command of Lt. Col. Harry Liversedge, a former enlisted Marine.

* * * * *

Back in southern California the Fourth Raiders were being formed under the command of Majaor Roosevelt. Both Third and Fourth Raiders would ship to Espiritu Santo in February 1943. In March 1943 the First Raider Regiment was formed, encompassing all four Raider battalions. The new Col. Liversedge would command.

* * * * *

Guadalcanal would plague Merritt Edson for the rest of his life. When he could sleep, when he was drunk, the nightmares would return. Screaming Japanese soldiers, hundreds of them, attacking the ridge his men held adjacent to Henderson Field, the island's airfield. Always at night. First Washing Machine Charley would drop a few bombs on Henderson Field, then a fierce Naval artillery bombardment would pound them from the sea. Then the Japanese would come, hundreds of screaming, yelling little men, waving swords, shaking bayonet fixed rifles. Toward the end they had homemade spears. Trip flares and mortar rounds impacting, and the occasional artillery flare from Henderson would light them up like a parade of ghouls on Halloween night. The Raiders would pour fire into their ranks until they broke the attack. Then the Japs would fade into the jungle and snipe at the Marines. Invariably, the Raiders would send out a combat patrol and clean them out, but always at the cost of a man or two.

The Matanikau River fights were even worse. The Japs would try to slip across the river and storm Henderson Field. The Raiders and some First Marine Division units set up defensive positions along the river bank adjacent to Henderson Field.

On the nights of September 27th and October 8th the Japanese broke the line by sheer numbers when the Machine Gunners ran out of ammo. Lucky for the Marines they had built an in-depth defense. There were breaches the length of the line. Vicious hand to hand fights broke out. The Marines would not retreat. One Machine Gunner beat a Japanese officer to death with an empty ammo can after the Jap stabbed him in the shoulder with a sword. Another Gunner got three Japs with his sidearm before being bayoneted to death. A Marine Sgt. emptied his Thompson submachine gun into the enemy, and being out of ammo, dropped the Thompson, picked up a Browning 30 cal., water cooled 1917L1A1 machine gun that held a live ammo belt but had a dead Gunner. The Sgt. cradled the barrels water jacket in his left arm, walked up and down behind the line of defense, mowing down groups of Japanese who got through the line, heading for Henderson Field. He was awarded the medal of honor for this action. When the President asked him why he did this instead of staying under cover, the Sgt. replied:

"God was with me, protecting me, I had nothing to fear."
The President looked surprised and said:
"You're quite right, young man, God bless you anyway,"
"Thank you, Sir."

* * * * *

THE LONG PATROL - November 4th to December 4th
Finally the Raiders were going on the offensive. This is what

they were created and trained for. The would reconnoiter the whole island, cut enemy supply and communication lines, kill the enemy whenever possible, employ enemy weapons and supplies if needed. The jungle became their ally. They found trails the enemy was using. They set up ambushes. If a large body of troops walked through the kill zone, they would let them go by and take the rear element, then melt away into the jungle. The pursuing forward element would follow the ambushers right into another ambush and be wiped out. Small groups of two or three would be killed quietly and buried. Japanese food caches and supply lines from ships and submarines were favorite targets. Hence the Japanese re-named Guadalcanal "starvation island." More Japanese died of starvation and disease than in battle on this island.

* * * * *

Petty Officer James and Corp. Fairbanks met on the beach in the center of the fjord, as planned. They signaled the Derby, lying silently off-shore, waiting to disembark her charge of Commandos. The men loaded their rubber rafts and headed for shore. Once on shore they hid the rafts in the woods adjacent to the beach. A three man security team was left with the boats in case a German patrol found them. Any such patrol would have to be eliminated before making contact with their headquarters. The Commandos moved inland, using map and compass and taking bearings every five hundred yards as they had been taught. They arrived at the rendezvous point ahead of the Paratroopers. Forming a defensive perimeter near a clearing in the woods, they waited. The men of the English First Airborne, the same men who would later fight the Germans in the Pa de Calais region of Normandy, France on D-Day, were approaching the field. Gunnery Sgt. Rawlins could see dark forms moving through the trees across the small clearing. It might be the Troopers or it might be a Kraut patrol. He picked up the field telephone and called the CP.

"This is Rawlins. I have movement in my forward."

"Jolly good, old man. It must be the Paras. They do like to sneak about and jangle the nerves a bit."

"It could be a patrol, Sir."

"Yes, yes, you're quite right, Sgt. Offer the password and if they don't answer toss them a grenade."

"Aye, Sir. Over and out."

Rawlins put the phone receiver in it's cradle and pulled a grenade off his web gear. He straightened the safety pin for easy, fast removal and called out the password.

"London."

The reply, in a distinct English voice:

"Piccadilly."

Then the voice said:

"Hold fire. We're coming in."

Now the Troops were mixing, shaking hands, talking in low tones, and trading gum and cigarettes. Their morale was high, knowing they were finally going to hit Jerry where it would do some real good. Rawlins got the word:

"Officer and NCO call in five minutes."

A tent was erected for use as the CP and the meeting was held there. Col. Wakefield addressed his men for the final briefing:

"Gentlemen, this young man is with the Norwegian underground. He will lead us to the target and out of here after the raid. If anyone is left behind he will help him escape and evade. He is known as Ge Org and that's all you need to know about him. Capt. Simmons will lead First Platoon; I will lead Second Platoom; Sgt. Rawlins will assist the Capt. By the way, good work back there at the clearing, Sgt. Glad you didn't blow up any of our Paras. Frightfully embarrassing, you know. Sergeant Rothchild will assist me. Any questions so far?"

"That's Color Sergeant, Sah."

"Yes, Rothchild, we are all aware of that. We will form two columns, platoon strength, infiltrate from the north and west, set time delay charges with composition B plastic and acid pencil fuses, break fuses for five minutes, destroy anything that looks useful. Half the Airborne men will fall out three hundred yards from target and form and ambush perimeter; the other half will remain here, prepared to defend against attackers. This will be the rally point for the exfiltration. Any questions?"

"Can we expect support?"

"We will support each other like we were trained to do. The RAF and the Navy have a few surprises planned for Jerry during our exfil. Any more questions?"

No response.

"Right, Then form your men, check your kits and form a column of twos and prepare to march. Dismissed."

* * * * *

Ge Org led the men through the dark forest to the power plant. The Paratroopers dropped off and set up an ambush position three hundred yards out. The Commandos abandoned the trail and moved through the woods until they reached the north and west fence lines. They watched the guard houses as they cut through the fence and entered the compound. Sgt. Rawlins and Corp. Fairbanks disposed of the first guard house contingent. The Corp. pulled a German helmet out of his kit bag and fit it to his head.

"What the hell is that?"

"Jerry headgear. Borrowed it from one of the blokes on the beach. He didn't seem to mind. Thought it might come in handy."

He then pulled out his 22 Colt pistol and jacked a round into the chamber. Opening his battle jacket, he hid the silenced pistol inside.

"Sgt., I'm going to walk up to the guard house and take out as many as possible with this pistol. Walk behind me and watch my back. OK. Go."

Fairbanks and Rawlins headed straight for the guard post until challenged.

"Halt. Vo biss du."

The Corp. answered.

"Commarad Gebensie ien cigaretta und kaffee mit milsh bitta. Ich bin Oberfeldvebel Strouse."

The sentry eyed him curiously and grabbed the pistol grip of his MP40 machine pistol. Sgt. Rawlins threw his dagger, striking the German's chest. He then rushed the sentry, tearing the machine pistol from his grasp and knocking him down. He pulled the dagger from his chest and drove it in his throat before the Nazi could make a sound.

"Good show, old man. I was getting a bit nervous. He had the drop on me and my German's not that good."

"Better than mine, Corp. I was completely lost."

They walked into the guard house and the Corp. shot two guards in the head with his 22 pistol before they could react. Rawlins killed a third Nazi, who was in the radio room, with his knife. Now the rest of the Team was through the fence, entering the compound, looking for things to blow up. The other sentries had been eliminated by the other Team. Luckily, there were no workers here at this time, and the security contingent was bivouacked in the town a quarter mile away. Charges were placed on fuel tanks, oxygen and acetylene tanks and nitrogen tanks. Any pumps, cooling towers, pipe lines or other apparatus for production were mined. When the charge detonated the Commandos were back in the woods watching the show. Great sheets of flame erupted from the compound, shaking the ground. Green and blue flames from chemical reaction spread through the plant. The fire was so hot steel beams and girders were bending like fish hooks in the intense heat. The Commandos watched and cheered. Hitler's plans would be ruined for a long time to come.

"Right. Let's get moving, people. Jerry will be after us any time now. Sgt. Rawlins."

"Yes, Sir."

"Can you devise a surprise for Jerry and maintain a rear guard action?"

"Yes, Sir."

"I'll give you Color Sergeant Rothchild, Corp. Fairbanks and four other lads, with Capt. Simmons commanding."

"Aye, Sir."

"Hold them as long as possible to give our chaps a head start on Jerry. Pip, pip, cheerio, old man."

Off went the Col., leading his men to the rendezvous with the Paratroopers. Roosevelt's men were busy laying contact mines in the road and adjacent woods. Grenades were taped to 60mm mortar rounds to act as detonators. Their safety pins had been straightened and nearly removed. Trip wires were attached to the loop in the pins.

Two rounds, laid ten yards apart, connected by trip wire, would be devastating. Trip flares with trip wires connected to trees or underbrush would illuminate the enemy so the Bren guns and Browning light machine guns could do their deadly work. The Commandos took positions in the woods on the high ground overlooking the compound. When the Germans came it was obvious that these men were combat vets. They advanced by squads, maneuvering to cover each other and avoiding the dirt track the Commandos had mined. Color Sergeant Rothchild spotted them first.

"Here they come, lads. Let them get close. No firing until I say so."

There was a ripping explosion as half of a German rifle squad went down, killed or wounded. Two of the 60mm mortars had done their job. An SS Trooper stepped on a land mine, blowing off his legs, sending his torso into the air and falling, dead from shock. The Deutsch Shutz Staffall Soldatan began to fire wildly in the direction of the high ground, knowing their enemy had to be there.

"Hold fast, lads. I'll say when."

The Germans were getting close. They were finding the range. One man was hit in the shoulder, putting him out of action. Trip flares were popping and drifting on their tiny parachutes.

"Make ready with grenades."

The woods looked like a cheap horror flick with dark figures running to and fro in the bouncing flare light.

"Throw grenades."

The multiple explosions forced the Nazis to take cover. This is just what the Color Sergeant was hoping for.

"Give 'um hell, lads. Fire."

The fusillade was intense, killing many of the hated SS Troops with the first volley. The rest withdrew in an orderly fashion, covering each other as they descended the hill. This is when Color Sergeant Rothchild was hit.

"Bloody hell, Capt., that damned Jerry got me with his burp gun."

Rothchild had two 9mm 124 grain slugs in his abdomen and one in his left arm. As the medic worked on him the Color Sergeant lamented:

"Leave me, Capt. I'm no good any more. All shot to hell."

"Color Sergeant, shut up. You're in the company of U.S. Marines. We don't leave our men behind."

"But Capt., I'll slow you down."

"What makes you think you're that important. Medic, give the Color Sergeant morphine and put him out. I don't want to hear him whine all the way home. Now let's get the hell out of here before the mortars come in."

The Commandos had traveled two hundred yards down the track when, as expected, the mortars came crashing down on their previous position, tearing up the forest with high explosives and shrapnel. The rear guard finally reached the rendezvous site and passed through the Paratroopers who were waiting to ambush the Nazis who would be following.

"Right, lads. They will be coming soon so no fidgeting about. We want to surprise them"

Fortunately the Paras were formed in an inverted tee because the SS Grenadiers who were sent after them advanced in platoon formation in company strength, through the woods flanking the trail.

"Here come the bloody bastards, lads. Let 'um have it."

The line exploded with fire from automatic weapons and mortars. Now the big surprise for the Nazis.

"Piccadilly calling. H.M.S. Repulse fire mission."

"Repulse calling. Go ahead."

"Request fire mission. Enemy infantry company strength."

"Request received."

"Proximity fuse air burst anti personnel co-ordinance map reference: Grid section four, alpha romeo tango fire spotter round, will adjust."

"Roger, Piccadilly. Over."

Seconds later the eight inch shell landed with an ear splitting roar.

"Repulse. Up fifty, right twenty five."

Another shell came in and air burst in the center of the SS advance.

"Right on the money. Fire for effect. Walk it back and forth."

The Repulse fired a full two minute barrage with her main

batteries.

"Cease fire, Repulse. Cease fire. Well done, Repulse, and thanks. That's one less company of SS Grenadiers to worry about."

"Glad to be of service, Piccadilly. Cheerio."

There were dead Germans and pieces of dead Germans everywhere. The medics did what they could for the German wounded and the small force headed for the beach to be picked up by the Navy with the Commandos.

* * * * *

Back in the village the SS Panzer Lear Grenadiers were boarding armored half tracks to renew the attack, this time in battalion strength. Two Mark Three Panzers (tanks) would accompany them. The 88mm cannon and heavy machine guns would make short work of these invaders. The Germans didn't know it at the time, but there was a plan to deal with this action they were undertaking. Three Royal Air Force Mosquito Fighter Bombers would bomb and strafe the road, destroying any force trying to attack the landing force. This would be Dunkirk in reverse. Germany's turn to be humiliated. The Commandos were boarding their rubber boats and the Paratroopers Naval launches from the destroyer squadron on station at the fjord's mouth, when the first 88mm H.E. rounds landed in the tree line near the beach. Soon afterwards three fighter bombers zoomed over the disembarking troops in attack formation etalon right. A half mile inland sheets of flame could be seen and the rattle of machine gun fire and the thump of automatic cannons was heard. The armored vehicles were bombed and the infantry columns strafed.

"Never mind, lads. The R.A.F. will see to them. We have a date in Piccadilly tonight. Mustn't be tardy."

* * * * *

Back on board the H.M.S. Derby the Naval surgeon did emergency surgery on Color Sergeant Rothchild. Capt. Simmons was informed that Rothchild was expected to live and was doing well.

"I knew it. You can't kill that old rooster. He's too ornery.

He'll be here for the next war and the one after that."

* * * * *

After returning to Scappa Flow and the train ride back to base with much singing and celebrating, the men were given three day passes. This meant much hell raising in London for the Brits and boarding ship for the Yanks. Back to the States and back to the war. This time in the Pacific.

Chapter Three

THE KRIEGSMARINE

Between Nova Scotia and England in 1942 the German Kriegsmarine submarine force ruled the North Atlantic. Any Allied shipping in that area was at risk. Convoys would steam from the Canadian port of Nova Scotia. Ships would rendezvous there from as far away as Galveston, Texas or even South America on their journey to Russia or England. The Canadian and U.S. Navies and the U.S. Coast Guard would protect them from commerce raiders such as the German battleships, Bismarck and Prince Oigen. The Merchant Marines worst fear was the unterwasser boats or U-boats. The German fleet submarines caused terrible death and destruction among the merchant ships that helped keep England and Russia alive during the war. Kriegsmarine Unterwasser Boat Capitan Rolf Crueger, Captain of U-241, shadowed a convoy heading for America. It had left England two days before carrying German prisoners of war from North Africa. The war was over for these men of Gen. Rommel's Africa Korps. They would spend the duration of the war in a POW camp in Arizona, U.S.A. There were also U.S. Marines in the convoy, going home after intensive training with British Commando.

* * * * *

Capitan Crueger would make his attack at night, on the surface. Conditions were perfect for such an attack. Overcast sky and calm seas.

* * * * *

In the bowels of the ship where the Marines were, there was much activity. Card games, crap games, letter writing and in-depth discussions.

"Hey, Gunny."

"What, Collins."

"Why we gotta wear these life jackets? We're Marines. We ain't swabbies."

"Somebody saw a periscope."

"Yeah. So?"

"Any periscope out here is attached to a Kraut sub."

"Oh, shit. How the hell we supposed to fight that?"

"We ain't. That's the Navy's problem. I heard from the Colonel that the lead ship broadcast in plain language that we're carrying German POWs, in the hope that they won't fire on us."

"That's pretty good. The Krauts get to go where we want to be and sit out the war they started, and we gotta go to some shit hole and fight."

"That's war, Collins. Get used to it."

* * * * *

Dark now, the convoy is a mere 800 meters away on the starboard beam.

"Blow main ballast. Surface the boat. Prepare for surface action."

The Capitan opened the conning tower hatch and climbed onto the bridge. He could see the ships in the distance, like ponderous elephants all in a line looking for a water hole. The escorts, British and Canadian corvettes and American destroyers, raced to and fro like gazelles on an endless prairie. Crueger thought:

How ridiculous. How do these so-called "Allies" hope to escape us with their lumbering whales on the surface of the sea when we can go anywhere and apprehend them.

"Hans, bring me the target data machine."

"The First Officer obeyed his Captain, giving him the data machine and a reminder.

"Capitan, there are German POWs on those ships."

"Yes, Herr Luitnen. I am aware of that fact. I am also aware of the fact that those POWs are expendable. If they had done their duty to the Fatherland they would not have surrendered. I will not allow them to damage the war effort any more by showing them pity.

Is that clear, Herr Luitnen?"

"Javoll, Herr Capitan."

Verdamt Nazi, Hans thought to himself. He hated them all.

The Nazi Submariner made ready for the attack.

"Con, this is the Capitan. Give me a relative target bearing."

"Target bearing 270 degrees, 800 meters, speed 8 knots."

"Forward torpedo room."

"Torpedo room. Aye."

"This is the Capitan. Load tubes ein, svie, drie, fere. Set depth to funf meters, fuses to contact. Launch at my command. Con"

"Con. Aye."

"Steer 315 degrees true."

"Torpedo room."

"Torpedo room ready, Sir."

"Con. Do you have a firing solution?"

"Yes, Sir. Steer 300 degrees at flank speed. Use a full spread at 5 degrees deviation."

"Very well. Make it so."

The Capitan watched the escorts through his binoculars, echo ranging, searching for him even before he fired. Close now. Almost too close, but that's how he liked it. The bigger the risk the bigger the prize. After firing he would dive the boat under the convoy and fire from his stern tubes and hopefully confuse the enemy escorts.

"After torpedo room."

"Torpedo room. Aye."

"Load tubes funf, sex, und zeben. Set deviation at 10 degrees, surface run, contact fuse."

"Aye, Capitan."

Finally all was ready. Torpedo rooms fore and aft, flood tubes, open outer doors. When the Capitan felt that everything was just right he gave the command.

"Octung, octung. Torpedos eins, drie, svie, fere. Torpedo loss."

The U-boat vibrated and geysers of compressed air broke the surface of the calm sea. Forty five seconds later there were two horrendous explosions, shooting flames one hundred feet in the air when the torpedos found their mark. The escorts immediately spotted the U-boat in the firelight.

"Alarm, alarm, dive the boat and rig for depth charges."

U-241 slid beneath the surface with the little escort ships in hot pursuit. The sonar operator shouted,

"Capitan, wasserbombs off port quarter."

The explosions were so close, the pressure wave was so intense that rivets from the inner hull shot through the air like bullets. Men's teeth were broken from the concussion. The Capitan grabbed the intercom mike off the bulkhead and yelled above the noise of exploding depth charges.

"After torpedo room. Torpedos funf, sex, und zeben. Torpedo loss."

The explosion was deafening as a torpedo found it's mark and blew the bow off the H.M.S. Fearless. The British corvette sank very quickly, taking most of her crew with her to a watery grave. The U-boat crew didn't cheer or celebrate. They were very quiet. Some even prayed for their fallen enemies. They knew that today they were lucky and tomorrow they might be the ones sinking to their graves, never to return home again.

* * * * *

"Son of a bitch. What the hell was that?"

"Torpedo hit. Stay calm and put on your safety gear."

"F..k this. I'm getting outta here."

Rather than have a mass panic on his hands, Rawlins punched the private between the eyes and knocked him out cold. He would deal with the consequences later. He then pulled the 45 pistol out of its shoulder holster and told the men:

"The next guy to try that gets a bullet. So far we're all right. The torpedos missed us and got the ship behind us. If we have to abandon it will be when I say so and not until."

* * * * *

The ship's Master at Arms gave Rawlins the order from the Captain.

"Gunnery Sgt. Rawlins reporting as ordered, Sir."

"Rawlins, this man claims you struck him and then threatened him with a pistol. Is that true?"

"Yes, Sir."

"May I ask why?"

"During the U-boat attack the Private panicked and had to be subdued before mass panic infected the whole Marine complement, Sir."

"I see. Private. Is that what happened?"

"Well, kind of, Sir."

"Yes or no, Private."

"Yes, Sir. But he didn't have to hit me so hard, Sir."

"Private, you're lucky he didn't shoot you."

"Yes, Sir."

"When we reach port, Private, you are on report to First Marine Division Headquarters at New River Training Facility for re-assignment."

"But, Captain, Sir."

"That is all, Private. Dismissed."

"Aye, Sir."

After the Private left the Captain opened up on the Sgt.

"Dammit, Gunny, what the hell is wrong with you. Answer me when I speak to you."

"The Gunnery Sgt. does not understand the question, Sir."

"What? Don't give me that Boot Camp NCO School lifer bull shit. One of these days those fists of yours are going to get you in big trouble. We're not the Old Guard in China, Rawlins. These kids are different and you can't bully them. Am I understood?"

"Yes, Sir."

"Any more bull shit from you and I'll kick your ass myself. Is that understood?"

"Yes, Sir."

"Fifty dollar fine and restricted to quarters. Now get the hell below and don't let me see you until we're off this scow."

"Aye, aye, Sir."

* * * * *

Rawlins hated wearing dress blues. But to gain entrance to the Navy Marine Corps Officers Mess in Washington, D.C. they were required. Also a letter of Admittance Recommendation for NCOs from an officer. The letter came from his Navy Captain father-in-law and would get him in. Somehow he felt nervous, like the foreboding feeling just before combat. Something was wrong. He could feel it. He hadn't seen Susan in months and she would be here. How would she act? What would she say?

The cab stopped at the front door of the club and Rawlins stepped out, giving the driver a five. He showed the door man the letter and was taken inside. A Navy Chief Quartermaster led Rawlins to the Captain's table.

"Ken. It's really you," Susan blurted out as she jumped up from the table to embrace him.

"My God. So skinny. What did they do to you?"

Then the Captain said,

"Welcome home, Ken."

"Thank you, Sir."

"As they shook hands it was plain to see they were fond of each other."

"When I heard you made port I took the liberty of calling your parents and letting them know you were back safe."

"Thank you, Sir."

"I told your father, in confidence, about your raid on the Hun and how successful it was."

"You knew about that, Sir?"

"Oh, we Captains get around. A bottle of Scotch in the right place can do wonders for information gathering. By the way, your father is very proud of you and hopes you got a couple of Hun bastards for him."

"How about a whole battalion of the Panzer Lear Division destroyed?"

"Outstanding, my boy. No wonder Winston was so thrilled when he called the President."

* * * * *

Susan was acting strange, Rawlins thought. *Normally she would dominate the converstion but tonight she was very quiet.*

"Captain. Who's the J.G. at the bar that keeps staring at us?"

"That's Susan's friend. He's an Airdale from Pensacola. Just got his wings. He's here waiting for assignment. They play tennis and go swimming together at the Officer's Club."

"Think I'll go get a beer."

The Captain grabbed Rawlins by the arm.

"Be careful, son. He has deep connections."

"Aye, Sir."

* * * * *

"Hey, Marine."

"Yes, Lieut."

"Are you Rawlins?"

"Yes, Sir."

"I know your wife."

"You're drunk, Lieut."

"You know, Sgt. Gunnery Rawlins, you should never leave a woman like Susan alone. Anything could happen."

"What did happen, Lieut.?"

"Let's just say she's got no use for a burned out old jarhead when she's got me taking care of her needs. And I mean all of them."

Rawlins hit the Lieut. so hard his jaw broke in three places. He lay on a table out cold. Rawlins grabbed him and threw his beer in the Lieut.'s face to wake him up to continue the fight. The lights went out for Rawlins when two Marine Guards beat Him to the floor and hauled him to the brig.

* * * * *

"Attention on deck. The Judge Advocate's Group will now proceed with the General Court Martial of Gunnery Sgt. Kenneth Rawlins, United States Marine Corps. Gunnery Sgt. Rawlins is accused of striking a superior officer, Lieut. Junior Grade Wayne Douglass, United States Navy. How do you plead, Gunnery Sgt.?"

"Guilty, Sir."

"Gunnery Sgt., take the stand."

"Aye, Sir."

The prosecution may question the accused.

"Thank you, Sir."

"Gunnery Sgt. Rawlins. Are you in the habit of beating and attacking people whenever the mood strikes?"

"Only if they're German or Japanese, Sir."

This induced a laugh from the old salts in the court room.

"In your file there is reference to you beating and then threatening a Private with a pistol. Is this true, Mr. Rawlins?"

"Yes, Sir."

"Would you care to explain why?"

"We were on board ship coming home from training in England when a Kraut U-boat attacked the convoy. The Private panicked and had to be subdued."

"Are you a psychologist, Sgt.?"

"That's Gunnery Sgt., Sir. The answer to your question is no. But I do know what can happen when men panic in combat."

"I see. Please explain to the court why in 1939, while serving in China as an advisor to Chang Kai Chek's army, you beat two Chinese coolies almost to death."

"They were giving the Japs fire direction for their 90mm mortars."

"Oh, really, Sgt. And how did we determine that little gem of information? Or did you just assume it to be true?"

"I watched them pace off yardage from the C.P. to the compound fence. Then I found their radio transmitter tuned in to a Jap frequency."

"Why didn't you just shoot them, Sgt.?"

"We needed them for intel, Commander. But of course you wouldn't know that since you weren't there (more laughs)."

"That's enough sarcasm, Gunnery Sgt."

"Aye, Sir."

"The prosecution rests, Your Honor."

"Very well. The defense may question the accused."

"Is it true the while in England you participated in a raid with

British Special Forces against the Heavy Water Facility in Norway?"

"Yes, Sir."

"Was a senator's son, Captain James Simmons, on this mission?"

"Yes, Sir."

"You may step down, Gunnery Sgt."

"Aye, Sir."

"The defense would like to call Captain James Simmons, United States Marine Corps, to the stand as a character witness."

"Captain Simmons. Do you know Gunnery Sgt. Rawlins?"

"Yes, Sir. Very well, Sir."

"How long?"

"Since 1939. We met in China."

"What is your opinion of him?"

"Finest combat Marine I've ever known."

"How was his performance during the Norway operation?"

"Outstanding."

"How, Sir?"

"Gunny Rawlins eliminated four enemy Soldiers single handedly, making it possible to set demolition and withdraw properly. He then acted as rear guard, holding back the Germans long enough to evacuate the wounded. He was personally thanked by Winston Churchill, Air Marshall Dowding and Sea Lord Mountbatten. His actions may have shortened the war and saved countless lives on both sides. Mr. Rawlins is also scheduled to meet with my father, Gen. Marshall, Admiral Nimitz and the Commandant of the Marine Corps to be debriefed."

"Is it true that your father is a Senator of the United States?"

"Yes, Sir."

"Thank you, Captain. You may step down. I would like to call Captain Robert O'Hare, United States Navy, to the stand."

Now Rawlins felt really low. He liked the old man and he had been through enough. Losing his only son at Pearl, which he never recovered from, and now the shame of his daughter's infidelity being dragged into this court room. The old man winked at Rawlins and gave him a curt smile. He was telling Rawlins that he could still take the heat. He wasn't washed up yet.

"Captain O'Hare. Please, in your own words, describe Rawlins to us."

"That's Gunnery Sgt. Rawlins, Commander. Is that understood?"

"Ah, yes, Sir. I'll ask the questions, Captain."

"Yes, Commander. I assumed that was your function while you're standing there trying to impress the Admiral."

"Captain O'Hare. Please answer the question."

"Yes, Admiral. Gunnery Sgt. Rawlins is the finest combat NCO of any service I have ever known in my career, including the Great War, and to incarcerate him over this trivial matter would definitely hurt the war effort."

"Do you know the Gunnery Sgt. personally, Captain?"

"Yes. He's my son-in-law."

"Were you at the Naval Officer's Club when the incident occurred?"

"Yes, I was."

"Any special reason."

"Yes. It was a homecoming dinner for Mr. Rawlins."

"Captain. Please tell us what happened."

"The Lieut. was at the bar drinking heavily. He then began staring at our table. Primarily at my daughter Susan and the Gunnery Sgt. I was then forced to explain the relationship between the Lieut. and Susan."

"What relationship, Captain?"

"They were having an affair."

"Was Rawlins aware of this?"

"Not until that moment."

"Then what happened?"

"He went to the bar to get a beer and the Lieut. engaged him in conversation."

"What was said?"

"The Lieut. informed the Gunny that he was all washed up and was of no use to Susan any more. He stated that he was taking care of all her needs. All of them."

"I see. And that's when Rawlins hit him?"

"Yes, that's right."

"What are your feelings about this matter, Captain?"

"I think the Lieut. is lucky to be alive in spite of his broken jaw and broken ego."

"Then you condone the Sgt's. actions?"

"I condone none of this, Commander, but I know what a jealous, distraught husband is capable of, especially if he's a Marine."

* * * * *

After a two hour deliberation the jury reached a verdict. Guilty with condition. It also recommended that Lieut. Douglass be charged with drunk and disorderly and conduct unbecoming a Naval officer.

"Lieut. Douglass and Gunnery Sgt. Rawlins approach the bench."

"Rawlins, since you're the accused I'll deal with you first. Brig time, time served. Reduction in rank to Buck Sgt., $500.00 fine. Report to Colonel Carlson's Second Raider battalion at Ocean View, California. Dismissed. Lieut. Douglass. Lucky for you we have a great need for pilots in the Pacific area. Report to San Diego Naval Air Station for deployment. Dismissed."

Chapter Four

TULAGI, GAVUTU, TANAMBOGO

While the first Marine divisions landing on Guadalcanal were unopposed, the smaller islands to the north, across Sealark Channel, were a different story. Tulagi had been the seat of British government in the Solomon Islands. A hospital, radio station and many wharves and buildings were there. This island was attacked on schedule by the First Raiders, followed by Second Battalion, Fifth Marines. Naval gunfire was delivered by destroyers USS Monssen and USS Buchanan (fire support group Mike). The initial landing was unopposed. When the Raiders reached the center ridges of the small island, they came under fire. Company C received heavy fire from hill 208 on the right flank. After an hour long fight, the enemy was destroyed with rifle fire and grenades. At the same time Edson was calling for Naval fire support against hill 281. The USS San Juan complied, delivering 280 five inch 38 caliber Naval rifle rounds on target.

* * * * *

The Raiders found a road intersecting the ridges and dug in for the night. They set up on both sides of the road and put out listening posts. This was the first time a U.S. attacking force would spend the night on a Japanese held island. In classic Japanese style, the Rikusentai Special Naval Landing Force troops (Japanese Marines) attacked the Raiders at least four times. They made penetrations in the Raider lines, only to fall back in confusion. Company C was nearly overrun, killing 26 of the enemy within 20 yards of the line. Infiltrators slipped through the line and attacked the former residence where Edson's command post was, five separate times. Each time the raids were repulsed. Two groups tried to outflank C and D companies on the beaches but were repulsed. On the morning of August 8th two companies of Second Battalion, Fifth

Marines reinforced the Raiders for the final push for this island. The Raiders laid down a 60mm mortar barrage and Second Battalion, Fifth Marines helped out with the heavy 81mm weapons. At 1500 the Raiders attacked with the help of Company G, Fifth Marines. All enemy resistance in the main ravine between the ridges was wiped out. Tulagi was secure by nightfall on August 8th.

* * * * *

Gavutu and Tanambogo are twin islands lying less than 1000 yards apart. The islands are flat with the exception of hill 148 (named for it's height) on Gavutu, and hill 121 on Tanambogo. There was a causeway between and connecting the islands that would prove useful for a night assault. TheJapanese used the harbor for a seaplane anchorage. It sould be mentioned here that these islands were invaded and secured by the First Marine Parachute Battalion, Companies A and B with C in reserve. The Raiders were still engaged with the enemy on Tulagi at this time. For historical correctness I would like to mention the fact that the First Parachute Battalion was deployed on the First Raider's flank during the battle of Bloody Ridge on Guadalcanal. The Paramarines took heavy casualties but held their end of the ridge while the Raiders were nearly overrun with much hand to hand fighting. Between Edson's First Raiders and the First Parachute Battalion, Henderson Field was saved and possibly the whole campaign. There was no surprise when the Paramarines stormed Gavutu. The Raiders had attacked Tulagi four hours before so any chance of a surprise raid was gone. Naval support fires from the San Juan consisted of 280 rounds of 8 inch Naval rifle in four minutes. Also, SBD Douglas dive bombers from the carrier USS Wasp. The Battalion landed in three waves. The first wave, Company A, got ashore with no casualties and moved inland against light resistance. Companies B and C were taken under fire from the front and flank when they came in range, being farther north than Company A. The Paramarines moved inland, still taking fire from Tanambogo. Major Robert Williams was wounded, and command was given to Major Charles A. Miller, the Executive Officer. By 1430 most of the island was taken. The Paramarines were still taking flanking fire and casualties from the neighboring island and defilalade fire from hill 148. Major Miller requested a Naval barrage of Tanambogo. The USS Buchanan and USS Monssen on station south of Gavutu fired an intense barrage with their 5 inch batteries as planes from the USS Wasp gave the island a ten minute strike, With a final sweep to clean out any enemy resistance, the Paramarines were ready to board their LCPs (Higgins boats) and storm Tanambogo.

* * * * *

TANAMBOGO

With the Raiders still cleaning out hidden enemy positions on Tulagi, the Paramarines took over the job of storming and securing Tanambogo. Six landing craft, carrying a company of Paramarines, guided by Australian Lieut. Spencer Raaf, attempted a night landing on a small pier on the northeastern tip of the island. Second Platoon ran aground on a coral reef off Gavutu and did not take part at this time. The first boat made the beach with no problem. A shell from the Naval bombardment landed in a nearby fuel dump and lit up the whole area. The Japanese opened fire with machine guns and mortars. The fire was so intense Marines and Sailors were being hit in the boats. In one boat the Navy crew suffered one hundred percent casualties. The Marines had to take over their duties. The machine gun platoon managed to set up two of their weapons on the pier and return fire. Because of their exposed position and the firelight they received a large volume of fire and were forced to withdraw. About 35 men made it to shore. There was so much resistance and so many wounded that they withdrew with the wounded and all but twelve of the Paramarines. The boats with the wounded went directly to the ships for evacuation. The other boats went to Gavutu. Two of the men left behind made it to Gavutu in a rowboat. Lieut. John Smith made it over the causeway with the rest of the survivors and back to Gavutu about midnight. At 2200, after being briefed on the situation, General Vandergrift and Admiral Turner decided to commit the First Division Reserves, Second and Third Battalions. Second Marines would disembark from Guadalcanal and join the action on Tanambogo.

The Third Battalion, under Lt. Col. R.G. Hunt, landed in three waves at ten minute intervals on Gavutu. These men would help clean up infiltrators that had swum to Gavutu from Tanambogo the night before. Then they would storm Tanambogo and destroy the enemy. This time there would be a ten minute interval bombardment by USS Buchanan and a machine gun platoon would support from Gavutu. There would also be two tanks from the Second Marines helping out. When the Naval barrage was lifted, the assault Company with the tanks went in. Lieut. Sweeney was killed while observing from one of them. The Japanese stopped the other tank with an iron bar jammed in the tread and set it on fire. Later, 42 Japanese bodies were found around the tank.

Company A landed and separated into two groups. One group moved on the southern slope of the hill; the other, moving inland, worked against the eastern slope. There, advances were met with heavy resistance from caves in the coral. Fire was also coming from Gaomi Island, a few hundred yards to the east. The USS Gridley laid concentrated fire on the island, ending the problem.

A supporting attack was launched across the causeway by First Platoon, Company K. These men secured the causeway and dug in for the night at the Tanambogo end. Through the night there were many small fights all over the island. Small groups and individuals attacked the Marines all night and into the next day. The Marines held their ground and by that evening the island was secure.

* * * * *

BUTARITARI ISLAND MAKIN ATOLL

Ten days after the First Marine Division landed on Guadalcanal and Edson's Raiders cleared Tulagi, Carlson's Raiders (Second Battalion) landed on Butaritari Island Makin Atoll. Two hundred twenty one Raiders journeyed from Pearl Harbor to Makin Atoll in eight days. The mine layer class submarines Nautilus and Argonaut transported the men. When the island was reached the

Raiders boarded rubber boats with outboard motors. Many of these refused to start. They had become wet due to high seas. The men were forced to paddle, many with rifle butts.

Just after reaching shore the Raiders engaged the Japanese garrison. A fierce firefight broke out between the Rikusentai troops (Japanese Special Naval Landing Force Troops "Marines") and Companies A and B, Second Battalion. The Raiders were outnumbered at least two to one. Because of their superior training and weapons, they refused to yield and unknowingly killed almost all the Japanese combat affectives on the island. The Japanese were now strafing and bombing the island and attempting to land reinforcements by flying boat and landing barge from nearby islands. Two Kawanishi flying boats were shot down by Raiders with a boy's anti-tank shoulder fired 50 cal. rifle and 30 cal. rifle and machine gun fire. The landing barges were destroyed by deck guns on the submarines assigned to the Raiders. The weather continued to deteriorate and the problems began. Radio communications were out and Lt. Col. Carlson could not raise the submarines to evac the men. The Lt. Col. with the Exec. Officer, Maj. James Roosevelt, in agreement, ordered the men to withdraw and try to get to the subs. Again they were plagued with a high surf overturning their boats, losing their equipment, and outboard motors that refused to run. A company sized group of men remained on the island, exhausted and many without weapons or equipment. To make matters worse the Japanese were still strafing by air and a patrol attacked the remaining men, wounding a sentry. Carlson believed he was facing a reinforced Japanese force, had no communications, didn't know if the submarines had left or were destroyed in the air attacks. Instead of facing annihilation he decided to surrender. The battalion Operations Officer delivered a note of surrender to a Japanese Soldier to give to his commander. Luckily for the Raiders the Soldier was killed before he could deliver the note.

At dawn of the second day things began to improve. Some of the men made it to the sub. Carlson made contact with the sub, using an electric torch and Morse Code. They arranged a pickup at the island's lagoon where there was quiet water. Eighteen Raiders were killed on Makin Atoll and nine captured. The captured men were taken to Kwajalein Island by the Japanese and beheaded. The reason for this raid was to relieve some of the pressure on Guadalcanal. It was hoped by Admiral Nimitze's staff that some of the replacements pouring into Guadalcanal would be re-routed to the Gilbert Island group. Also, after the losses at the battle of Midway in June it was felt that America needed a victory against the Japanese. The Raiders gave their country that victory.

Chapter Five

PEARL HARBOUR

The Second Platoon of Alfa Company, Second Raiders Battalion left the submarine wharf in Pearl Harbour by Army 6by6 truck and was taken to Fifth Marine Regiments Headquarters Company. There they took hot showers, were issued new uniforms and cleaned and stowed their gear. Next they were debriefed on the Toulabong raid, and each man received liberty in Honolulu.

It was May 1943. Sgt. Rawlins sat at the bar of the Aloha Hotel overlooking Pearl Harbour. He was shocked at the amount of wreckage still in the harbour. He had served on some of those ships lying half sunk or rolled over in the channel. They resembled great whales sunning themselves in the shallows of some huge reef like he had seen them do in Australia. He remembered all the Sailors and Marines entombed in those ships for eternity. Then he thought of his own life. He wondered how long it would last. Now that Susan was gone all he had was the war. Better to die in combat than to live alone for the next twenty or thirty years. He hoped the war would last long enough for that to happen. As the Johnny Walker burned his throat Susan's memory burned in his mind. He remembered her saying on their wedding night that she could never leave him no matter what happened. She just loved him so much. Yeah. Until the big, suave, jet set, tennis boy, Navy officer with his gold wings and white ducs entered the picture. He had heard that gold wings will get you in bed anywhere in the world.

Must be true, he thought. And the way she had disgraced her father in front of the Navy Officer Corps. How cruel. After losing his only son who now lies in the bottom on the Arizona, she tortured the old Captain further with her selfish indiscretions.

Ironic, thought the Sgt. *The Captains two sons killed in the same war, now entombed in the same place, one thinking of the other, and the other not thinking at all. What remains is the daughter, thinking only of herself. The war has not affected her. It has only served to entertain her with its lavish parties in Washington, tennis and swimming at the Navy Officer's Club, and cocktails at seven at the Admiral's Inn, by the Capitol Building. The people fighting the war were eating dog food out of cans, or whatever they could find, or each other. No, the war hadn't affected Susan yet. Not yet.*

"Hi, Sgt., a penny for your thoughts."

Rawlins looked to the corner of the bar where an attractive blonde woman of about thirty five sat smiling at him.

"Mind if I join you?"

"No. Not at all. But I may prove to be lousy company."

"We'll see," said the blonde. "Buy me a drink?"

"Yeah, why not. Barkeep, another Scotch and whatever the lady wants."

"Okay, Mac, that's three bucks."

"Kinda steep, ain't it?"

"You don't like it, there's the door."

"What's on your mind, Sgt.?"

"Oh, the war, you know. By the way, the name is Ken."

"I'm Joan. You married, Ken?"

"Not any more."

"Get the 'dear John'?"

"Yeah, something like that. How about you, Joan?"

"My old man got killed on Guadalcanal during some river battle or something."

"What outfit?"

"First Division, Fifth Marines."

"Must a been the Tenaru."

"Yeah, that's it. Were you there, Ken?"

"Yeah."

"Same outfit?"

"No. Second Raiders."

"Oh, yes. The Makin Island Raiders."

"Yeah, that's right."

"That was bad, wasn't it?"

"Not as bad as the Canal. We lost a lotta good men there. Sorry about your old man."

"We weren't that close. Just lonely, that's all."

"Yeah, I know how that can be."

"The drinks are a lot cheaper at my place if you're interested."

"Let's go."

After too many drinks and too much conversation they went to bed. Unfortunately, the artillery just wouldn't muster. Susan kept interrupting and he couldn't shut her out.

"What's wrong, Ken" Don't you like me?"

"I like you just fine. It's just ..."

"It's your wife, isn't it?"

"I told you I'm divorced."

"She may be out of your bed but she's still in your head. You better go now. Look me up when you're feeling better."

Rawlins felt like hell. This wasn't supposed to happen to Marines. Susan was still taunting him, dominating his every move and thought even though she was thousands of miles away.

* * * * *

Samson's Post Bar was named after Senior Chief Petty Officer John Samson, U.S. Navy Retired, the owner. Ironically, the same name of the lash down device attached to docks or piers to moor ships in safe harbour (Samson Post).

Samsons was situated near Pier 32 on Harbour Street. A favorite hangout for Sailors, Marines and whores. The drinks were cheap and so were the women. Rawlins squad spent most of their off-duty time there. Ramirez and Russo were sitting at a small table with some Fifth Regiment Marines.

"We heard you guys really kicked ass on Toulabong."

"We were lucky. There were more Japs than were reported. Somebody screwed up. It's a good thing they were amateurs. Probably 18th Division replacements from Rabaul, re-routed from the Canal. If they'd been Rikusentai it might have come out different."

"You think they're as good as us?"

"Better. They don't surrender. They fight to the death, they kill their own wounded, so they won't waste C-rats or water on 'um.

They don't take prisoners, and they're damned good shots. We ran into some on Makin Island and had a tough time with 'um. Let's face it. Marines are Marines even if they are Japs."

The bar was small and decorated like most bars near military installations at the time. Japanese battle flags adorned the walls, along with Samurai swords, Japanese helmets, even some Japanese pictures. All donated by the local Marines, trophies of battles already fought.

The Joker sat at the bar, drunk as a lord.

"Barkeep. Gimme a shot and a beer."

"You had enough. The Shore Patrol's gonna pick you up."

"Yeah, and my mother-in-law's gonna pick you up. If you weren't so ugly that is."

"The other patrons were becoming aggravated with Joker's mouth and began to speak up.

"Stow it, Jarhead. We don't wanna hear it."

"Yeah. Kiss my ass, deckape."

"We better get Joker outta her, Ramirez, before the Shore Patrol shows up."

"Too late. The Joker just punched out the Sailor with the big mouth."

As usual on liberty weekends the bar exploded into a giant free for all. The Harbour brig was full to capacity with drunk, beat up Sailors and Marines. Colonel Carlson was called to retrieve his Raiders. They were escorted out to the parking lot by the Shore Patrol where they were turned over to the custody of the Colonel pending further action.

"Stand at attention until your name is called, then board the truck and keep quiet."

Dumb ass Joker. Another liberty shot to hell. Probably a fine too, thought Ramirez. *What a pain in the ass he is. He can't even decide who the enemy is. The Japs or the Navy.*

* * * * *

Reveille at 0500 hours, punishment tour, 20 mile hike with full field gear and rifle. Form up on parade ground in five minutes.

"Attention on deck. For last night's disruption and destruction of civilian property, each man will be fined twenty dollars and receive punishment tour as described by the Commanding Officer. Form a column of twos, right face, forward, march."

The battered and bruised Second Platoon marched off into the hills of Honolulu, overlooking the town and harbour. Platoon Gunnery Sgt. Parker called off cedance,

"Yer left, yer left, yer left right left."

Buck Sgt. Rawlins began to sing in his well practiced gravelly drill instructor voice.

"Yer Momma don't want ya no more."

and the men answered,

"Yer right."

And so it went, as marching songs always have.

"Yer baby don't know ya no more."

"Yer right."

"Joby's at the front door."

"Yer right."

"Sound off."

"One, two."

"Sound off."

"Three , four."

"Sound off."

"One, two, three, four, one, two, three, four."

SECOND VERSE

"The Marine Corps gave you a home."

"Yer right."

"So you're never really alone."

"Yer right."

"Sound off."

"One, two."

"Sound off."

"Three four."

"Everyone knows your name."

"Yer right."

"But it's still all the same."

"Yer right."
"Sound off."
"One, two."
"Sound off."
"Three Four."
"The Japs are waitin' for you."
"Yer right."
"They wanna see what you can do."
"Yer right."
"Sound off."
"One, two."
"Sound off."
"Three, Four."
"Sound off."
"One, two, three, four, one, two, three, four."
Finally they reached the half point.

"Column of march, halt. Left face, ten, hut. This is your bivouac area. We will spend the night here. And remember this is a war zone. Anyone caught sneaking off can be shot for desertion. Fall out."

The Captain hoped his scare tactic would curb any mischief his boys might want to get into. The Raiders put their shelter halves together and made two man pup tents. Then they were allowed to have a fire, and the Captain mysteriously found four cases of G.I. 3.2 beer and two cases of coke buried in the ground, packed in ice. On top of these were four crates of steaks marked: HANDS OFF - U.S. Navy Officers only. There was an old, green tarp covering the feast and dirt was shoveled over it. Captain Roosevelt called a "gung ho" meeting, which had become tradition to the Second Raiders.

"Men. Washington has been talking about us. They are impressed with our performance and are forming two more Raider Battalions like ours. Even the Japanese have shown respect by calling us "jungle devils" that can appear and disappear at will. They say we fight like Samurai, which is a big compliment from a Jap."

"When we goin' back in, Captain? We didn't sign on to march around this cemetery our whole tour."

"Don't worry, Smitty, I know you're bored. We ship out in

two days. You'll get the details on board ship. And this time it will be an extended operation. I can tell you that much. On a happier note, the President sent me this letter to read to you men.

Dear Second Raiders;

I want you to know that we are aware of the outstanding job you have been doing out there in the Solomons. Your contributions to the war effort are well noted. The sacrifices all of you men have made for your country and humanity will never be forgotten., I assure you. Every one of you is a fine American and we and your friends and families are very proud of you. Because of you Raiders, and other Marines like you, the Marines are sure to survive for a thousand years. Please accept this small token of our appreciation.

Franklin Roosevelt, Commander in Chief.

"Whats he mean, Captain?"
"I need two men with E tools and I'll show you."
The two men uncovered the pit, and dragged away the tarp, and a rousing cheer went up when they discovered the contents. The whole platoom built a bon fire, barbecued steaks, drank beer and coke and had a great time. At the insistence of the men the officers even joined in. After all, that's what "gung ho" (work together), the Raider battle cry, is all about.

* * * * *

The march back to Fifth Regiment Headquarters Company was uneventful. The men enjoyed the rain-free, somewhat cool weather for the tropics. Seventy eight degrees with a slight breeze. Perfect for marching. When they reached the company parade ground, they were instructed to stack arms and drop packs, then proceed to the company mess for briefing. Once inside the platoon was given instructions for its next mission.

"Gentlemen. Your target is Ruwawa. We have information from Australian coast watchers and local natives that the enemy is massing troops and supplies and building an air strip in the center of the island. The island is approximately sixty square miles in diameter. There are two major rivers and most of the troops and supplies are billeted between them. Now I would like to introduce Australian Captain Sir Howard Lansby, Australian Royal Forces. He will be your guide on this mission and I want him returned the same way he's going. All in one piece. Captain, take over."

"Right then. Men of the Second Raiders. My country sends best wishes and well done for the Makin Island and Toulabong raids. Outstanding. I have spent the last two months with a Coast Watcher on Ruwawa and I can tell you the Nips are up to something big. Our greatest fear is an invasion of Australia or a very large suicide attack on Guadalcanal. What we propose to do is a reconnaissance in force and interdiction and harassment as long as possible. We want to keep them busy until we can free up enough troops for a full scale invasion."

"Thank you, Captain. The platoon will split into two groups. First and Second Squad will be Team Alfa, Third Squad will be reinforced by a Squad from Third Platoon. They will be Team Baker. You will disembark from Guadalcanal by P.T. boat at dusk, travel the fifty two miles to Ruwawa, then proceed up the Ibu and Zimbu Rivers under cover of darkness. You will leave the boats before light so they will have time to exfill to the open sea before dawn. At the same time a company of Paramarines from the First Parachute Regiment will be jumping on the southe side of the airfield. That will be their objective. After scouting your area of insurgence, you will link up with the Paras and continue operations with them. Your call signs will be Alfa One and Baker Two respectively. The Paras will be Echo One. Exfiltration will be by a combination of A.P.D. destroyer, P.T. boat and submarine. We expect the pickup to be hot. That's why all the fire power. We will try to arrange air support from the fleet and maybe a destroyer or two for fire support but we can't promise. Stay in as long as possible. If you need supplies we'll bring them in by sub or air drop them. If you have wounded we'll get them out by sub or P.T. Now I would like to introduce our newest asset, Lieutenant William Matsumo, First Lieut., 442 Combat Infantry Team, U.S. Army. Don't be so shocked. He's an American just like us. Born in San Francisco, he spent the last three months fighting the

Germans in Italy and won the Silver Star for valor above and beyond. The Lieut. volunteered for this mission because he knows the language and the culture of the enemy. He feels that because of his knowledge and abiltiy, casualties may be reduced. We concur. Any questions. Corp. Hays."

"Colonel, Sir. How do we know the Lieut. will fight?"

"May I answer the Corp.'s question, Colonel?"

"Yes, of course, Lieut."

"I know I'm a Soldier and not a Marine, Corp., but my combat record will speak for itself."

"With all respect, Lieut., we ain't fightin' Krauts right now. And you look just like the enemy we got here."

"Corp. Hays. Shut your mouth. You're one step from the brig and bread and water, Mister."

"Colonel, please allow me to answer the Corp. I was prepared for this."

"Go ahead, Lieut."

"Corp. Hays and the rest of you men. I understand your animosity toward me. I'm pissed off too and so is my family. We are totally disgraced by the actions of the old regime of Japan. We all pray for the day our United States takes Japan from the warlords and forms a democracy. Oh, one other thing. If you men are captured you will be taken to Cabanatuan Prison on Leyte Island in the Philippines. If I'm captured I'll be beheaded on the spot for being a traitor to the Empire."

"Sorry, Lieut. Welcome aboard."

"Gung Ho, Corp."

* * * * *

The transport to Guadalcanal by LST (Landing Ship Tank) was uneventful, except for a possible I-boat (Japanese submarine) sighting. The two destroyer escorts protecting the small convoy began echo ranging and presumably chased off a sub.

When Guadalcanal came into view Sgt. Rawlins was sitting in the starboard anti-aircraft gun cupola sunning himself. When he saw the long white sand beach and palm trees he felt sick. What looked like a picture postcard of some South Pacific Paradise to the average person, looked like the island of death to him. The other Raiders were looking too from any vantage point they could find on the superstructure of the oddly shaped ship.

"So that's the Canal," said one of the new men.

Ramirez answered.

"You're lucky you missed it. Bad ass place. Half of Edson's Raiders and half the First Parachute Battalion got greased just off that beach on the other side of the airfield. Bloody Ridge they called it. I hear there's still Japs hidden in the jungle that refuse to give up."

"I heard that too."

"They steal food sometimes or try to blow up a plane or snipe at a work party. The Army even tried taking Jap prisoners around the island, talking through megaphones, trying to get them to surrender with no luck."

* * * * *

The LST beached itself on what had been Red Beach during the invasion the year before. The two personnel bow ramps descended to the beach and the huge bow doors opened with the tank rated bow ramp dropping to the beach. The Raiders and their equipment, along with some equipment for the Navy Seabees maintaining Henderson Field, disgorged from the amphibious ship. They were glad to feel land under their feet after the eight days at sea their voyage from Pearl Harbour had taken.

"Second Platoon Second Raiders form up here."

The Raiders did so and were told that this was their bivouac area. An Army Major told the Marines not to leave their area and to post guards. There were still Jap infiltrators around.

"Hey, Sarge. I thought this island was secure."

"It is."

"I thought you guys wiped out the Japs a year ago."

"We did."

"That ain't what that Major just said."

"The Major said 'infiltrators.'"

"Yeah. So."

"Our Japs are dead. These guys gotta be new Japs coming in by submarine at night."

The Raiders spent a nervous night under the palm trees between the Tenaru and Matanakau Rivers; the place where so many brave Marines had died the year before, taking this miserable island with its airfield from the Japanese. The same enemies who were now threatening Australia.

In the morning after PT and chow, some of the men went on a sight seeing tour. They visited the Tenaru River battle site first. Looking for some souvenirs, they found a rusty 45 pistol half buried in the bottom of an old fox hole. They also found broken bayonets, knives, ammo belts, human bones, grenades and mortar rounds that had failed to explode. The junk of war.

Next was Edson's Bloody Ridge. More of the same. Hundreds of spent rifle cartridges, pieces of shrapnel from artillery rounds, and two Japanese Soldiers who had been left unburied. The Raiders buried them and kept their papers and ID for the Red Cross.

Last stop was the cemetery. Some men looked for friends left behind; others just stared in awe at all the white crosses and Stars of David. One man whispered:

"Well, at least it's over for them. No more suffering."

Back at the bivouac area they were told to make ready for departure. They would be leaving tonight.

* * * * *

The strike force boarded PT (pursuit torpedo) boats off the long pier the Seabees had built to accommodate supply ships. Three boats, two to ferry the Raiders and one for fire support in case they were spotted by the enemy and had to fight. The PT Sailors were a motley crew compared to the clean cut, highly disciplined Marines. They had long hair and beards; most wore only shorts and sandals. Even the officers had beards and went shirtless.

"Hey, Sarge, how do they get away with that?"

"They ain't Marines. And so many of 'um got killed that they tend to leave them alone. When one of these plywood boats gets hit, they go up like a bomb. Plywood and aviation gas make a hell of a fire. If they manage to abandon the Japs machine gun the survivors. What the Japs miss the sharks get when they smell blood."

* * * * *

The throbbing cadence of the twelve cylinder Chrysler engines relaxes the Sgt. The Marines above and below deck take this time to write a last letter home, clean weapons, or just relax. Sgt. Rawlins, nearly asleep, is jolted awake by the sound of Susan's voice!

"Ken I will always love you no matter what happens."

Son of a bitch. Here we go again. Another peaceful day ruined. I wonder if Mister Romance, the Navy slob, is in the area. I'll have to look him up when this op is over.

* * * * *

The Sgt. noticed that the three V12 Chrysler engines were reduced to an idle. He climbed the ladder to the bridge to see what was happening.

"Request permission to enter the bridge."

"Permission granted."

"What's up, Lieut.?"

"Target dead ahead. The Ibu River."

Rawlins could see the river mouth in the moonlight. He noticed the other boat headed up the coast to find the Zimbu River. The third boat lay dead in the water one hundred yards behind them, standing in reserve. The engine noise at 700 turns per minute (idle) was barely discernible. The Sailors manned the boat's guns and the Marines were at the ready with their small arms. The river ran through a mangrove swamp and triple canopy jungle. The boat's Skipper, Lieut. Jenkins, was nervous. He preferred the open sea if he had to fight. This was a great place for an ambush. No room to maneuver, their only defense from incoming fire in these plywood coffins.

"Sgt., where do we drop you off?"

"At the edge of the swamp where the kuni grass starts."

"Roger."

Ancient banyan trees and huge cedars stood like sentinels on the river banks protecting the land beyond from intruders from the sea. Jungle birds screamed and hundreds of tropical bats dipped and dove above the river and through the trees, sometimes colliding with an unseen Sailor or Marine.

"This place is giving me the creeps, Sgt."

"Relax, Skipper. Those feeding bats and jungle birds raising hell are a good sign. That means there's no Japs in the area waiting to ambush us."

"There's your grass, Sgt."

"Aye, Sir. That's the spot."

Jenkins slid the bow of the boat up to the grass covered river bank and called for all stop through the com tube. The Raiders jumped off the deck into the grass and set up a defensive perimeter. After unloading their equipment the Raiders bid farewell to the PT crew. The Skipper of the boat reversed engines and backed into the river's main stream. He now idled the craft back the way they had come just fast enough to maintain steerage. Sparks, the radio man, climbed the ladder to the bridge and informed Jenkins that the other boat was in trouble. They had run aground on a sand bar, unseen by the Aussie Coast Watchers during their previous recon of the area. Probably due to the tide which controlled the rivers depth. Boat 94s Skipper was asking for a tow or they would have to abandon before dawn.

"Tell 94 to hold on. We're on the way."

* * * * *

When Jenkins boat arrived at the 94 boats location she was fast amidships on her port chine on a sand bar. Marines were deployed on both river banks for security. Her Skipper, J.G.LT. James Stewart, Mobile, Alabama grandson of Confederate blockade runner Captain Andrew Jackson Stewart, C.S.N., was in the water, 45 pistol in hand, surveying his predicament. Four of his crew were with him. Jenkins leaned over the gunwale of his boat for a conference with Stewart.

"Listen, Stew. If we lash a block and tackle to that banyan

tree on your starboard beam, lash that to your forward 50 cal. mount and stern 20mm mount with a double pulley, one line fast on the tackle block and one line fast on my bow Sampson, it should work. When I full reverse you forward with your starboard engine and reverse with your port. With the opposing force it should wrench the boat free. If not we'll have to scuttle and burn her. That will alert every Jap on the island. Hopefully, they will think we came in here to make repairs. We'll spray it with the twin fifties to simulate battle damage. And to destroy it."

It was just breaking light when all was ready. Lieut. Jenkins gave the signal to commence and amid a great shower of mud and spray the 94 boat was pulled free. The mighty Confederate's grandson was saved the shame of losing his first command and the Raiders continued on their mission undetected.

Chapter Six

RUWAWA

"**Joker. Take point,** steer clear of the airfield and head for the jungle at the end of this kunai field. When you get there, hold up. We'll assemble on your position. Don't engage. If you have to try to do it quiet and hide the body. Remember there is at least a full division of Nips on this island and we're not ready for 'um yet. Johnson."

"Yeah, Sarge."

"Gimme the radio. Alfa One calling Baker Two. Come in, Baker Two."

"Yeah, Sarge. Go ahead."

"Proceed with infill Plan A - assemble and join up with us at map reference Delta Tango Two Niner. Got that?"

"Got it, Sarge. Delta Tango Two Niner."

"And don't engage. Got that?"

"Got it, Sarge. Don't engage."

"Alfa One out. Joker, shove off. We'll see you in the jungle."

* * * * *

Back at Guadalcanal Colonel Carlson was briefing Major Hinsdale, First Parachute Regiment, on their part of the operation. They were camped on the edge of Henderson Field five hundred yards from where they and the First Raider Battalion, better known as Edson's Raiders, had fought the battle of Bloody Ridge. That battle, which had taken place just a year before, was to hold this ridge. Japanese General Kuribyoshi committed fifteen thousand crack infantry troops from the elite Sendie Division, reinforced by Rikusentai Special Naval Landing Force troops. That battle was one of the bloodiest of the Pacific War.

"Your mission, gentlemen, is to jump into this flat area

behind these ridges, below this jungle area. The Raiders will have a secure landing zone ready for you."

"What if the L.Z. is hot, Colonel," asked a young lieutenant.

"In that case you will abort. If the Raiders aren't there or you take fire your mission is compromised. There would be no point in risking your lives any further."

* * * * *

Corp. Hays ducked a Jap patrol at the edge of the rain forest by hiding in the grass. He then regressed to report to Rawlins.

"Sarge, there's a Jap patrol up ahead and they're big and their uniforms look different."

"Probably those Manchurian conscripts we heard about or maybe Special Commando Force troops."

"I don't know but they're big for Japs and they had what looked like a German with 'um."

"You sure it wasn't a Dutch or Aussie prisoner?"

"No, Sarge. This guy had weapons. Some kinda sub gun and a pistol. And he was wearing a khaki tropical uniform like the Krauts in Africa that we saw in the news reels. Remember?"

"Yeah, I remember. Captain, you know anything about this?"

"There have been reports of German speaking people seen with the Japs but we dismissed these as Dutch farmers working with the Japs to keep their families alive. But there was no mention of uniforms or weapons."

"Echo One calling Baker Two."

"Go ahead, Sarge."

"Be advised that there may be Jap Commandos with a German advisor in your A.O."

"OK, Sarge. We'll be careful. Baker Two out."

Ramirez sounded the same no matter what the situation. Confident almost to the point of boredom. Always reliable.

"Captain. Would you like to have a talk with this resident Nazi?"

"Why yes, Sgt. That would be simply grand."

"Lieut."

"Yes, Sgt."

"Let's get the big advisor and one of the Japanese if we can take one alive."

"No problem, Sir. That's our specialty."

"Corp. How many?"

"Looked like six and the Kraut, Sir."

"Short for an infantry squad. Might be Special Commando or Rikusentai. Good work, Hays."

"Thank you, Sir."

* * * * *

The Sgt.'s squad waited until dark before hitting the Japanese patrol. The squad encircled the Jap night outpost silently and commenced the attack. Rawlins eliminated one sentry by placing two 22 cal. rounds behind the enemy soldier's right ear at 1100fps, destroying his medulla, killing him instantly. The Suppressed Colt Woodsman 22 pistol given to him by the Office of Strategic Service (OSS) which he had served so well in Europe, claimed another Jap with a slug through the left eye as he approached the sentry position to relieve his comrade. The other Japs were either clubbed or bayoneted with the exception of a Jap officer and the German. They were gagged and bound and taken to the rendezvous point for interrogation. Ramirez looked at the prisoners and spoke to Rawlins.

"That the Kraut you spotted?"

"Yeah, that's him. Looks like an officer. That white piping on his collar means Warmackt Infantry Lieutenant, I think. And the Jap is an officer too. Let's find out. Hays, form perimeter security while we interrogate the prisoners. Herr Hauptman, vass ist die nama, vass ist die regament? Sprecken die Englase? Du sprecken Dutchen sere gut Feldwebel. But my English is better I'm sure."

"You may address me as Herr Lietnen of Infantry. I am not a Captain. My unit is the 356 Warmackt Regiment of the Imperial German Army. And that is all I am required to tell you by the rules of the Geneva Convention."

"We'll see about that, Herr Lietnen. Lieut., can you talk to the other prisoner and see what you can find out about his unit?"

"With pleasure, Sgt."

There was a storm of Japanese oaths and curses from the Jap Sub-lieutenent who lay bleeding on the ground near death.

"Lieut., what happened?"

"I untied his hands and gave him a D ration bar and some water. He said he hadn't eaten in two days and he would talk if I fed him. He had a knife inside his pants and tried to stab me. I got him with my bayonet instead."

"Doc. See what you can do for him."

"He's dead, Sarge."

"Bury him and bring his papers. You're in charge of the Kraut. If he tries to escape, kill him but keep it quiet. Use your Ka-Bar or a rock."

"Okay, Sarge."

"Johnson, help him out."

"Right, Sarge."

Non-typical orders for a Navy Pharmacist Mate (doc) but he was a Raider. Navy or Marine all the same (the Marines loved their Navy Corpsmen (docs) and still do to this day). The German Lieut. had a look of disdain on his face after hearing this order concerning his mortality and that's what the Sgt. was hoping for.

* * * * *

"Russo, take point, head due south and get us out of this jungle. When you reach the hills hold up and stay out of sight."

"Got it, Sarge."

"Move out."

* * * * *

Ruwawa looked big on the topo map the Paramarines studied before boarding the C47 Dakota transports that had been waiting for them at Henderson Field. Four U.S. Army Lockheed P38 Fighter Interceptors stood at the ready for escort duty. This same squadron would later shoot down and kill Admiral Yamamoto, Chief of Naval Operations, South Pacific. They had received intelligence that the

Admiral's private Betty Bomber would be flying to Truk Lagoon from Rabaul, New Georgia for an inspection of the large Naval base located there. During that same time period the JN 25 Japanese Naval Code was broken. In 1942 the New Zealand destroyer, Kiwi, rammed a Japanese submarine and recovered its cipher machine and code books. The Japanese High Command thought the I-boat was lost with all hands due to lack of radio contact and failure to return to port. This huge stroke of luck may have shortened the war by as much as two years.

Ironically, in June 1944 a battle in the South Atlantic between a U.S. Navy submarine hunter, killer group, and a German Unterwasser Boot (submarine) netted the same results when the U-boat surrendered and a U.S. Navy boarding party disarmed the scuttling charges found in the sub after the crew was removed. The boat's Enigma Machine and code books were saved and given to the U.S. Navy's most trusted ally, British Intelligence (M15). The code was broken and the secret kept, even from the Abvere (German Intelligence) until the end of the war. Admirial Doenitz, Kreigsmarine Unterwasser Boot Fuhrer was mystified at the horrendous losses his U-boat fleet was suffering. The Allies now knew every move the boats would make ahead of time. In 1944-45 one in three U-boats and their crews would not return from patrol. By wars end thirty five thousand U-booten Kreigsmarinen were killed.

* * * * *

The platoon strength force broke into a clearing at the edge of the jungle and stopped, taking up defensive positions. Soon Russo made his presence known.

"Russo, comin' in."

The Corporal stood up not twenty feet from the C.P., covered in grass and jungle vines.

"You look like something outta Flash Gordon."

"Yeah, Joker, and you're as ugly as ever too. Maybe you'll scare the Japs to death so we won't have to waste ammo on 'um."

"All right. Stow the crap and listen up. We gotta break through these hills when it gets dark and form an L.Z. for the

Paramarines we're gonna link up with. We gotta be quiet so tie down your equipment and either fill or empty your canteens. Check weapons and break out a C rat. We shove off in twenty. And remember there's patrols out by now looking for us after their buddies didn't come back. So be quiet.

* * * * *

The Paramarines were doing their final equipment check and beginning to board their transports. All were quiet and serious, knowing very well that this might be their first and last combat jump. If they ran into Jap Zeros (Mitsubishi Zero Pursuit, Attack Unit) their only hope of survival would be the P38s. Even escaping a shot up, burning transport didn't always guarantee survival. The Jap pilots had a nasty habit of machine gunning anyone in a parachute. Each Paramarine carried an M1 rifle, Thompson submachine gun or M1 carbine. Also a 45 cal. pistol, two knives, 782 gear, extra 30 cal. bandoleer or machine gun belt, 180 rounds of personal weapon ammo, one 60mm mortar round. In addition to his personal effects, two full canteens, rations, med kit, hidden weapon, reserve chute. Average weight - 150 pounds. Needless to say, exiting a burning, sinking aircraft full of men and equipment, carrying this kind of load, would be quite a feat.

* * * * *

The Sgt. waited for full dark to envelop their position before giving the order to shove off. Luckily, it was a dark, rainy night and there was plenty of cover if needed. Ramirez was at point, Thompson sub gun at the ready. The area was covered with low hills, kunai grass, and small stands of cedar and banyan trees. The elevation steadily increased as the Raiders marched. At 1400 hours they arrived at the edge of a long, flat plain covered with grass and a few trees. A small creek flowed along its edge where the hills ended and the land flattened out. A perfect place to set up a defensive position, in depth if need be. The Aussie Captain and his Coast Watchers found an ideal location for the Paramarine drop zone.

"Russo, drop off here with the first squad and dig in. Place the M.G. Team on that rise and make that the center of your line."

"Aye, Sarge."

"Joker, take second squad across the field and dig in. Set the B.A.R. Team in your center."

"Aye, Sarge."

"Eyes, take your team and the grenadier to that small group of trees 200 yards down the field. If you see infiltrators, take out as many as you can before being overrun. When they get close lay down a grenade barrage and fall back to this position. Third squad. Captain Lansby and Lieut. Matsumo will act as a roving force and cover your flanks if necessary. That is, if the Captain and Lieut. agree."

"Jolly good, Sgt. After all, you are in charge. We'll give the bloody sots a good thrashing if they show up in our LZ, won't we, Lieut.? Tally ho, Captain."

This brought a laugh from the surrounding men. Good natured officers the men could talk and laugh with was a much admired tradition of the Marine Raiders.

* * * * *

"Stand up and hook up."

The Jumpmaster gave the order when the red light, mounted on the forward bulkhead of the passenger-cargo hold of the C47 Dakota, came on. As the plane passed over the end of the island from seaward, he spotted the four strobe lights, one on each corner of the LZ.

"Check the man's chute and dragline standing in front of you."

The first man in line, a very pale looking Corp., the Jumpmaster told to stand in the door. The paleness was either from nerves, since this was his first combat jump, or malaria, which almost every Marine in the South Pacific suffered from at some time in his tour of duty.

As the nose of the plane edged over the LZ approach the pilot switched on the green light.

"Go, go, go, yelled the Jumpmaster."

One after another they tumbled out the door into the black silence two thousand feet above the island. It was almost peaceful as the Paramarines drifted to the surface of the enemy held island. They knew many of their number would never leave this mysterious place.

Captain Joe Krenshaw, First Paramarine Regiment, First Battalion, from Kansas City, Missouri hit the ground and rolled, bending his knees as he was trained to do to lessen the shock of impact. He rolled up his chute and buried it with his E-tool while his men gathered around him and did the same.

* * * * *

"Any casualties, Gunny?"

"One, Sir. Pvt. Jarvis. Got hung in a tree and broke his neck."

"How bad?"

"He's dead, Sir."

"Damn, Take his personal effects and weapons and bury him. Make sure you mark it on the map for Graves Registration."

"Aye, Sir."

"Captain, this is Sgt. Rawlins, Second Raiders. He's the ranking NCO of the Raiders contingent."

The Captain stepped up and shook Rawlin's hand.

"Gunnery Sgt. Thanks for keeping the LZ open for us."

"Our pleasure, Sir. We appreciate the help. And it's Buck Sgt., Sir."

"Your Colonel informed our Major and myself about your episode with a Junior Officer overstepping his position and making a grand ass of himself. Lucky for us your misfortune placed you right in our laps. Lucky for you, you didn't kill him like your reputation would indicate. After considerable debate we came to the conclusion that you rate a battlefield promotion to the rank and pay grade of Gunnery Sgt. Congratulations, Rawlins. You deserve it."

"Thank you, Sir. And please thank the Colonel when you see him."

"I'll do that, Gunnery Sgt. With pleasure. Now let's set up our C.P. in the middle of this field."

"Aye, Sir."

Raiders and Paramarines worked together in the spirit of Gung Ho, digging slit trenches, two man foxholes, machine gun and 60mm mortar emplacements and a well dug in command post. As it was breaking light the officers and ranking NCOs began to plan the operation in detail. The riflemen finished their dugouts and defensive positions and cleaned their weapons. They expected to be attacked at any time. The enemy had to know they were here by this time.

* * * * *

"Gunnery Sgt. Rawlins. Since Gunny Parker is in sick bay with malaria and Lieut. Pruit is still recovering from wounds, you will assume command of the entire Raider detachment."

"Aye, Sir."

"You will split your men into two mutually supporting forces, head north, recon the airfield, and try to get an accurate count of forces in that area. After this is accomplished, raise hell with every enemy unit you encounter as long as it's not too big to handle with your small force."

"Aye Sir," replied Rawlins.

"Gunny Alverez."

"Sir."

"Take two platoons, mutually supportive, south, and map out major trails, waterways, and beaches. Avoid contact until your recon is done. Then give 'um hell. Captain Lansby. Would you consider going with the Paramarines and acting as a guide?"

"It would be an honor, Captain. After the jolly good thrashing the Paras gave the bloody blighters on Gavutu and the Canal I would love to engage the Nips in their company."

"Captain, I must remind you that you're a guide only. Not a combat effective. I have orders to return you in as good or better condition than I found you."

"Bloody hell, Captain, these bloody slummers are threatening my country. They bombed Melbourne just like Pearl Harbour and Manila."

"Captain. You're too valuable to get killed. We really need

you for Intel. You'll do far more for Australia and the Crown and our Allies by giving us intel instead of killing the enemy. By the way, Captain, what's that strange looking weapon you have there in addition to your sidearm?"

"It's a German Shmissere MP40-9mm Machinen Pistol (submachine gun), more commonly called a burp gun. I became intimately familiar with them in North Africa while sparring with Rommel's boys in the desert."

"Where did you find it. Rawlins, did you give it to him?"

"No, Sir. He took it off the Kraut prisoner."

"You have a German prisoner?"

"Yes, Sir. He was an advisor to a patrol we jumped on the way here."

"Any more?"

"We had a Jap officer but he killed himself."

"Too bad, but he probably wouldn't have talked anyway."

"No, Sir. The officers never do. Lieut. Matsumo I.D.'d him as Samurai Warrior class and the unit looked like Special Commando."

"Where's the German now, Gunny?"

"Pharmacist Mate Smith is watchin' him, Sir."

"All right, Rawlins. Tell your doc to drop him off here and good work. Captain Lansby, can't you rely on that 455 Webly for protection?"

"Can't hit a bloody thing with it, Captain. I carry it with shot loads to kill snakes."

"Rawlins. You allowed this?"

"I wouldn't want to be the man to try to take it from him, Captain. I think it would be a bad idea. Besides, Captain Lansby is an old salt and we need all the help we can get."

"Bravo, Sgt. Rawlins. Well said. Your top NCO trusts me, Captain. Wot say I keep my little toy? After all, a man has to defend himself."

"All right, Lansby, but for defense only. No leading the charge with the damn thing. Understood?"

"Quite right, old man. Jolly good show."

"Lieut. Matsumo."

"Sir."

"Will you accompany Gunnery Sgt. Rawlin's Team? If

Rawlins is killed or wounded you will assume command. Now you know what's expected. Are you up to it?"

"Yes, Sir."

"Good man, Lieut. We'll make a Marine out of you yet."

"Semper fi and gung ho, Sir."

Everyone in the CP laughed at the Soldier turning Marine.

"All right men, you have your assignments. Now brief your men and check equipment. Jump off at 0700 hours. God bless and good luck."

* * * * *

"Joker, Ramirez, Russo. We break into two units, mutually supportive. We recon the airfield and surrounding area and get a count. Then we harass the enemy and keep him busy as long as possible. This is base camp. We return to this position. Joker and Carlos, take Team Able. Vito, you're with me with Baker. We'll head out on a northern vector. Try to stay within five hundred yards of each other. The Paras are goin' in the other direction so we're on our own. If one Team gets in trouble the other Team will hafta help out. You guys clear on that?"

"Yeah, Sarge, we got it."

"All right. Saddle up. We move out in ten."

* * * * *

The jungle was hot and wet in the morning light. Dew covered everything. Bougainvillea hung from giant cedars like fish nets trying to escape a violent sea. A huge boa constrictor hung from a banyan watching the Raiders slip by, absolutely silent like jungle phantoms in the rising mist. The Raiders hated heavy jungle because a sniper could be twenty yards away and they would never see him. The Japanese felt the same way because when the American jungle demons were in the area people tended to disappear without warning.

Able Team found a small river and decided to follow it downstream. It wound its way through the triple canopy jungle and emptied into the sea. Near the mouth, adjacent to the beach, they found a Jap bunker complex, abandoned but still in good repair. This find was marked on the map as a defense and exfil by sea location if things got really hot and they had to bug out. Baker Team found a road through the jungle to the airfield. They decided to watch for armour escorting trucks to the airfield. If found, the armour would have to be eliminated before the invasion.

Gunny Alverez and the Paramarines found a small village being used as a Jap R & R Camp. There was a very large cook house and mess, a bath house, movie theater, and geisha house. A number of fuzzies were there, being used for slave labor (fuzzies was a name given to Polynesian Solomon Island indigenous people because of their long curly hair).

"What do you think, Captain?"

"I've heard of this place. It's the officer and senior NCO resting area for the Sendie Division. If we hit them here it would really muck things up for their invasion defense."

"Aye, Sir, wouldn't it though. I say we bypass for now and continue our recon and come back later and destroy the place."

"I agree. We need the intel for the invasion."

* * * * *

"Sarge. I hear trucks."

"I hear 'um too, Vito. They're coming from the airfield. Must be headed inland with supplies."

The Raiders were well hidden in the jungle underbrush near the road.

"I count four Mitsubishi Type One trucks, two troop carriers, loaded, and two TOMAs (Japanese light infantry tank), one field car with three officers."

"Got it, Sarge."

"OK, Vito. Let's move closer to the airfield."

All at once the droning of an aircraft engine could be heard.

"Jap Zero. Hit it."

The Raiders knew instinctively to find cover quick and hit the deck while the Zero passed low over the road looking for the unseen enemy. When the killer from above was out of sight, Russo spoke up.

"Sarge. We gotta get that bastard before he gets us."

"When we hit the airstrip we gotta get 'um all, Vito, or the invasion forces will be in trouble."

* * * * *

Rawlins and Russo decided to follow the road in the direction the convoy had gone. After two miles of slow progress in the jungle along the shoulder of the road, Baker Team found a regimental size encampment. As they hid at the jungle edge they surveyed this new find.

"What you think, Vito? Regimental strength, Regular Army, probably Sendie Division. Joseph, call it in to the CP."

"OK, Sarge. Baker One calling home plate. Over."

"Go ahead, Baker One."

"Be advised. Regimental base camp, coordinates map reference delta tango two two niner. Over."

"Message understood. Delta tango two two niner. Home plate over and out."

* * * * *

Joker and Ramirez found Jap rations, ammo, and a field radio stored in the abandoned bunker complex. They kept the canned salmon, crab, lobster, and sake (rice wine); also, some loaded Nambu magazines for the shortpecker. The radio might come in handy later with Lieut. Matsumo.

Able Team headed north, parallel to the beach, fifty yards inland so as not to be caught on the open beach by the enemy. And then it happened. After traveling a half mile or so they ran into a Jap patrol taking a break. There was a small clearing in the jungle bordered by the sea. Half the enemy were in the water swimming, some were heating rations, others were sleeping. Flanking sentries were visible so they could not be bypassed. If they reversed course the enemy would be in their rear and swoop down on them at the slightest noise. And worst of all it would be dark soon. This would be a bad place to be in the dark with the enemy close by.

"We gotta take 'um, Joker. No way around it."

"Yeah. Like it or not there's no choice."

"All right. Listen up. The Corp. and I will take the sentries. Then we'll grenade the ones on the beach. When you hear the genades, hit 'um hard and fast and make sure you get 'um all. After the attack we'll rendezvous back at the bunker complex and set up our NDP (night defense position) there."

One swipe from Ramirez' kukri slashed the throat of the Jap perimeter guard, killing him silently. The flanker went out when Joker's K-Bar was driven into the enemy's thoracic cavity, cleaving his heart. The two Raider NCOs met at the far side of the clearing near the beach. Ramirez lifted an M2 frag from his web gear and straightened the safety pin. Joker did the same. At the same time they pulled the pins and heaved the grenades toward the beach. The safety levers discharged, popping the fuses as they flew.

At the detonation there was a great eruption of sand, sea water, and mud. The two seasoned warriors jumped up, sprayed a twenty round magazine into the Japs that were still up, then hit the deck and rolled into the underbrush to reload.

The rest of Able Team was pouring heavy fire into the enemy in the clearing with their M1s and B.A.R. (Browning Automatic Rifle 1918A1, a great favorite of all Marines and Soldiers due to its fire power, accuracy and small amount of recoil because of its gas operation).

The Japanese were all down with only a few scattered shots delivered toward the Raiders position.

"Check 'um out. Make sure."

A muffled pistol shot rang out just as the Team entered the clearing. The Sub-lieutenant leading the patrol had put his Nambu in his mouth and pulled the trigger rather than be taken alive and disgraced. According to Bushido, a Japanese officer if obliged to commit seppuku (ritual suicide) rather than fail or be captured. A shot rang out here and there administering the coup de grace.

"Check 'um for papers and let's get the hell out of here. Any Japs in the area that heard the fire will be lookin' for us."

* * * * *

Sgt. Rawlins and Baker Team rose from their holes in the mist covered jungle floor like ghouls on Halloween night. Their camouflage dungarees and black striped faces lent intrigue to their appearance.

"Vito, take point. Head for the airfield."

"OK, Sarge."

"We gotta recon the area. Move out."

The jungle was waking up. Birds were screeching overhead, gibbons were following their progress, screaming and throwing sticks and the odd mango at the Raiders, making the men nervous. The apes were like miniature enemy mercenaries sent in the jungle to harass any human invaders.

"Hey, Sarge."

"What?"

"These damn monkeys are giving me the creeps. Can I shoot one?"

"No, you dummy. You want every Jap on the island to know where we are?"

"No, Sarge."

"Besides, they ain't monkeys. They're gibbons. They're different."

"Whatta ya mean, Sarge? They look like monkeys to me."

"That's because you're a dummy. The monkeys on the Canal were monkeys. These ain't the same thing."

"Okay, Sarge."

"Lieut., would you please explain to our zoologist here the difference?"

"OK, Gunny. The gibbon is a higher species of primate compared to the common spider monkey which you are accustomed to. They are not as high as the chimpanzee or gorilla. Gibbons are territorial and highly intelligent and known to attack people without provocation."

"What's he sayin', Sarge?"

"He's sayin' that that big ass monkey is gonna tear you a new ass if you don't get the hell out of his jungle."

"No shit."

"No shit."

"Hey, Lieut. You called the Sarge Gunny. How come?"

"Because he received a battlefield promotion to Gunnery Sergeant."

"No shit, Lieut."

"No shit, Private."

"Hey, Sarge. Why didn't you tell us?"

"You didn't ask."

"How come I never got no battlefield promotion. I been in the Corps longer than you."

"Cause you're a dummy and you talk too much. Now shut the hell up and go find Russo. Then report back to me."

"OK, Gunny."

* * * * *

"Russo, Truesdale, comin' in."

The two Raiders hid in the tall kunai grass, mapping the airstrip. There were perimeter guard towers at each corner with mgs fighting trenches parallel to the strip, both sides. Company barracks, officer quarters, center east end. EM and NCO mess behind at jungle edge. Officer mess west of red shack. Sick bay and commissary south side, jungle edge. Main hanger and pilot shack north side between two gun towers. Machine shop and ordnance depot west of hanger. Six Mitsubishi Zero fighters, two Kawanishi reconnaissance float planes visible.

"Let's get this back to the Sarge before some Jap spots us."

* * * * *

"There's the layout, Sarge."

"Good work, Vito. You too, Truesdale."

"Sarge, I got an urgent return to CP, ASAP."

"OK, Joseph. Let's move out."

* * * * *

"Gunnery Sgt. Rawlins reporting as ordered, Sir."

"Rawlins, come in. How was your patrol?"

"Good, Sir. We mapped the airfield, Sir, and found a Sendie Division Regimental bivouac with their H.Q."

"Very good, Rawlins. Give my compliments to your men."

"I will, Sir. Thank you, Sir."

"I'm afraid I have bad news, Gunny. You're going stateside."

"Why, Sir?"

"Funeral duty. Your father-in-law, the Admiral, passed away two days ago. Sorry, Rawlins."

"Oh, no. Oh, shit no. Son of a bitch. Not him. Is this confirmed, Captain?"

"I'm afraid so, Gunny. A sub will pick you up at the mouth of the Ibu River at 0300 tonight and drop off your replacement. A Lieut. Pruit. You're supposed to know him."

"Yes, Sir. He is our platoon C.O. Caught a bayonet on Toulabong. Sure glad he's OK."

"Then you feel he's up to leading your unit?"

"Yes, Sir. He's a fine officer. Plenty of guts and smarts. Good in a fight."

"OK, Rawlins. With your recommendation I'll give him your Team."

* * * * *

Three Sailors and Leiut. Pruit paddled into the mouth of the Ibu River. The attack sub Halibut lay off-shore, decks awash, waiting for Rawlins. The tiny boat crew all had Thompson submachine guns at the ready in case of ambush. They knew the only real chance for survival in the event of an ambush was to swim back to the sub or to the surrounding jungle where they could try to make it to the Marines base camp for a future sub or PT boat pickup. Surrender meant death in one of a hundred different ways and rubber boats were far from bullet proof.

Rawlins flashed his electric signal torch twice seaward. The boat crew responded with one flash and beached their tiny craft. Rawlins was standing up to his knees in water near the boat.

"Lower the Tommy gun, Sailor. I ain't the enemy."

"You Gunny Rawlins."

"No. I'm Tojo's old lady, dummy."

"That's Rawlins. I'd recognize that Marine Corps voice anywhere."

"That you, Lieut.?"

"Yeah, Rawlins. It's me."

"We thought you were dead."

"Not yet, Gunny. What's the drill?"

"Lotta Japs, Lieut. Sendie Div. Rikusentai and some Special Commando."

"No shit."

"No shit, Sir."

"Sounds like something big happening."

"Yes, Sir."

"Seen much action?"

"Just some patrol skirmish. Nothing big. Mostly recon. They know we're here, though. We took some prisoners and shot up a couple a patrols."

"OK, Rawlins. You better shove off, and sorry for your loss. The Admiral was a good man."

"Thanks, Lieut. and good luck.

* * * * *

Lieut. Pruit's egress to the base camp was uneventful. The Lieut. and the security team ducked a Jap patrol setting up an ambush by a large trail. The Japs were hoping the invaders were amateurish enough to use these precut easy walking avenues. Anyone making that mistake would be cut to pieces by automatic weapon fire, contact mines and grenades.

The Lieut. put this area on his map as off limits.

* * * * *

"Lieut. Pruit, Second Raiders, reporting as ordered, Sir."

"Welcome aboard, Lieut."

"Thank you, Sir."

"Lieut. Pruit, meet Lieut. Matsumo, Nisie Regiment 442

Combat Infantry, U.S. Army."

"Pleased to meet you, Lieut."

"Likewise, Lieut."

"I've heard of your exploits in Italy. Your unit was very popular back in college."

"Why thank you, Lieut. I hope I don't disappoint you now that I"m here."

"I've been told already that you're an asset."

"Gentlemen. With your permission I would like to continue the briefing."

"Sorry, Sir."

"Lieut. Pruit, at this time Lieut. Matsumo is in command of Baker Team. With your permission, Lieut. Matsumo, I would like to make this a joint command."

"Very good, Sir."

"Lieut. Pruit, what say you?"

"I agree, Sir."

"Good. Well, that settles that. Gentlemen, I suggest you stand down your men. They have gone without sleep for two or three days. That's long enough."

"Yes, Sir."

"Aye, Sir."

* * * * *

"Captain Lansby. Take a look at this. Looks like the bloody Melbourne thoroughfare. Must be a major supply line to the sea."

Gunny Alverez' Team followed the road to the sea and sure enough camouflage piers and docks were visible in a small cove that could not be seen from the air.

* * * * *

"Charlie three to home plate. Over."

"Go ahead, Charlie three."

"Main supply drop seaport, map reference victor tango five able two five."

"Got it, Charlie. Three victor tango five able two five.
Charlie three return to base, repeat, return to base."

"Roger, home plate. Wilco and out."

* * * * *

Ramirez and Joker followed the beach in the opposite
direction from where they had gone the day before. Able Team was
very quiet and moved slow, expecting to run into a Jap patrol any
time. They found an old abandoned village on the edge of the jungle
by the sea. There were signs of Japanese habitation everywhere.

"Where's the fuzzies, Corp.?"

"Japs either took 'um for slaves or killed 'um. Shit. Look at
that."

Four shrunken Japanese heads were hanging from a pole in
the center of the village.

"I guess they got some revenge on the bastards. Joker, tell
'um to break out a C rat and the smoking lamp is lit. We'll hold up
here for a while."

"OK, Carlos."

* * * * *

Ramirez and Joker decided to set up an ambush.

"The Nips gotta be tracking us by now. We better set up an
ambush and get them off our backs. We don't wanna lead 'um back to
the CP."

"I agree. The far side of the village in the tree line would be a
good place. This clearing will offer a good open field of fire. I just
hope they're dumb enough to walk into it."

Able Team dug in and made fighting positions in the edge of
the jungle. Flankers were hidden twenty yards behind and adjacent to
the line in case the enemy tried to encircle the Team.

Two hours of silent waiting paid off. Two Japanese Soldiers
with their odd looking kepi tropical campaign hats, split toe boots and
leggings, and extra long Arisaka 6.5mm type 38 rifles crept into the
village like lunar explorers afraid of being caught by space aliens.

"Hold on. Wait for the main body."

The Raiders held fire and watched the curious spectacle unfold twenty or so yards away. The enemy Soldiers would charge into a hut with fixed bayonets, screaming like banshees at an unseen enemy. Then they would exit the same and attack whatever else lay in their paths. The Raiders tried not to laugh at the performance of the enemy.

"Joker. Here comes the main body, all bunched up like a flock of turkeys. OK. Grenades first, on my mark. Then we charge 'um and finish 'um. Everybody ready? OK. Throw grenades."

While the last of the M2 frags were detonating Joker yelled:

"Up and at 'um, Raiders. Gung ho."

The Japs were stunned and easy prey for the experienced Marine combat vets. The platoon sized Japanese patrol was destroyed in a vicious hand to hand fight which was a typical Japanese tactic and one which the Raiders were more than happy to employ against them.

As the Able Team NCOs expected, the Jap officer and radio element were at the rear of the column. They decided to flank the Marines and counter-attack from the rear. Pfc. Simmons spotted the two officers. Radio man and Senior NCO first.

"Here they come," he told his two comrades. Simmons shot the Jap Captain in the head with his M1, dropping him stone dead. The man next to him threw a grenade, killing another. The other two disappeared into the underbrush.

"Simmons. We gotta find the other two. If they report to their command we're in deep shit."

"Yeah, I know."

"All right. You two go toward the dead officer and I'll check by the grenade blast."

"Nothing here, Simmons."

"Come over here. I got a blood trail and tracks. Looks like one's dragging the other."

The three men followed the trail, finding more blood and discarded equipment as they went. A pistol shot rang out and the followers hit the deck. This was answered by a frag thrown in the area the shot had come from. The three men cautiously advanced and spotted the radio man on the ground. There was crashing in the underbrush and Simmons emptied an M1 clip into the brush in the direction of the noise. After looking another fifty yards, Simmons decided he had missed. The Jap Senior NCO was gone. The radio operator was riddled with grenade shrapnel and had an 8mm Nambu hole in his head. Executed because of his wounds.

"Corp., we got three of 'um but one got away."

"OK, Simmons. We better get the hell outta here before Sgt. Tojo comes back with a whole company. OK, Joker?"

"Agreed."

"Ramirez. Form up. Column of twos ten yard intervals. Move out."

Ramirez took the point and steered Able Team in the direction of the LZ, knowing they wouldn't make it back before nightfall. It was too dangerous to travel in this unforgiving jungle at night with its snakes, ravines, and swamp sinkholes. And with the enemy looking for them an ambush was a good bet now that they had their AO (area of operations).

"All right, Raiders. It's getting dark. Form a perimeter and dig in. Two man fighting holes. No smoking. No lights. If we get infiltrators, no firing unless we're attacked in force. Use grenades instead. Don't give away our position. Go hand to hand if a Jap gets close."

After digging in the jungle became dark and very quiet. The screeching birds, chattering spider monkeys and howling gibbons were quiet now. The later it got the more restless the Raiders became. All that could be heard was the buzzing of the ever-present insects and a tree frog croaking.

"Corp., I gotta shoot that frog. It's driving me crazy."

"You heard Joker. No shootin' allowed. Go after it with your bayonet."

"Out there? There's Japs out there."

"Really? I never woulda guessed it if you hadn't said so. You know, brave heart, it might be a Jap frog. I hear the Japs trained 'um and brought them to these islands just to mess with Marines."

"No shit."

"No shit. If you could capture one with the Jap battle flag

tatooed on his back you'd get a medal."

"How come?"

"Cause he's an officer frog."

"Yer bull shittin' me."

"Would your Corp. do such a thing?"

"I don't know. You might."

"If it turns out to be an officer frog, try and catch the whole platoon or company even. You might be the next Sgt. York."

"You think so, Corp.?"

"Why not. It could be your lucky day."

"I think you're shittin' me."

"Never know till ya try. Now pipe down. Every Jap frog in the AO will hear ya. I'm going to sleep. Wake me up when the Japs get here."

* * * * *

Ramirez didn't have long to wait. A Manchurian Scout employed by the Japanese picked up the Raiders trail at the village.

"Corp. Wake up. I hear something."

In the jungle, thirty yards away, the rustle of foliage and the rattling of equipment was heard. Then muffled voices. Then sounds of a struggle in the perimeter. A Jap with a knife jumped in a hole occupied by two Raiders. The enemy managed to stab one man in the shoulder and was promptly beaten to death with an M1 rifle owned by the wounded man's ship mate. Joker grabbed a Jap crawling by his hole and pulled him in.

"Come here, ye slant eyed shitbird."

The Soldier held an armed grenade in one hand and a knife in the other.

Corp. Hays managed to relieve the enemy of his deadly gift and heave it into the jungle. As the Jap tried to stab him, Hays pinned him to the floor of his hole, overpowered him, and turned the Bushido dagger around in the Japs hand and drive it into the would be killer's chest to the hilt. The fourth generation Samurai warrior died without a sound as was their custom. Happy to join the land of the rising sun for the emperor.

Another Marine was jumped by two of Hirohito's henchmen. The first tried to bayonet him. The Marine parried the plunge and chopped the infiltrator in the head with his jungle machete. The other Jap butt stroked him with his Arisaka rifle and tried to take him prisoner. It would bring him great honor to capture an American jungle demon alive. When the Raider came to, the would be hero of the emperor was standing over him, bayonet at his throat and in perfect Berkeley, California English, said:

"You're coming with me, American. Any wrong moves and I will kill you. You are my prisoner."

The Marine twisted his body, grabbed the rifle, and kicked the Jap in the groin all at the same time. Out of reaction the Jap dropped the rifle and grabbed his crotch. That was his last mistake. The Marine, still on the ground on his back, kicked the attacker in the face hard, making him drop. He then grabbed the Arisaka and drove the bayonet into the neck of its owner, ending the fight.

Dumb bastard. What did he think I would do? Go with him so some officer could behead me for fun like they did to our guys on Kwajalien? F..k them.

* * * * *

The enemy probe seemed to be over. Corp. Hays decided to find Ramirez.

"Carlos. Joker, comin' in."

"OK, Joker."

"Well, the gig is up. They know we're here and our strength. It's only a matter of time before they overrun us."

"Maybe not. I had Holmes give the CP our position at the last sitrep. They said they would send a patrol out to link up with us."

"How long?"

"Five hours give or take. I'm sure they will hear the firing to guide them in."

* * * * *

Then it started. Japanese psychwar, their favorite night tactic before an attack.

"Maline, you die. We gonna cut your livers out and eat them. We gonna kill you slow. We gonna rape your whore sisters and mothers. We make them slaves."

This proved to be too much even for the combat hardened Raiders.

"Come out and fight, you chicken shit bastards. C'mon, you slope headed, cross eyed, fish suckin' sons a bitches. Let's see what you got."

The Raiders and the Japanese traded insults and oaths like school children.

The pop of Type 89 grenade dischargers (knee mortars) was heard and a few seconds later parachute flares hung in the night sky, casting an eerie glow over the Raider position.

The enemy opened fire with everything they had. Nambu L.M.G.s and Arisaka rifles chattered and blasted at the Raiders.

The sound of heavy shells rushing through the air toward their position offered a new threat.

"Incoming. Hit it."

The Raiders crouched in their fighting holes as the 90mm mortars struck the earth around them, shaking the ground and detonating with a horrific blast.

Corp's Ramirez and Hays were in the same hole discussing the situation when the mortars came in.

"Shit, Joker. Those are nineties. They're gonna chop us up but good when they find the range."

"Yer right, Carlos. I think they're set up in the clearing in the villa. I'll take two men and clean 'um out."

"OK, Joker."

"Thomas, Simmons. You're on me."

When they had crawled out of the perimeter away from the beaten zone, Corp. Hays briefed the men.

"We gotta get that ninety. We think it's in the clearing back at the villa. Let's head that way. Thomas, lead off."

Almost at the villa, the three Raiders ran into a Jap LP (listening post). Joker clubbed one Nipponese with his Thompson. Simmons did the same with the steel butt plate on his M1 rifle. And

Thomas knifed an enemy with his K-Bar (Marine Corps fighting knife). As the three men drew near the clearing, they could hear the muzzle blast of the big mortar as the shell left the tube.

"We're getting close. I can hear the launch blast when they drop a shell."

Joker motioned to his men to hit the deck and low crawl to the jungle edge. And there it was, silhouetted against the night sky. The big tube with its four man crew. Two loading and firing; two fusing and arming the shells.

"Let's take 'um from here. Grenades first; then recon by fire."

At the sound of the grenade detonations the three Marines opened up. Joker burned a 20 round magazine into the mortar position. And his comrades spent their M1 rifles 8 round clips.

"Reload and we'll check 'um."

The mortar team were all dead but one, and a bullet from Joker's 45 cal. pistol dispatched the sneering son of Nippon.

"Anybody got a willy peat?"

"Yeah, Corp., right here (white phosphorus grenade used for melting metal)."

Joker placed the grenade on the transverse and transit site mechanism and pulled the safety pin. There was an audible pop as the fuse lit and the grenade melted into the steel, rendering it useless.

"Let's make it hot for the Nips back at the perimeter. Grab a couple a those mortar rounds. Let's give 'um a real surprise."

The Corp. removed his boot laces and boondockers and used the straps to attach grenades to the mortar bombs, leaving the safety handles exposed. He straightened the safety pins for easy removal.

"Gimme yer laces."

He then tied the laces together and tied the loose ends to the grenade pins. This provided a perfect trip wire and the grenades the perfect detonator for the mortar shells. Hays knew the Japs would pull back for the mortar attack so he would sneak into their attack position where they would surely return. There he would set his trap. Just for good measure he placed a live M2 frag under the mortar rounds, waiting to be fused. When a round was picked up the grenade would discharge, setting off the mortar shells.

Hays and his men set the mortar round trap thirty yards from the Raider perimeter on a trail they knew the enemy would have to use to advance against them. The three men heard the Japanese talking and laughing no more than twenty yards away. The mortar rounds were tied to tree trunks four feet off the ground on each side of the trail for maximum effect. The bootlaces became an invisible trip line across the trail, unseen in the dark jungle. The first Jap on the trail would catch the trip line, discharging the grenades which would ignite the high explosive charges in the mortar shells and eradicate any enemy in a twenty yard blast zone.

Hays decided not to rejoin the Raider position, but rather to fall back to the clearing edge and flank the attacking Japanese. He would try to break their ranks and cause confusion.

"Make sure your weapons are fully loaded. When the mortars blow we're gonna infiltrate the Jap flank and see if we can take some pressure off the Team. Got it?"

"Yeah, Corp., we got ya."

"OK. Be ready to move out fast when you hear the blast."

* * * * *

"Corp. Ramirez."

"Yeah. I hear 'um out there."

"They gonna hit us?"

"Yeah."

"Where's Corp. Hays?"

"He's up to something."

"Wadda ya mean?"

"He musta got the mortar with the firin' we heard. He should be back by now. He's out there doin' something to help us out."

"He's gotta be nuts. The Japs catch him they'll skin him alive."

"They won't. Not alive anyway. They're getting close. They'll rush us any time now. Get ready."

Flares popped overhead and a ghostly, greenish white glow was cast upon the Raiders and the surrounding jungle. The enemy Soldiers could be seen in the trees forming a banzai attack. Their green and brown uniforms glowed in the dim light.

"Tennco banzai Samurai." screamed their officer, waving a sword over his head. Kill the American gangsters. A well placed bullet from a Raiders M1 caused the pep rally to abruptly end when a 150 grain M2 ball round at 2900fps exploded Mr. Banzai's thoracic cavity. The hero of the empire fell over as dead as the fish heads he had had for lunch.

"Here they come. Let 'um have it."

"There was a deafening roar when the Raiders opened fire. The phantom Soldiers in the eerie half light with their extra long bayonet fixed rifles dropped like flies under the heavy fire. Then there was a thunderous explosion in the treeline. A whole squad disappeared, bunched up on the trail as they were, trying to attack all at once. Smashed rifles and body parts were all that remained of a full infantry squad of the Sendie Division.

"That's it. Let's go."

In the shadows and projected light the three Raiders walked up to the attack force and picked their targets. Joker burned down three rising sun hopefuls ten feet away. Then he nailed two more who were trying to save their dead friends. Now he was empty. He quickly ducked behind a tree and reloaded. His two partners were firing and loading in relay, putting their Ranger training to good use. One fired eight aimed shots and when the empty clip sprang from the receiver and locked open the bolt body the shooter yelled empty. Now the other Marine would fire his eight rounds while the first reloaded. With practice this technique was devastatingly effective. The attackers were confused with firing coming from two directions and with their officer dead they were beginning to scatter.

Just then the Baker Team came into range. They formed a defensive line two deep and prepared to engage.

"Lieut. Matsumo. Do you speak Japanese?"

"Like a champ, Lieut."

"Good. Do you think you could get 'um to come our way?"

"Let's find out. (In Japanese): This is your senior officer, Nipponese Soldiers. You will report here immediately or be severely punished and dishonored."

They came on the run looking for an authority figure to lead them to victory.

"Open fire."

The devastation was terrible. The grouped up Soldiers were slaughtered by the platoons withering fire. Automatic weapons at fifteen yards or less tore the Japanese apart. Few got away to tell their comrades about the jungle demons. It was just breaking light and the attack was over.

"Lieut.'s Pruit and Matsumo. Boy, are we glad to see you."

"Joker. How are you?"

"Better now, Sir. We were getting a little worried there for a while. We're low on ammo and we were gonna start using enemy stuff."

"Well, I'll be. You didn't say Jap."

"No, Sir. Don't wanna hurt no feelings or nothing."

"My God, Lt. Matsumo. I think Corp. Joker's in love."

"You don't hafta rub it in, Lieut. I'm tryin' to be good."

This broke up the whole platoon.

* * * * *

Baker and Able Teams joined forces for the march back to the CP.

"Ramirez. Good to see you."

"Thanks, Lieut. Glad you're back. We worried about you."

"How'd you make out last night?"

"We got two dead, four wounded."

"Can they travel?"

"Yes, Sir. Doc's fixin' 'um right now."

"Make stretchers for the kias. We ain't leaving them here."

"Aye, Sir."

"Pick five men, give them two frags apiece when we re-distribute ammo. And have them set up a rear guard action on this trail when we pull out. Tell them we need a ten minute lead off."

"OK, Lieut."

The jungle was coming alive as they took to the trail. Birds screeching, lizards scampering across the trail and mist rising like a two bit horror flick.

Corp. Russo stayed behind with the shortpecker (Nambu

1mg) to guard against flankers against the rear guard element. He would act as squad automatic weapon and lay down suppression fire to keep the Japs down while the rear element retreated. The BAR Team would fire in relay and cover Russo's withdrawal. Before leaving, Able Team gave him the loaded Nambu magazines they had found in the bunker complex, where they had also found more ammo on dead enemy gunners and loaders. Russo had enough ammo to start his own private war. Just like back in Chicago. Able Team also left all their remaining grenades. Baker Team kept theirs in case of trouble on the trail.

* * * * *

Lieut. Pruit decided to leave the trail and dead reckon to the LZ. On the Canal and other islands the Japanese mined and booby trapped the trails causing high casualties. This would also save time affording the wounded less pain and suffering.

Wham! an intense explosion sounded through the triple canopy jungle and reverberated around the one hundred foot high cedars and coco bolo trees.

"What the hell was that?"

"That would be the little surprise I left for the Nips back at the villa. I buried a live frag in a pile of unfused mortar rounds just for the fun of it."

"Sounds like it had the desired effect."

"Yes, Sir."

"All right. Take ten. Smoking lamp is lit."

The exhausted Raiders collapsed on the jungle floor and those that had them, passed out Chesterfields, Luckys and Camels. Wounded first, then the rest of the men shared their last butts.

"Aw, shit, that's good. Been a long time. If I get killed I hope it's right after my last butt."

"You get killed you won't know the difference, you dumb bastard."

"Kiss my ass, shitbird. Who the hell invited you anyway?"

"Pipe down, dummies. You wanna pull in every Jap on this island?"

"Lieut. What's goin' on with the Sarge? Why did he get pulled out?"

"Death in the family. Father-in-law cashed in?"

"How's he rate a furlough?"

"Funeral duty. The old man jsut made Admiral."

"I thought the Sarge caught his old lady whorin' with a swabbie flyboy and divorced her nasty ass."

"Separated. Now he's under orders to escort her like nothing happened."

"No shit. What a raw deal that is. Don't she have a brother or something?"

"Brother's dead. Got greased on the Arizona."

"How about the swabby?"

"He's missing. Presumed dead. Shot down over Truk Lagoon."

"Gee, that's too bad. I bet the Sarge will get all misty eyed when he hears about that."

"Just as well."

"Whatta ya mean, Joker?"

"Better the Japs kill him than the Sarge doin' it."

"You think he would?"

"Without a doubt. Somethings been botherin' him lately. Must be what it is. By the way, Gentlemen, for your information, it's now Gunnery Sgt. Rawlins. He was given a battlefield promotion just before he left."

"Hey, that's great. It's about time. He sure deserves it. Hey, we got a new Gunny. Rawlins got promoted."

And so it went throughout the ranks until the whole platoon knew. And every man was happy about the news.

* * * * *

All of a sudden the point lookout man came running through the jungle, back to their position.

"Lieut. Matsumo grabbed the Raider as he ran."

"Japs, Lieut. Sorry, Sir."

"That's OK, Collins. What did you see?"

"A hundred yards down the trail a platoon a Japs headed this way."

"OK, Collins. Good work."

"You heard the man, Lieut. Pruit. Do we avoid contact or fight?"

"We fight. Take up positions along the trail. Fix bayonets. Don't fire till I do unless attacked."

The three man point element rounded a bend in the trail, out of view of the main body. They were grabbed and dispatched quietly without making a sound. Now the main body came into view, completely unaware that their enemy was a scant ten yards away. They marched along, rifles slung, right shoulder arm as if they were on parade in Tokyo. Lieut. Pruit stepped onto the trail with his Browning Auto five 12 gauge shotgun loaded with 2.75 inch double 00 buckshot. The Japanese halted their march and stared in shock at the crazy American gangster with his bird hunting gun, blocking their way. It was as if they were at a loss and didn't know how to react.

It was like a gun fight in a wild west movie. Lieut. Pruit waited until they unslung their rifles and began to cycle bolt bodies to chamber a round for firing. Almost trying to give them a fair chance like in a western movie. He then opened fire with his new sawed off A5 and turned the four closest enemies into fertilizer. Dropping the empty shotgun, he pulled his issue 1911 45 auto from its shoulder holster and droppped two more bad guys with 230 grain death at 830fps. He then hit the deck and rolled off the trail to reload. The din from all the high velocity weapons firing was deafening. When the Lieut. was reloaded he rose to one knee, A5 at the ready, and looked for targets. But there were none. All the enemy that had not run away were down.

Raiders were stepping onto the trail now to check the enemy for papers and of course souvenirs. One man liberated a gold plated Bulova watch, two Nambu type 14 8mm pistols and one Smith & Wesson military and police 38 special revolver. Probably taken from a dead or captured American or Australian pilot.

As the force was getting ready to move out there was the faint but distinctive report of a BAR, then M1 rifles and finally the chatter of a Nambu type 96 6.5mm L.M.G.; then three grenades. Then scattered pistol and rifle shots.

"That's Vito and the rear guard. Ramirez, take Second Squad and head back down the trail half way to Vito's position and set up an ambush. The rear element will be withdrawing under fire and may need support. I'll send First Squad ahead with the wounded and wait for all of you here. I'll place flankers parallel to the trail in case the Japs try to sweep around to your rear. When you meet with Russo leap frog back to this position. If you're still in contact when you get here I'll call in 3.2" mortars. We should be close enough to the CP to call in a fire mission by now."

"OK, Lieut. See you in a while."

"Good luck, Carlos."

"Gung ho, Lieut."

Ramirez and his squad found firing positions on either side of the trail. No time to dig in. Ten minutes later Russo's rear guard came running up the trail, Japanese in hot pursuit. Two or three man rifle teams stopped and fired in relay slowing the enemy advance. When the Marines entered their position Ramirez yelled,

"Raiders down."

Instinctively, from months of training, the pursued Raiders hit the deck to a man. Second Squad opened up with a clear shot on the jungle trail fifty yards away. This very rarely happened in dense jungle fighting. The enemy pursuers fell like ripe wheat before a hot sickle. The trail was littered with dead and dying Soldiers. A few were lucky and ran away unscathed.

"Finish 'um off and let's get the hell outta here."

"Vito, you all right?"

"Yeah. Caught some grenade shrapnel."

"Yer bleedin'."

"Doc, take care a Corp. Russo."

"OK, Lieut."

Pharmacist Mate Second Class Smith (Doc) cleaned and applied sulfa powder to Russo's shoulder and left arm. Then a battle dressing and a syrette of morphine.

"That will do till I get you evacced outta here, you lucky stiff. Clean white sheets and hot and cold running nurses for you. The war is over for you for a while."

"Thanks, Doc."

"You deserve it, Corp."

The squad and rear element returned to the main body without incident. It seemed as though the enemy had had enough for a while.

* * * * *

On the way back to the LZ Gunny Alverez' Team was ambushed. The enemy allowed the three man point element, led by Corp. Rogers, to pass by and waited for the main body to appear.

The first burst from the Nambu Type 99 7.7mm machine gun (woodpecker) dropped three men. One killed, two wounded. The cries of the wounded could be heard above the firing.

"Corpsman. I'm hit. Get yer ass over here. I'm bleedin' like a stuck pig."

The Marines poured fire into the ambush position with everything they had, but to no avail. The prepared dugout position with its coconut log reinforcements and cover was too much for small arms fire. And the Paramarines were pinned down tight and could not advance or flank the position. Amazingly, the Japanese forgot the point element who were now in their rear.

"Corp., we gotta do something. Our guys are gettin' chopped up bad."

"All right, listen up. We're gonna hit 'um with grenades , then take 'um hard and fast while they're still stunned. Got it?"

"Yeah, Corp., we got it."

"Fix bayonets. This is gonna be close work."

The three Marines crawled through underbrush across the jungle floor. When they were close to the emplacement grenades were made ready and when the NCO gave the order they tossed the miniature bombs into the dugout and rolled away. Amid Japanese screams and curses there were three muffled explosions.

"Give 'um hell."

And the three Marines jumped into the trench, weapons blazing. Corp. Rogers cut down three Jap gunners with a burst from his Tommy gun. Pfc. Lawrence shot two at close range. Then his M1 ran dry. No time to reload. A Jap officer attacked him with a katana (sword). The blow was so strong that when he parried it with his rifle, the stock was nearly cut in two. Lawrence was knocked to the ground. The Jap came at him again, screaming like a wild demon from hell, and tried to decapitate him. The Pfc drove the bayonet on the end of his empty rifle into the Japs gut as the man stood above him. The officer grunted, dropped his katana and stood there impaled on the bayonet. Then he somehow began to draw his Nambu 8mm pistol when he was blown down by a burst of 45 cal. death from the Corp.'s Thompson.

Pfc. Andrews was holding two prisoners at bayonet point, wounded from grenade shrapnel but alive. Two others that lay at his feet were not.

* * * * *

When the grenades blew, Gunny Alverez realized what was happening and yelled at his men,

"Up and at 'um, Marines. Let's go."

The Team raised a war whoop and charged the position. They jumped into the trench, stabbing and slashing the enemy as they went. Those without bayonets such as BAR and Tommy gunners used their weapons as clubs, fearful of hitting their own men in this close action.

"Damn, Gunny, am I glad you and the boys charged when you did. There were more of 'um than I expected."

"Bloody good show, old man. You and your men surely saved our bacon."

"Thank you, Sir."

"Gunnery Sgt."

"Yes, Sir."

"I'm all for putting these men in for a decoration. What say, old boy? Are you with me?"

"Yes, Sir. I agree."

* * * * *

Sgt. Rawlins arrived at Arlington National Cemetery, having taken a D.C. yellow cab from his room at the Ambassador Hotel. He was feeling very apprehensive, almost sick, knowing she would be there. Rawlins had not seen Susan in sixteen months. He wished he could dodge this detail but no such luck. The Sgt.'s friends in Washington that could countermand the order would not speak to him after the embarassment at the officer's club two years previously. He felt like he was going into combat where he was sure he would die but he would make it through somehow. Rawlins felt a yearning for his parent's who lived in Buffalo, NY and his pre-war hangouts on Hertal Ave. Stepping out of the forty one Packard into a light rain, the Sgt.'s Class A dress blues were soaking up the water like a sponge. They had been in long term storage in the sea bag he had left at Pearl Harbour Marine Corps barracks months ago.

* * * * *

On his way to Higgins Field to board a C47 Dakota transport bound for San Diego, Rawlins had stopped by the wreckage of the USS Arizona to pay his respects. The Admiral's son, a twenty year old ensign, lay entombed in her bowels with one thousand, one hundred forty of his shipmates. They had died defending their ship when a Jap five hundred pound bomb penetrated her forward main deck by number two forward gun turret, blowing out her bottom and killing her crew. Rawlins prayed that the Admiral and the ensign were together now, in a better place.

* * * * *

As the Sgt. walked into the Arlington Chapel he could see the Navy issue casket with the U.S. flag draped across it and the Naval officer's sword and full dress cover lying on top. He had really liked the old man and the first pangs of grief hit him.

And there she was, sitting in the front pew alone. Her long blond hair and thin shoulders marked her from across the room. Rawlins panicked. He wanted to leave but could not, so doing the Marine Corps thing, he sat down beside her just for show.

"Ken. My God. When did you get in?"

"Twenty one hundred last night."

"You should have called."

"Didn't want to impose. How are you feeling?"

"Like hell. First I lose Daddy and then I hear Doug's been shot down. Do you think he's alive, Ken?"

"Probably. The Japs treat officers pretty good."

"Do you think he was captured?"

"That's what usually happens with downed pilots," Rawlins lied, somehow feeling sorry for this woman who had broken his heart. In reality the Japs executed pilots on the spot.

"Ken. Let's go have lunch. I have to get out of here for a while."

During the ride to the NCO Club in Susan's Stuts-Bearcat, compliments of Daddy, Rawlins noticed she still had the best legs in D.C.

"Ken. What do those new ribbons on your suit represent?"

"This is a uniform, not a suit."

"O, whatever."

"These are battle ribbons. Guadalcanal, Toulabong, Ulithi, Southwest Pacific Area."

"You really get around, don't you?"

"Wherever the Japs go, I go."

"You still mad at me?"

Just then the waiter reached their table.

"I'll have a Johnny Walker and the lady will have a Bloody Mary."

"How cute. You remembered. You know, Ken, I never loved him. It was only sex."

This drove through Rawlins gut like a hot Jap bayonet.

"Why?"

"All those long deployments. You left me alone too much. It started when you were in England playing with those Commandos, fighting Germans. I started to play tennis at the Officer's Club and met Doug there. One thing led to another because you weren't there."

Rawlins didn't know what to say or do. Should he feel guilty; should he feel rage or remorse. He was very confused. Here sat the woman of his dreams and he was afraid of her. For the first time in his life he felt fear.

Rawlins returned to his hotel by cab and got very drunk. Dealing with women was worse than war. At least in war you knew where you stood.

Later that night the Sgt. had a terrible nightmare about his squad being overrun by screaming Japanese and being wiped out to the last man. He had to get this over with and get back to his men.

* * * * *

Sgt. Rawlins sat in the rain, under a steel gray sky, with the woman he did not understand, next to the Admiral's casket. They were surrounded by high ranking officers and officials from many Allied countries. Most noteworthy were Great Britain, Denmark, Canada, Free France, Free Poland, Russia, South Africa, New Zealand, Australia, China. The Sgt. had had no idea the old man was so well respected. Six enlisted Sailors brought the casket to the grave and stood nearby as an honor guard. Seven Marine NCOs stood as the firing party for the twenty one gun salute. The Senior Chaplain for the Navy gave the eulogy. All Rawlins heard was the tail end. *The Lord giveth and the Lord taketh away. Blessed be the name of the Lord.*

* * * * *

He couldn't stop thinking about his men reconning that God forsaken island for the coming invasion. He knew that if they were caught they were as good as dead. There were two full divisions of Nips, one being Naval Special Landing Force, the dreaded Rikusentai (Jap Marines). The other the Seventeenth Army's Sendie Division. Hard core vets of the China campaign, looking for a fight. Rawlins had tangled with both of these units before so he knew how tough they were.

* * * * *

"Preeesent arms," bellowed the Gunnery Master Sergeant as only a Marine could.

"Fire."

At the command, the M1 03 Springfield rifles fired three rounds of blank ammo.

"Ooorderr arms," commanded the old NCO. Next the Master Chief Boatswains Mate of the Navy played taps on his bugle. All military personnel came to attention and saluted.

After the funeral luncheon was served at the Naval Officer's Club in honor of the Admiral, a British Royal Marine Colonel addressed Rawlins.

"Sorry about your loss, old man. I know you and the Admiral were close."

"Thank you, Sir."

"By the way, Sgt., splendid job with Royal Commando in Norway. Caused Jerry to act like blithering idiots. May have shortened the war by years. They're still speaking of it in Whitehall. Quite smashing, old man."

"Thank you, Sir. Glad to help."

"What are you up to now, if you don't mind?"

"Fighting Japs, Sir. I was pulled out of combat to be here."

"Bloody buggers. Bad enough we have to deal with Jerry. Now the Japs are becoming a serious problem."

"Yes, Sir."

"Well, Rawlins, when you're done with them we would love to have you back with Commando."

"Thank you, Sir. I'll keep that in mind."

"Well, carry on, Sgt. and good luck."

After the Colonel walked away Susan blurted out,

"I didn't know you were a hero."

"I didn't either. I just did my job and got lucky. The Germans didn't expect us."

"While I was having fun here in D.C. you were in Europe fighting half the German Army."

"Just one Schutzstaffel Panzer Division in Norway. Like I said, we were lucky."

"That's my Ken. Full of surprises.

* * * * *

Gunnery Sgt. Rawlins' return trip from D.C. was filled with nightmares and sleepless hours of foreboding thoughts of war. He was plagued with apprehension and self doubt about his ability to take care of his men. It was obvious that he had failed as a husband. Maybe he would fail as a Marine Senior NCO as well.

The train was filled with servicemen of all types. Some going to war, some coming home. He noticed a one armed Sailor in dress blues staring out a window. The victim of some long forgotten battle, on some unforgiving sea or island.

No one will remember but he will fight for the rest of his life.

He's probably better off, Rawlins thought. *He's home and alive and it's over for him. More than can be said for many of his shipmates.*

"Gunny, what's it like?" a young Marine Pfc. asked Rawlins.

"Not what you would expect."

"Whadda ya mean, Gunny?"

"Lots a noise. Like the Fourth of July only worse. Confusion. Nobody knows what's goin' on till it's over. And lights at night. Their tracers, mortar and grenade flashes, rifle muzzle flashes enough to blind a man."

"How much combat you seen? I see you're a Raider."

"Too much. There's just no end to them Japs and they all wanna die for the emperor. Don't worry, kid, just do what the old hands tell ya and you'll be fine."

Poor kid will be dead in a week, naive as he is.

* * * * *

Rawlins de-trained in San Diego after a three day ride cross country. He then took a bus to El Toro Marine Air Station and boarded a Dakota transport headed for Pearl. There he boarded an SBD destroyer (shallow draft, high speed) for Guadalcanal. Upon arrival Rawlins found Colonel Carlson and reported for duty.

"How are you feeling, Rawlins?"

"Fine, Sir."

"Ready to go back in?"

"Yes, Sir."

"Good. Things are heating up on Ruwawa. And one of your squad leaders in wounded."

"Who, Sir?"

"Corp. Russo."

"How bad?"

"Shoulder and arm. Shrapnel. We're going to try to evack him tonight. He will leave on the PT that takes you in. Good luck, Rawlins."

"Thank you, Sir."

* * * * *

The scruffy PT crewmen bothered the high and tight shipshape Marine. But they were not his problem. He had enough trouble keeping his Marines in line.

The purple orange sunset on the majestic blue green sea was awe inspiring as the patrol craft left the dock at Guadalcanal. After running through a squall it bacame so dark and quiet that the sea and sky looked the same. The crew watched for enemy ships in the slot as the Skipper navigated toward Ruwawa. Rawlins was on deck enjoying the cool night air. He was glad to be back. Life was so much simpler here. He often thought he would like to return here when the war and his tour with the Marines was over.

* * * * *

Wham! Fire everywhere. Men screaming. What happened? Rawlins found himself in the water, thrown clear from the explosion. He pulled the cord in his lifebelt and it inflated with CO_2. He could see three Sailors in the water but no one else. The boat was burning furiously and so was the gasoline from fifty five gallon drums lashed to the deck for the return trip. The four men swam for their lives, escaping the burning gasoline that was spreading across the water like an evil tide. Finally, the boat slipped beneath the surface and the burning gasoline began to dissipate. The Sailors and Marine stayed together, having a better chance of survival that way, according to their "abandon ship" training in boot camp.

As dawn broke, the four survivors were exhausted and in need of fresh water. They noticed many small islands around them. God knew how far they had drifted in the last twelve hours. They swam for the nearest one, about a half mile away.

"Gunny, I can't make it."

"Shut the hell up, Swab. You don't have permission to die on my watch. If I can make it so can you. What the hell kinda Sailor are you anyway? This ain't even tough goin.' Wait till we're on that island and we run into Japs."

"We'll just hafta surrender, Gunny. We don't know how to fight on land."

"Like hell we will. Marines don't surrender."

"We ain't Marines."

"You're in the Naval Service, ain't ya?"

"Well, yeah."

"We'll be on land, won't we?"

"Yeah, Gunny."

"Then you're Marines and you gotta do what I say. Now swim and belay the whining. We gotta make that island before a Jap patrol barge spots us and we get machine gunned."

The beach was white sand and palm trees like a Hollywood movie. Rawlins dragged one Sailor off the beach and the other two helped each other. They opened coconuts with the Ka-Bar survival knives. Most above deck Sailors carried these knives in case they found themselves in the water. The four men drank the contents greedily and ate the meat from inside. Mangos were also consumed.

"What's your name and rating, Sailor?"

"Gunner Mate Second Class Tony Rizzo."

"Able Seaman Joe Clark."

"Motormac Third Class Alvin Holms."

"Gunnery Sgt. Rawlins, Second Marine Raiders. I guess I'm ranking NCO in this lash up so listen up. We ain't surrendering so forget that idea right now."

"Better than starving, Gunny."

"The Japs have been killing all the shipwrecked personnel

they find. You wanna lose your head, Sailor."

"Well, since you put it that way I guess you're right."

"And don't worry about starving. We'll find food. There's plenty of stuff to eat in these islands. Anybody have a weapon?"

The Gunner Mate spoke up:

"I have a 45 and a Ka-Bar and they both have Ka-Bars."

"OK. Let's clean and oil what we have in case we run into trouble."

Rawlins pulled out a small vial of GI gun oil and a folded rag stored in an oilcloth pouch.

"Boy, Gunny. Just like a Boy Scout."

"You never know when you might get stranded on a desert island."

Rawlins pulled his pair of 1911 al 45 autos from belt and shoulder holsters and the Gunner Mate pulled his. They both expertly field stripped the big pistols and replaced sand and water with gun oil. Then they stripped the magazines of their ammo and cleaned each round of ammo.

"Either of you two know how to handle a 45?"

"Yeah, Gunny. I had my own I carried on the Canal 'cause of infiltrators. Now it's at the bottom of the sea."

"Here, take this one."

"Thanks, Gunny. Why do you carry two?"

"Banzai charges. They're great for breaking up an attack when the enemy is close. Lots of fire power, lots of knockdown. And if one jams, breaks, or runs dry you got backup. Better than a rifle in a close fight."

"What else you got?"

"Thompson, same caliber. Lots a knockdown."

"Yeah, but I hear they jam."

"Not if they're clean. Just like these pistols. Gotta be clean. We better recon this island and see what we're up against. And if we can find anything useful to help us survive. I'll take point. If you hear firing or see Japs the best thing to do is hide. We only fight if forced to. Our main concern is survival and finding a way outta here."

Rawlins found a trail inland on the small island. He paralled it in fear of booby traps and mines. The palm trees gave way to jungle. After an hour or so he broke into palm trees in rows, and rubber trees in rows. In the center of the plantation stood an old Colonial Dutch two story planter's house. Rawlins waited here for the misplaced Sailors to catch up. Soon he could see them walking up the trail in tight formation. He let them pass and walked up behind the group and grabbed the closest one by the neck from behind. The Sailor fell to the ground and almost passed out from shock and fear.

"Gunny, what the hell are you doing?"

"Trying to keep you alive, you dummy. If I was a Jap you would be dead now. Could have taken you all, no problem. Don't bunch up like that. You make yourselves prime targets. And stay off the trails. They could be mined or booby trapped."

The only reply to this jungle warfare lesson was,

"F..kin' Marines. They're all nuts."

The house had been destroyed by the Japanese some time before but there were usable items remaining. The kitchen contained a wood burning cook stove and a few pots and pans. The well in the yard had a pump that still operated. The castaways drank and drank the clean, clear water, rehydrating their depleted bodies.

In the cellar, hidden, buried under the stairs, they found tins of Australian bully beef, potatoes, carrots, Japanese crab, lobster and mackerel.

In the yard a pineapple patch supplied some much needed fruit. The men would eat well until the food ran out. Then they would have to forage in earnest.

Next, they began to explore the island. The jungle gave way to grass fields and low ridges. Near the opposite shore was higher ground with volcanic caves and craggy peaks. Many species of bird life lived there, supplying eggs for their diet. The men found a bay hidden among lava caves that was protected from the sea and perfect for fishing. They also found a lean-to built from bamboo and palm fronds, fish drying on a bamboo rack, hanging over a fire and small plantain bananas and kiwi in a basket woven from kunai grass.

"Gunny, we ain't alone on this island paradise."

"Yeah, I see that."

"What we gonna do?"

"Let's get up there on that high ground and watch from

there."

They didn't have long to wait. Two Japanese came walking down the beach like they owned it, carrying a palm frond and a kunai grass woven net full of fish.

"They're Jap Sailors, Gunny. Look at those uniforms."

"Well, I'll be. Jap Sailors in the middle of a Jap ocean on a Jap island. How mysterious."

"Ya know, Gunny, you're a real prick."

"Stow it, Swab. This ain't the time. We gotta take out those two beach bums and see if there's any more around here."

"Why, Gunny? They ain't hurtin' anybody. They're shipwrecked like us. Why don't we just let 'um be?"

"You forgettin' we're at war with the Jap Navy? You forget Pearl already. How about your mates? All killed by Jap Sailors, dummy. They could be the ones. We'll wait till dark and take 'um quiet. Don't wanna make noise or waste ammo on 'um."

"F..kin' jarheads. Always gotta kill something."

"I heard that, snow cone. Stow the crap. The Japs will hear you. There could be Rikusentai on this island."

"Who?"

"Jap Marines."

"Oh, great. One regular Marine is bad enough. Now you're saying there's Jap Marines around here."

"That's right. And they patrol these islands looking for survivors from local sea and air battles. If those two spot us they will tip them off when they get picked up."

"What happens if they catch us?"

"If we're lucky they will use us for bayonet practice."

"That's lucky?"

"If we ain't they will rape us, skin us alive and feed us to the sharks."

"We ain't women."

"Don't matter. We saw in on the Canal. They ain't particular. See, deck ape. I'm not such a prick after all."

The only reply was, "shit."

* * * * *

Full dark. Rawlins and Gunner Mate Rizzo crept down to the jungle edge, keeping well back from the edge of the high bluff so as not to be sky lighted. They slid through the jungle foliage like hunting serpents preparing for the kill. The enemy Sailors sat around a fire like surfers at Huntington Beach, seemingly oblivious to the war around them.

Rawlins pounced on one like a jungle cat, grabbing the enemy by his long hair and pulling his head back over his own leg, exposing the Jap's neck. Rawlins drove his stiletto into the Sailor's neck, severing the carotid artery. The Jap slid to the ground and died.

Rizzo was in trouble. The son of Nippon he had attacked was on top of him, choking the petty officer with one hand and trying to stab him with his own Ka-Bar with the other hand. Rawlins threw his prized stiletto, striking the enemy in the back, burying itself in his shoulder. The only effect was a grunt of pain and surprise. Rizzo was getting weak from lack of air. The Jap was killing him. Rawlins rushed the would be victor, knocking him off Rizzo, and gave the Jap a spear point strike to the throat with his extended fingers, crushing his larynx. He then grabbed the almost victor's menacing hand, still holding the Ka-Bar, and smashed his elbow with an inside knife edge strike with the outer edge of his free hand. He now drove the Ka-Bar with both hands into the Jap's chest to the hilt. The imperial Naval Seaman staggered back a few steps, his eyes rolled back in his head and he fell over dead.

"Rawlins, you saved my ass. That fish eatin' bastard almost killed me. I owe you one."

"Forget it. Let's bury these stiffs and get outta here."

About that time the two other Sailors walked up.

"Gunny. That was some show. Where did you learn to fight like that?"

"Raider school."

"Damn. I'm glad you're on our side."

"Go through their stuff and take whatever you can use. We gotta get outta here with this fire and all."

"Aye, Gunny."

The stranded Americans took the dried fish and fruit the enemy had prepared. They headed to the far end of the island to avoid

Japanese shore parties. The planter's house was off limits also
because the enemy would surely check it for survivors.

     The four men found another bay, this one uninhabited. They
built a lean-to between two palm trees, lashing bamboo stalks
together with kunai grass and bougainvillea vines. A roof and
sleeping mats were made from palm fronds. A nearby stream
provided fresh water.

     "Gunny, how we gonna eat?"
     "We fish, we hunt."
     "What about the food from the house?"
     "We save that for emergencies."
     "Why you diggin' that hole?"
     "For a fire."
     "For what?"
     "For our pig."
     "What pig?"
     "The one we're gonna catch and eat."
     "Really?"
     "Really."

     Rawlins removed a spare magazine from it's pouch and slid
one round of ammo from the feed lips into his hand. He then pried
the bullet from the case with his Ka-Bar. After gathering wood for a
fire, half the powder charge was sprinkled over the wood. The bullet
was replaced in the case, making a subsonic round. The beginning of
a silencer. A piece of bamboo slightly bigger than the forty five's bore
was split at one end to slide over the pistol's muzzle and a series of
holes were cut into the shaft to create a muzzle vent. Then a Sailor's
Dixie cup (hat) was placed over the bamboo contraption, making the
perfect expansion chamber. This was tied fast to the pistol slide and
frame with water soaked vines that grew tighter as they dried in the
hot sun, making the perfect silencer.

     "Gunny. What the hell is that?"

     "It's a noise free pig getter. It will kill a wild pig with hardly a
sound, if I can get close enough to use it. And it's a one shot deal."

     Rawlins found a game trail in the jungle, kunai grass edge,
and followed it until he found a place where wild pigs had been
rooting for taro root. He hid in the oversize roots of a banyan tree and

waited for his prey. The Sailors prepared a smokeless fire in the hole Rawlins had dug, using dry drift wood and gun powder. The Gunnery Sgt. left a small piece of flint that he always carried in his blouse to start the fire. By striking the Ka-Bar against the flint a shower of sparks ensued, causing the gun powder to ignite. This in turn lit the dry wood and a smokeless fire burned vigorously in the hole. Next, volcanic beach rocks were placed in the fire.

Three pigs came loping down the trail into the Raider's ambush. They were rooting and snorting, oblivious to the hunter ten yards away. The human predator picked the smallest of the three, took aim as best he could with his single shot pig provider and fired. All that was audible was a thumping sound and the locking back of the slide. The pig exuded a woofing snort when the bullet struck it's chest, walked in a half circle and fell over dead. Rawlins jumped up and charged the animal, sticking his Ka-Bar into its neck to make sure it stayed down. The other pigs ran off in a panic.

Rawlins walked into their camp site, the pig, dressed and skinned, over his shoulder.

"Well, I'll be. He really did it. Look at the jarhead, mates, we're gonna eat good tonight."

The four shipmates placed the pig in the hole on top of lava rock and drizzled a mixture of coconut milk and crushed pineapple inside and over the pig. Palm fronds covered the pigs upper side and dirt and sand covered these.

"Four hours, gentlemen, and we can eat."

The men busied themselves collecting what fruit they could find and making their camp more livable.

The roast pig was exhumed from its Polynesian oven and placed on a bamboo rack. The meat was sliced off and devoured.

"Gunny, this is really good. Where did you learn this trick?"

"Watching natives on Palau. And deer hunting back home in New York State."

"There's deer in New York?"

"Lots a deer. Both two and four legged."

* * * * *

"Rawlins is missing."

"Son of a bitch. What happened?"

"PT boat disappeared on its way here. Search and rescue came up empty."

"No bodies or wreckage?"

"No, Sir. Nothing."

"He's not dead."

"How do you know, Sir?"

"Because I know Rawlins. If there's no bodies it's because he's not dead."

* * * * *

The Paramarines were playing cards and shooting the bull with the Raiders when the inevitable happened. Sgt. Evans from First Platoon, Third Squad, Company B, Third Battalion, First Paramarines, was struck in the chest with a 7.7 Arisaka bullet, killing him instantly. The Rikusentai sniper with his 6 power Nikon scope sighted Type 99 Arisaka rifle was deadly from two thousand meters. This was an easy kill at four hundred meters.

Next, the mortars came in.

"Incoming. Hit the deck."

The Marines scattered and jumped in their holes and dugouts. An intense 90mm barrage pounded the Marines for twenty minutes. When the fire lifted the Marines watched the enemy moving in by squad and platoon in the trees below their hillside positions, preparing for a frontal attack. At the CP the officers were busy.

"Joseph, get the Chicago on the horn."

"Aye, Sir. Tay due noc ta hey new sy eto ruto sayto (USS Chicago. Fire mission. Over)."

"USS Chicago, Go ahead."

"Request anti-personnel proximity fuse ten foot airburst H.E., over."

"Roger, home plate. Send coordinates."

"Roger, Chicago. Coordinates are as follows: delta, X-ray, 2-9-9 north end of grid."

"Roger, home plate. We have coordinates and are ready to

fire."

"Fire smoke salvo, will adjust."

"Roger and wilco, home plate."

The smoke rounds sounded like a freight train racing through a tunnel as they screamed in from seaward ten miles away. They slammed into the ground on the southern edge of the jungle covering the Marines with an eerie white curtain of phosphorous smoke.

"Raise one fifty, fire eight inch salvo H.E."

The four Naval artillery shells slammed into the jungle detonating ten feet off the ground for maximum effect.

"Right on the money, Navy. Fire for effect. Walk 'um back and forth."

The barrage was devastating for both the attackers and the jungle. A whole company (130 men) of Imperial Naval Special Landing Force Marines (Rikusentai) was wiped out to a man. The jungle looked like a strange planet, scorched and almost void of vegetation from the big Naval shells. The devastation was complete.

When the Marines crawled out of their holes they were shocked.

"Man, I never saw anything like that. There's nothing left. Reminds me of the Canal a year ago. The Japs did that to us every night for a week. Then the Navy finally drove 'um off."

The Command Section of the mixed unit agreed that they should disperse and conduct guerrilla operations until relieved. A large force would surely arrive any time and overrun their position now that their base camp had been discovered.

A night raid on the airfield was the first order of business. But first the Marines put some miles between themselves and the main force Japanese.

* * * * *

"What's wrong, Susan?"

"I received a telegram today from the Dept. of the Navy."

"Bad news?"

"Ken is missing in action, presumed dead."

"Oh, well, so much for tonight's good time."

"You son of a bitch. How dare you? Ken is twice the man you will ever be."

"So what. You're done with him. Now it's my turn."

"You 4Fjoby bastard. Get away from me and stay away."

"All right, princess, if that's the way you want it. But you're bound to get lonely waiting for a dead man."

Susan threw her drink at her escort and screamed,

"Get out, you bastard, and stay out."

After an appropriate cooling off period a Navy Commander approached Susan with a fresh drink.

"Mind if I sit down?"

"Please. Do I need the company right now. And the drink. And you are?"

"Commander Bill Lynch. And you're Susan Rawlins."

"How did you know?"

"Your husband told me you have the best legs in New Orleans. I see he was right. And I also saw you and Rawlins at the funeral. Sorry for your loss. The Admiral was a great officer."

"First my brother, then my father, now Ken."

"He's alive."

"How do you know?"

"Because he's the toughest Marine s.o..b. I ever knew. We got in some scrapes in China together and always came out on top because of him. I know you're not together any more but I know he still loves you. And I think it's mutual after watching you tear up that 4F shitbird. Rawlins said you're a real spitfire just like your Dad."

"Well, Commander, I guess it runs in the family."

"Yes, Ma'am. I'm shipping out for the Pacific soon. When I see Rawlins I'll tell him you're waiting for him."

"Are you sure you will see him?"

"I'll make a point of it, Ma'am."

"There's no point in trying to convince you otherwise, is there, Commander?"

"No, Ma'am."

"I see. Why are you doing this, Bill?"

"I owe your husband at least that much, Ma'am, and I know how he feels. I lost my wife to a Sailor too."

* * * * *

"I will always love you. "

"Shit, she's back. Won't even let me die in peace on this lousy Pacific rock."

"Hey, Gunny. You all right? You look all shook up."

"Just a bad dream. Nothing serious. Let's wrap up our food in palm fronds and tie it with vines and find a place near the stream and bury it."

The four survivors found an under-cut bank full of tree roots and stuffed the packaged dried meat, fish and fruit into the center of the roots suspended above the stream. It would stay cool and protected from the hot sun and easier to retrieve in a hurry if need be this way.

"Gunny, why are we stashing food like this?"

"In case we have visitors. We can't hide, fight and forage all at the same time. This way we won't starve."

Gotcha, Gunny, I used to think Marines were dumb. Silly me."

On their inspection of the beach they ran into the unthinkable. Slipping around the jungle edge where it touched the sea, the Americans were horrified to see a Jap landing barge disgorging troops one hundred fifty yards down the shore.

"Son of a bitch. We're in for it now."

* * * * *

"Corp. Ramirez."

"Sir."

"I want you to set up a rear guard action and cover our withdrawal. Take the Second Raider Platoon and set up a flanking ambush in those low hills adjacent to the trail. When the enemy appears let them get close and give 'um hell. Then get to the jungle quick so you're not overwhelmed when they counter-attack. Bug out and move fast. Head for the airfield. We'll meet you there in two days. Dig in and keep quiet. We'll find you."

"Aye, Sir."

"Your two Lieutenants will remain with me so you're in command."

"Aye, Sir."

"Semper phi, Marine."

"Thank you, Sir."

* * * * *

Two miles down the trail the Major held an officer call.

"Lieut. Pruit."

"Sir."

"Is your Scout Sniper Team available?"

"Yes, Sir."

"We are nearing the jungle edge, which will slow our progress when we enter. I want your Team to take position on that hill above us and harass the enemy and slow their advance. Tell your men to break off and withdraw at the first sight of a flanking maneuver."

"Aye, Sir."

* * * * *

Gunnery Sgt. Rawlins and his Naval companions headed back to the stream on the double. Sometimes the best place to hide is under water. The four castaways, now on the run, found two undercuts in the stream bank similar to their food hiding place. Two men lay under each undercut with just their heads about the surface, allowing them to breathe. The cold water felt refreshing in the midday heat. Then the fear crept into their bodies. Japanese voices, very close. Laughing, talking, one even singing some Nipponese ballad about Japanese world domination. The patrol was taking a break right on top of the stranded, hiding men. One son of Nippon was urinating three feet from Rawlins. The Gunny wanted to give this unpotty trained crusader for the empire a big surprise but he knew the Sailors in his charge were not up to a close hand to hand fight with these trained killers.

* * * * *

"Here they come. Get ready."

A company sized force was walking down the trail and through the hills. Second Platoon was well hidden in the tall grass on the hills. A Mitsubishi Zero fighter plane was flying above them, looking for a target. The Corp. let the enemy get so close the Raiders could smell them. Then he stood up and killed three Japs with a burst from his Thompson. They were ten feet away.

The noise that followed from all the weapons firing in unison was deafening. The enemy Soldiers fell like wheat before a huge lead sickle. The Raiders famous "aimed fire in relay" technique with automatic weapons wrought devastation on the Japanese infantry. They barely fired a shot and more than half their number was down.

The Raiders broke contact and headed for the tree line pronto. The Zero pilot added insult to injury by returning and machine gunning his comrades by mistake, guided by a radio message from Lieut. Matsumo.

"Wow, Lieut., you gotta teach us some a that lingo sometime."

"Sometime I will after we get the hell outta here."

"Aye, Sir."

Range 600 yards. Enemy flankers were closing on the column of Marines. They advanced in a wide sweep, trying to out-maneuver the fast moving enemy.

Eyes readied his rifle for the work ahead. He loaded five 3006 M2 ball rounds into his 1903 Springfield rifle and closed the bolt, chambering a round. Using his rucksack for a rest he placed the crosshairs of the Weaver telescopic sight on the nearest target.

"Range."

"Range 450 yards."

Eyes raised the elevation by turning the knob on the side of the scope an audible four clicks. This changed his zero point of impact from three to four hundred yards. This is where he would engage the enemy.

Eyes steadied the crosshairs on a Japanese Captain waving a sword over his head, admonishing his troops, spurring them on. Eyes could see red and blue ribbons bordered in gold on the Japs chest. And a gold anchor and chain embroidered on the right sleeve of his green blouse. His brown tropical kepi (hat) revealed the same gold insignia. The Captain's brown bloused pants and hand tooled brown leather knee high boots were a dead giveaway. Rikusentai Samurai Class Shogun Warrior.

At the report of the shot the officer looked shocked, grabbed his chest with one hand, dropped to one knee, drove his katana (sword) into the ground, and fell over dead. His Sub-Lieutenant Aide rushed to his side to help him and received a 150 grain reason to join his Shogun master in the imperial hall of fallen heroes.

The rest of the flanking platoon stood around their fallen officers in dismay, not knowing what to do. They weren't trained for this. Japanese officers were not permitted to abandon their troops. If killed they were to lead in spirit. This officer's spirit must have left town because it wasn't leading worth a damn. A senior NCO tried to take command and form the troops in line but to no avail. The men were too spooked to listen. Eyes placed a bullet in the NCO's left ear, removing most of the right side of his head, ending his "lack of command presence" problem.

"Range."

"Range 300 yards. All weapons fire. Fire at will."

The spotter and three man security element all opened fire with their M1s with devastating effect. Three hundred yards was the perfect range for an open sighted M1 Garand rifle in open country, being fired by a highly skilled Marine rifleman.

The Rikusentai warriors were broken up, retreating from the beaten zone of the heavy aimed fire. They barely returned fire as they ran for cover, leaving their dead and wounded behind them.

* * * * *

Rawlins and his charges waited for the enemy patrol to move on and gathered their hidden food. Their course was obvious. They had to leave the island or be captured and/or killed. The enemy landing barge would serve as transportation off the island. The stranded men headed back to the place where the jungle met the sea.

The lagoon where the lightly guarded barge was beached.

"Can you guys run that scow?"

"Yeah, Gunny, if its got an engine, we can run it," answered the Motormac.

"Guns, you take the one on shore. I'll get the one in the barge. Just sneak up on him from behind, grab his mouth and nose with your left hand and shut off his air. At the same time stick him in the back with your Ka-Bar, twist it and pull it out, then stick him again. Now this is important. Grab and stick at the same time or he could turn on you and get you instead. Got it?"

"Got it, Gunny."

"You guys stay outta sight till it's clear."

"OK, Gunny."

Rawlins followed the jungle edge to the sea. Waiting for dark, he low crawled into the water and swam toward the enemy barge. From his position he could see the two guards. As he neared the barge Rawlins submerged and surfaced at the stern of the enemy vessel. The Soldier in the beached craft was leaning against the gunwale half asleep. The man on shore was using his rifle for a prop as he leaned against it. The combat tough Marine grabbed the Soldier standing above him by the neck and dragged him over the side of the barge. At the same time the Gunner Mate grabbed the shore sentry and drove his knife into the enemy's back. The Japanese Marine spun around and broke the Gunner's hold, knocking him to the ground. The Rikusentai, mustering all his strength, tried to bayonet the American Sailor. Rizzo grabbed the wounded Jap's rifle and tried to wrench it from his hands. The warrior of the sun would not give it up. Finally, Rizzo pulled the 45 pistol from his waistband and clubbed the enemy with the heavy weapon. This knocked the Jap senseless just long enough to pick up the Ka-Bar, now lying on the ground, and shove it into the Jap's chest, ending the fight.

Rawlins broke the sentry's neck as he pulled him over the side and held him under water with his knee on the back of his neck to make sure he would not revive when his mates found him.

Now the other stranded Sailors ran down the beach and joined the men at the barge.

"Start this thing and let's get the hell outta here before the rest of those smiling, singin' assholes show up."

The Motormac started the engine, engaged the hand clutch
lever and slid the transmission in reverse. Increasing throttle and
easing out the clutch lever caused the barge to back into the surf,
using the torque of the Howa Diesel engine. Once deep water was
reached the forward gear was activated in the same manner.

"All right. Listen up. Let's check this tub out. Anything you
find that's usable, pile in the middle of the deck."

* * * * *

The airfield was needed for a forward base to strike Truk and
Rabaul on New Georgia. Also to defend Australia and Guadalcanal
from future invasion.

"All right. Listen up. There will be no artillery or air strike
before we attack. We need the strip intact. We'll wait here in the
jungle until 0300 hours, then jump off. Lieut. Pruit, take Second
Squad. Lieut. Matsumo, First Squad. Third Squad will be in reserve
under Corp. Ramirez. I'll lead the Paramarines. I want you Raiders to
take position on the far side of the compound in the tree line. We will
attack from this side. Three minutes after the first shot, when we have
their attention, you will attack their rear and destroy them. Pick your
targets carefully. We don't want any friendly fire incidents."

The Raiders crept through the silent jungle, not making a
sound, as they had been trained to do. No rucksacks or steel helmets.
They might make noise, so they were left behind. Even dog tags were
taped together so they wouldn't rattle. Slings were removed from
rifles for the same reason.

Three hours later they were in position. They signaled the
Major that they were in position by clicking the button on the radio
handset twice, breaking static. No talking.

The attack commenced with the elimination of guard tower
personnel from well aimed M1 Garand fire. The Paramarines rushed
the compound, engaging every enemy they encountered. The Raiders
waited until the enemy defenders were well engaged with the Paras
before attacking.

"Up and at 'um, Raiders. Gung ho."

The Japenese security and support troops were no match for the well trained and combat hardened Raiders and Paramarines. In the light from burning gasoline storage tanks the Marines could see the enemy troops trying to load their rifles as they were cut down. The fight was close and intense but over quickly. Three prisoners were taken. Lieut. Matsumo discovered that they were Manchurian conscripts waiting to surrender.

A Japanese officer, hiding under a barracks building, watched as the Japanese American interviewed the liberated support troops. The Imperial Naval Air Force officer worked his way close to the American Lieut. and charged.

Die, you traitorous swine. Matsumo spun around and blocked the vicious swipe from the Samurai's katana. His carbine was nearly cut in two. Next the enemy officer tried an up-sweep which Matsumo side stepped and countered with a kick to the solar plexus. Then Matsumo tried to bayonet the attacker but the enemy Captain deflected and disarmed Matsumo in one jujitsu rolling block. The Lieut. pulled his Ka-Bar from a leg sheath and the enemy Captain produced his ceremonial dagger. Matsumo plunged at the enemy's chest and missed. The Captain caught him in a running arm bar threatening to stab him with his own knife. Matsumo dropped the Ka-Bar and grabbed the Captain's knife wielding arm. Now they were in a mutual lock position. Neither could do anything. Gunnery Sgt. Alverez ended the stand-off by driving his Ka-Bar into the Captain's neck, sending a shower of blood over the Lieut. The imperial officer went limp and Matsumo let him fall to the ground.

"Damn it, Lieut., don't dance with 'um. Just kill 'um and be done with it.You're gonna get killed playin' around like that."

"OK, Gunny. Thanks for the help."

* * * * *

At the airfield, there were Mitsubishi Zeros and Kates. Also two Kawanishi Float Recon planes in hangers and on the runway. They were destroyed, using composition B plastic explosive taped to the fuel tanks.

"We better get the hell outta here, Major. Every Jap on this island knows our position now, Sir."

"OK, Gunny. Lieut. Pruit, get your men ready to move."

"Aye, Sir. Where we going, Sir?"

"To the area between the Ibu and Zimbu Rivers. We're to hold that area until relieved."

* * * * *

The Sailors found a water tank, rations, ammo and two bottles of sake (rice wine).

No wonder those sentries were half asleep. They were loaded.

"By the way, Guns, you did good back there."

"Thanks, Gunny. I damn near got killed again. I was lucky. These Japs ain't the pushovers they led us to believe back in the States. They're tough bastards."

"They're Rikusentai, the best the enemy has. And a lot of them are Samurai Warrior Class. They spend their whole young lives preparing to die with honor for the emperor."

"Look at this, Gunny. It's a chart with our island circled in red."

"According to this Ruwawa should be over here in this group. Too bad it's all written in Jap. Do you think you can get us over there to those islands?"

"Look up in the sky, Gunny. See the Southern Cross?"

"Yeah, I see it."

"Just like the First Marine Division's shoulder patch. If we reverse course, head south by west, keeping the cross on our starboard beam and if we don't run out of fuel, we'll find Ruwawa in the morning."

"Make it so, Coxwain. And good work."

* * * * *

The Raiders and Paramarines on Ruwawa found the area they were to hold at all cost. They were then told that the first wave of the main assault would land behind them and advance through their position.

"Dig in and make 'um deep. We ain't leavin' till relieved."

The Marines formed an inverted tee with the center leg pointing into the grass field and the main line forming against the tree line near the beach. The CP was positioned in the trees near the beach for protection. Flanking skirmishers dug in along both rivers on the ends of the tees main line. The fighting holes were staggered three deep with two men per hole. Sixty mm mortars were emplaced in four positions in the edge of the tree line behind the main line. Thirty cal. L1AL machine guns were placed in two positions in the main line and two B.A.R. teams were in the leg. Tommy gunners were with the skirmishers to break up any cross river infiltration attempts.

"Ramirez."

"Sir."

"I want you to take a Team and recon that road leading from the airfield. See it you can neutralize those tanks that were reported. And any other armour or heavy weapons you find. Take the Boy's elephant gun for the tanks."

(Boy's gun - 51 cal. anti-tank gun, shoulder fired. Developed by English Army Colonel Boys in 1936 to destroy thin skinned Italian and German armour of the time. Produced by Ingles Arms of Canada and adopted by the Raiders in 1942. Many units were converted to fifty cal. gov. and used for long range sniping. Called the elephant gun by Raiders).

"Eyes."

"Sir."

"Second Squad saddle up. Eyes, bring the elephant gun. We got tanks to kill."

* * * * *

The sea was so black and calm it was eerie. The reflections of the stars in the still water meeting the stars in the black sky gave a feeling of being suspended in time and space. No war, no killing, no pain, just millions of stars in a black galaxy, far, far away.

"Shit, there's a ship over there. What do we do?"

"Kill the engine. They'll see the wake we're making. And be quiet."

"What kind is it?"

"Looks like a destroyer?"

"Whose?"

"Australian or New Zealand in these waters. Or Japanese. Doesn't matter who they are. If they see us they will fire on us. The Jap Navy has been alerted by now that we borrowed their barge. And anybody else's Navy don't like Japs. If they hit this barge with anything bigger than the Captain's 45 we're done for."

The destroyer steamed north as they drifted south west. There were some tense moments as the ship was abaft their beam at four hundred yards. They would abandon the barge and take their chances in the black sea if fired on. A hit from a Naval shell or heavy machine gun, automatic triple AAA (anti-aircraft artillery) would mean certain death in this thin hulled water mule. It would surely burn and sink if hit. Better off in the water where you had some protection and the ability to hide in the wreckage.

"Looks like their leaving."

"Wow. That was close."

"Their lookouts must be half asleep. How could they miss us?"

"Low silhouette. They're looking down from above us and it's a dark night. No Sailor wants to send his mates to general quarters without being sure of what he sees."

"What now, Gunny?"

"I say we drift a while and watch the area around us. We don't need any more surprises. Try to get some sleep. I'll take first watch. Guns can relieve me in two hours."

"OK, Gunny. Sounds good."

Rawlins waited for the Sailors to doze off, then grabbed a bottle of sake and took a long pull. The burning liquid poured down his parched throat, almost making him gag. After a few minutes he felt warm all over and very relaxed. The first time he'd relaxed in many days. It reminded Rawlins of the morphine Doc had given him when he was wounded. Same feeling but more intense. He could understand how Marines and Soldiers got hooked on morphine trying to escape the horrors of war.

Rawlins felt like he was drifting through an endless abyss where the earth ended and the galaxy began. He was in the great planetarium of the South Pacific. Fascinating. The Southern Cross was above him and the black sky-sea all around. So still and peaceful in his alcohol induced state. He saw why Marines and Sailors always say:

"Until you see the Southern Cross you haven't lived."

The Marine also understood why ancient Mariners thought the world was flat and they would fall off it if they ventured too far. It appeared that way to him right now.

"Rawlins."

"Yeah, Rizzo."

"You all right?"

"Yeah. Just thinking."

"What the hell is eatin' you anyway? You get a dear John or something?"

"Yeah, something like that."

"Yeah, me too. A year ago. You, me and a million other guys. That's just the way it is in this lousy war. You think you got someone at home worth fightin' for and joby the 4F s.o.b. comes along and ruins everything. When this is over and we get home I think we should declare war on all 4F joby assholes that been stealin' men's women. Sign me up for that detail. I hate them as much as I hate the Japs.

* * * * *

Rawlins and his crew were all awake, wondering what to do.

"We can't keep drifting. It will be light in an hour or so and the Japs will be looking for us. We gotta find an atoll and hide this scow somehow. According to this chart we should be close to this group of islets. If we follow a course of 90 degrees true we should spot them at first light. It's our best chance to hide for the day. Do we agree or are there other ideas?"

"Sounds good, Gunny. Let's do it."

The engine was started and the barge was steered 90 degrees

true. Their wake was exposed but it couldn't be helped. They were racing against the clock, hoping to beat sun-up and detection by Japanese reconnaissance aircraft or the ever present motor launch and barge patrols in the area. One 6.5 pedestal mount Nambu light mg on the stern of this scow and three 45 cal. pistols was not much fire power to wage Naval warfare against heavily armed enemy Sailors and Airmen.

The stars began to fade and the sky turned purple and orange as the sun peeked over the horizon. And there it was. A mile or so to the southwest lay an atoll with a large lagoon with lava rock caves. The perfect place to hide a large boat in the middle of an ocean.

"Son of a bitch. There's a Jap battle cruiser."

"How can you tell?"

"It's over the horizon. Must be fifteen miles away. See the three pagoda masts and the forward superstructure almost sitting on the number two gun turret?"

"Yeah. I see it."

"That's Jap for sure."

"I guess it takes a Sailor to know."

The scow fit nicely in a cave at the far end of the lagoon. Her adopted crew managed to push her around a corner in the cave and lash her to the rocks. This way if there was a fight it would be close and surprise would be their's. Rawlins posted a guard near the cave entrance and rotated them every two hours. The rest of the men cleaned and reloaded weapons, ate Japanese rations, and waited for dark.

"Rizzo. You think they saw us."

"Probably."

"What will they do about us?"

"Depends on the Captain. First, he'll order a fly-over by flying boat. If that doesn't satisfy him he'll dispatch a motor launch with an eight man boarding party."

"Which do you think it will be?"

"If they saw us, both. Better get ready for a fight. I just hope it's late when they come so we can beat it outta here and get away from that ship in the darkness. If we can, we should commandeer their launch. It will have a lower silhouette and be much faster and

have full fuel and water tanks."
`   "Roger to that, Guns."

* * * * *

Corp. Ramirez and his squad followed the road from the airfield, keeping a descreet distance in case enemy patrols were in the area. They stayed in the jungle edge parallel to the road. Traffic was heavy as the enemy re-established a garrison at the airfield. The Corp. decided to ambush a column after dark. His men mined the road with anti-tank contact mines and the shoulders were booby trapped with grenade fused mortar rounds that were brought for this purpose. Trip lines were strung across the road, connecting the grenade fuses which would detonate the grenades, detonating the mortar rounds in turn.

After the ambush the squad would use the nearby Zimbu River for escape. They would enter the water after exfiltrating through a half mile or so of kunai grass, leaving no tracks in the hard earth. Then they would head in the direction the enemy was coming from to confuse the issue even further. The Japanese would beat the adjoining jungle to a pulp for the re-deploying Marines but would find nothing.

"All right. Find some cover but don't dig in. We gotta move fast when it's time. Check weapons and ammo. Use grenades first, then open up."

The jungle was quiet. The buzz of insects and the odd scamper of a lizard or chirp of a bat in the trees was all that could be heard. The night was so black a Raider couldn't see the man next to him, making things very uncomfortable. The men began to fall asleep from sheer exhaustion, having had little or no rest for days.

"Corp., I hear something."

"I think they're coming. Pipe down. They'll hear you."

The squad became restless and apprehensive. They knew they would be fighting for their lives very soon.

Fifty yards from the Raider position there was a horrendous explosion. A truck carrying troops to the airfield ran over a mine. The explosion threw the truck on it's side, spilling it's live cargo onto the road. The Soldiers who were still able to, ran to the shoulders of the road, detonating the mortar rounds. Destroyed, dismembered bodies flew into the trees like paper kites.

"Raiders. Throw grenades."

At the sound of the detonations Ramirez yelled,

"Let 'um have it. Open fire."

The ten man squad mowed down what remained of the enemy. Reloading their weapons, they merged with the enemy, silhouetted by the flames of gasoline fires. A few Japs tried to retaliate but were quickly dispatched by the Marines.

A Jap Sergeant, playing dead in the roadside ditch, shot Pfc. Jowarsky at point blank range. Eyes shot the Jap pretender twice with his 1911 45 pistol, making him dead for real.

"Doc. Get over here."

"Corp. I ain't gonna make it. Tell my wife I'm sorry."

"Shut up, Sky. You ain't that bad."

"Doc."

"We'll fix you. Then you can tell her yourself."

"Doc. Hurry up. We gotta go, Doc. C'mon. What's the holdup?"

"He's dead, Corp."

"Watta ya mean, dead. He barely got hit."

"Shock or an artery got clipped. Whatever the cause, he's dead."

"Son of a bitch. All right. Put him in a shelter half and pick two men to carry him. We ain't leavin' him here."

"Pfc. Jowarsky was buried a mile from the ambush site in a clearing on the bank of the Zimbu River. The spot was marked on the map for later recovery by U.S. Army Graves Registration personnel.

"Let's get back in the water. The Japs are looking for us by now."

The Raiders progressed silently upstream in the river until dawn broke. Then they chose a defensible position near the river bank; high ground with a good view.

"Dig in. Two man holes. Ten foot intervals. Semi-circle. Make 'um deep."

From this elevated position they could watch 360 degrees.

"Listen up. This will be our CP. We'll run patrols from here. Stay outta sight. Don't silhouette yourselves on top of the hills. Stay in the low areas. Wallace. Place your B.A.R. on top of that draw and cover the most likely route of attack. If we have to we'll bug out down the draw behind you and you and Eyes will bring up the rear."

"OK, Corp."

Ramirez led the first combat patrol to recon the area. After two miles of low hills and jungle the patrol found a road.

"Let's follow this and check it out. Stay in the jungle. The road may be mined."

After a mile or so of trying to navigate in the black jungle Ramirez was alerted.

"Corp., I see kights."

"Yeah. I see 'um too. Take a knee. I'll check it out."

The Raider NCO slid through the jungle like a reptilian predator; not making a sound. No enemy sentry was going to hear or see this professional. He even striped his face and hands with boot black to cut the reflection from the light. As he slipped past a large cedar a clearing came into view. And there they were. Three Tomas (light infantry tank), two batteries of 150mm heavy artillery and a multitude of trucks and support vehicles. Also two elevated guard towers with type 99 7.7mm Nambu heavy machine guns.

This must be the battalion lay down area they've been looking for. Those heavy guns and tanks must be destroyed or they will jeopardize the invasion.

Ramirez found his way back to his waiting men and uttered the pre-arranged password so he wouldn't be killed by his own people.

"Stutz."

and the reply,

"Bearcat."

The Stutz-Bearcat was a popular automobile of the time.

"Let's go."

Ramirez would fill in his Team when they reached the relative safety of the CP and not until. They all knew this and did not ask questions. Making any unnecessary noise of any kind could endanger the mission and lives of the Team.

Ramirez and his Team returned to the squads position near the river and made ready for the attack on the battalion bivouac.

"We hold up on the perimeter edge until 0300 hours. Stay outta sight and be quiet. If the enemy's alerted our surprise is gone and our mission compromised. And the Japs will be chasing us till hell freezes over. We gotta hit them hard and fast. Do what damage we can and get the hell outta here. Primary targets are the 150mm gun batteries and the three Tomas we spotted. After that destroy what you can and take off. Try and stay in two or three man Teams. Rendezvous here unless it's too hot. If so go to the river and head upstream until you're clear. We'll find each other up the river in the next couple of days. Then I'll arrange a sub pickup through the CP. Eyes, take two men and the elephant gun. Take out the tower guards with baby. Then go after the Tomas. Wallace, you and your loader with two riflemen go for the 150's. The rest of you guys watch their backs. You will be the perimeter fire support. Remember, the invasion could fail if we do. That's how important this raid is.

* * * * *

"Hear that, Gunny?"

"Yeah, I hear it. Kawanishi Float Recon plane. Gotta be from that Nip scow. He's making circles. Looking for us. Engine noise getting faint. He's gone."

"Wow, Gunny. You should be a sports broadcaster with that play by play action."

"Last year on the Canal Washing Machine Charlie would visit us from Truk Lagoon and drop a couple of five hundred pounders just to be friendly. Same plane. Might even be him."

In the cave entrance the Coxswain stood watch.

"They're coming, Gunny. Motor launch, six man party."

"All right, you guys. Get back here. Rizzo, get on that Nambu. You two check your 45s, make sure there's a round in the chamber and the thumb safety is off. When they come into view and they see us, open up. But not until they see us. That way they'll be as close as possible. Point the front sight at the middle of their bodies and keep firing until you come up empty. Then drop your weapon and go over the side quick. The water is deep here. Surface under the front of this scow just enough to get air. Keep your body under water. It will help protect you from flying shit. Guns, rake 'um port and starboard. Keep your muzzle high and level so we don't sink the boat."

Japanese voices could be heard talking at the cave entrance.

"This is it. They're coming," whispered Rawlins.

In an unnerving display of the oddity of war, friend and foe were within six feet of each other and the Japanese Sailors were oblivious to the fact. When the bow of the motor launch was four feet from the stern of the barge, Rawlins and his men, hiding behind a large rock, stood with all weapons raised. As the launch rounded the turn around the rock the enemies came face to face. The Japanese had shocked, horrified expressions, knowing they were about to die.

"Fire," bellowed the Gunnery Sgt.

The noise from the explosion of weapons firing point blank in the cave was astounding. And the devastation complete. All the Japanese were dead in a matter of eight seconds. They had never fired a shot. And the Americans had a new boat and supplies.

"Throw those bodies overboard. They're startin' to stink already. Swab this deck with sea water and get rid of the blood. Grab what's left of the rations and ammo. Guns, pull that chopper of it's mount and bring it along. Motormac, start this scow and let's get the hell outta here. Coxswain, man the tiller and steer 90 degrees true."

As the launch left the cave and rounded the corner of the lagoon and headed for the open sea sharks were already feeding on the dead Japanese Sailors.

"Look at that, Gunny. Didn't take long."

As the lagoon turned red with blood from the feeding frenzy Rawlins commented,

"That's why I'm glad I'm a Marine and not a Sailor. They're lucky they're dead."

* * * * *

The 6.5 inch Naval artillery shells sounded like a subway racing through a tunnel as they passed over the escaping Americans.

They crashed into the sea fifty meters ahead and to the left of the launch. A huge geyser of spray rose into the air where they struck. The smell of burnt cordite was in the air.

"Coxswain. Hard right rudder."

"Aye, Gunny."

The next salvo landed where the launch had been a minute before.

"Steer around those big rocks. Put them between us and the cruiser."

Just as the escaping Americans came abeam of the rocks another salvo slammed into the lagoon, spraying the small boat's occupants with mud and water.

"Son of a bitch. They have the range. Pour it on, Motormac. Flank speed."

"That's it, Gunny. We're all out."

The rock formation was falling astern when the next salvo struck. Rock chips and shrapnel screamed through the air, some striking the boat. Luckily sunset was casting a reddish glow across the sea and the rock formation was obscuring the enemy's view.

"I think they gave up on us, Gunny. Good thing it got dark and those rocks are there or they would have nailed us for sure. We better find land by daybreak or a Jap plane is gonna find us. We're taking on water, Gunny."

"How bad?"

"We can keep up with it as long as we man the bilge pump every half hour or so."

"Oh, no, Gunny. Look at that boiling water fifty yards off the port quarter."

"What the hell is that?"

"Gotta be a sub blowing ballast to surface."

"Well, I guess this is it. What you guys wanna do? End it here and go out fightin' or surrender and get raped and tortured?"

"F..k it. I would rather die fightin' than go through that and get beheaded anyway."

"Me too, Gunny. We have all heard what they do to prisoners."

"Guns, get on that chopper. You guys grab those Arisakas.

When they bunch up on the bridge let 'um have it. Maybe we'll get a couple of officers that way."

* * * * *

The USS Halibut broke the surface on an even keel and settled motionless on the sea fifty yards away. Men were seen opening hatches and scrambling to their stations as the boat was vented. From the bridge an American voice was heard.

"Ahoy, there. Drop your weapons and come aboard. This is an American vessel. Do not fire on us. We are Americans. This is the United States Naval vessel, USS Halibut. You have permission to board."

"Gunnery Sgt. Rawlins and Gunners Mate Rizzo reporting, Sir."

"Lieut. Commander Masters, gentlemen. Welcome aboard."

"Thank you, Sir."

"Your two Sailors are below being looked at by our Pharmacist Mate."

"Thank you, Sir. They're good men, Sir, and they've been through a lot."

"Yes, I agree. Tell me, gentlemen, were you going to engage us?"

"Yes, Sir. We agreed it was better to go out fightin', Sir, than face capture."

"Well, Gunny, I for one am glad you men changed your minds. It would be very hard to explain to Admiral Nimitz how I lost my boat to three Sailors and a crazy Marine I found doing battle with an enemy battle cruiser with three rifles and a Nambu in a 20 foot launch."

"Aye, Sir."

"Please report below for a checkup and a new issue. Then join me for dinner if you would."

"Aye, Sir. And thank you, Sir."

"Curtiss. Sink that Jap scow."

"With pleasure, Sir."

One short burst from the bridge mount 50 cal. AA mg. sent

the launch to the bottom.

* * * * *

"So tell me, gentlemen. What on earth compelled you to do battle with an enemy battle cruiser?"

"Well, Sir, it happened like this. We borrowed a Jap Rikusentai landing barge and left the island we were marooned on."

"How did that happen, Gunny?"

"I was being transported to Ruwawa by PT boat when we were hit and the boat caught fire and blew up. We were the only survivors. We were in the water for about twelve hours when we spotted this island and went ashore. There was no garrison, only a couple of Jap Sailors and we disposed of them. We did OK for a couple of days, finding food and shelter. A Rikusentai patrol showed up and searched the island. We knew they were too much for us, Sir, so we eliminated the sentries on and near the barge and escaped. At first light we found that lagoon with the caves and hid for the day. The cruiser must have spotted us, or a routine patrol with the launch found us, Sir, and we were forced to fight."

"Any casualties?"

"No, Sir."

"And the enemy?"

"All killed, Sir."

"Outstanding, Gunny. Then the men in your company fought well?"

"These Sailors are the best damn Marines in the Navy, Sir."

"Permission to speak, Sir?"

"Go right ahead, Guns. This is an open forum. Things are a little more relaxed on a sub than you're probably used to. Close quarters, long patrols."

"Yes, Sir. I would like to say for the record that Gunnery Sgt. Rawlins performed above and beyond at all times and without hesitation in the face of the enemy. Without his leadership none of us would have survived."

"Duly noted, Guns. This report will be amended with your statement. Yeoman."

"Aye, Skipper. Already done. It will go out with the morning report."

"Cookie."

"Sir."

"Take an order."

"Aye, Skipper. What'll it be?"

"Some real Navy coffee, then some more coffee. Any of that meat loaf left from lunch?"

"Yes, Sir."

"Sound good, men?"

"Been a long time since I ate that good, Sir."

"Well, enjoy. Nothing's too good for the crazy Marine and Sailor that attack cruiser and submarine with a motor launch. Rawlins. Where are you from anyway?"

"Marine Second Raiders, Sir."

"The Makin Island Raiders? Colonel Evan Carlson's group?"

"Same, Sir."

"Well, I'll be. It's true what they say about you Raiders."

"What's that, Sir?"

"Fight to the death, won't give up, won't surrender."

"Aye, Skipper. That's our creed, kinda like Submariners. They're nuts too."

This made everyone present laugh, including the Captain.

"How's Captain Hesscox, Sir?"

"You know him, Rawlins?"

"Yes, Sir. Damn good Skipper. Pulled us out of a few tight spots."

"Damn fine crew too. Far as I know he's OK. When we get back to Pearl I'll look him up and give him your regards."

"Thank you, Sir."

"Gunner Mate Rizzo."

"Sir."

"What am I going to do with you?"

"A vacation back at Pearl would be a good idea."

"Sorry, Guns, you're too valuable. I lost my Gunner Mate and two other men a week ago during an air attack. I could put a third stripe under that crow and give you a new home."

"Sounds good, Sir. I'm ready for a change. Lost too many friends in the PTs."

"Good man. You'll fit right in and do well, I'm sure. I'll contact your old Skipper and fill him in."

"Thank you, Sir. He'll be surprised to hear we're alive."

* * * * *

The Corp. and his squad were aware of the fact that they would be vastly outnumbered when they attacked. This was nothing new for the Raiders. Surprise was their ally. Confusion their greatest weapon. The Japanese were in a stand down situation at their bivouac and were not expecting to be attacked, especially by the small raiding party they knew was in the area. The Raiders would be outnumbered twenty to one. Also, the Japs had tanks, artillery and seasoned veteran infantry. These brash American gangsters in their lizard costumes wouldn't dare attack them in their base camp. It would mean certain death.

Mistake No. 1 - never underestimate the enemy.

As the attackers silently got into position they considered their own mortality. Each man knew the risks were high. But if they pulled off this raid, just like the airfield, casualties during the invasion would be light. The First Marine Division and the U.S. Army Forty Fifth Infantry Division would thank them later.

0300-

Eyes takes out guard tower occupants with two shots from baby. Range 400 yards. Rifleman from Scout Sniper Team eliminates gunners in closer tower using M1 Garand rifle. Range 150 yards. Sniper Team advances to first tower to engage tanks with Boy's rifle.

Three Tomas (tanks) are parked in compound 75 yards from tower. The closest is fired on with Boy's anti-tank rifle. Two rounds are fired which penetrate the thin armour. Muffled screams are heard as the target explodes into flames. The second tank is incinerated from heat and flames from the first. The third Toma lurches ahead, churning up the earth, turning right and left, searching for the enemy that killed it's friends. As the behemoth turned away from the Team, Eyes put a 51 cal. 750 grain, tungsten core armour piercing projectile through the juggernauts engine.

Shit. The bolt won't open. I can't reload this monster. Will have to finish it with grenades.

Two men headed for the tank. Eyes covered them with baby. They were almost there when the turret hatch lifted and out came a Jap NCO with a Type 14 8mm Nambu pistol. The tanker shot twice at the approaching Raiders. Then Eyes, with the help of baby, placed a 150 grain 30 cal. M2 ball fmj round at 2800 fps in the enemy's mouth, removing most of his teeth and the back of his head. The impact threw the Jap off the turret and on to the ground. One of the advancing riflemen shot him again just to make sure the dead Jap was really dead. He knew what could happen if he was only wounded. Then the Team member picked up the Nambu. They brought a good buck in New Zealand or back in Pearl.

The other Raider climbed on the tank, pulled his 45 pistol from it's holster, racked the slide and chambered a round, then pulled himself up on the turret, stuck the pistol in the hatch opening and fired seven rounds of 45 cal. 230 grain full metal patch at 830 fps. He then calmly dropped the spent magazine from the pistol and replaced it with a full seven round magazine, then addressed his partner.

"Hey, Bill, gimme a hot one."

A live smoking grenade was tossed to the pistolero which was caught and tossed into the tank's turret.

"Let's get the hell outta here before the fuel and ammo go up."

"Roger that."

Eyes and his Team, their mission completed, headed for the tree line and exfiltration.

Wallace and his Fire Team found a sliver of jungle protruding into the clearing near their objective. The 150mm batteries.

"I was afraid of this. There's a large security element around those guns. They gotta go first. Every man pick a target. When I fire you fire on that target. When all visible targets are down we rush 'um. When we're half way there hit the deck and throw grenades, reload your rifle and charge. Any questions? OK, let's do it."

At the sound of Wallace's B.A.R., three sons of Nippon

dropped like bad habits, then the ensuing 30 cal. barrage caused the rest of the very susrprised security force to disappear, either by being hit or diving for cover. As planned, the Fire Team ran for the guns while the enemy's heads were down. M2 fragmentation grenades were thrown with deadly accuracy into the sandbagged perimeter with deadly effect. The Japanese were stunned and disoriented.

"Reload," yelled Wallace.

"Charge."

Yells of "gung ho," the Raider motto and "semper phi," the U.S. Marine Corps motto, were shouted as the Raiders charged.

The Team breached the perimeter with hardly a shot fired. The Japanese defenders were either dead or too wounded to respond. One kind hearted Marine gave a dying Japanese Corp. water and a cigarette. These men were no longer a threat. The demo man with the Team placed thermite grenades on the trunions and turning gears of the big guns. Also in the breach blocks. At five thousand degrees Fahrenheit the high carbon steel would become molten destruction. The big guns were rendered completely useless.

"We're done here. Set a charge in that pile of stacked shells and move out."

A composition B charge with acid five minute pencil fuse was placed in the pile and the Raiders headed for the tree line.

Ramirez joined the Fire Support Team and directed fire. Pockets of enemy defenders were cut down as far as 400 yards from the tree line. The combination of M1 Garand and 1903 Springfield rifles in U.S. 30 cal. (3006 Springfield) were deadly at this range in the expert hands of well trained Marine riflemen. Targets were illuminated from the light of burning tanks and trucks shot up by Wallace's B.A.R. Team during their withdrawal.

The Infiltration Teams had done their jobs. Their targets were destroyed. Also many secondaries were eliminated. The two Teams were gone, back in the jungle heading for the river. The Fire Support Team was taking aimed fire from the battalion C.P., a type 99 Nambu heavy mg 7.7mm as they found the range. The Mission Fire Support Unit was taking casualties. One man was killed when three 7.7s ripped across his back while he was firing in the prone position. Another wounded from a Type 89 grenade discharger (knee mortar). It was time to go. The Corp. gave the signal and the Raiders melted into the jungle. They fired in relays as they retreated. Three men fired until weapons were empty. Then three more took their positions as they reloaded and retreated. This was done as long as their attackers tried to envelope their position. When the thick jungle was reached the Raiders threw grenades at the approaching enemy and ran like hell.

The next day, after a five mile hike up river, Ramirez' squad found a small clearing on the other side of the river and stood down for the day. So far casualties were light. Two dead, four wounded, one missing. A small price to pay for the amount of success so far. A battalion of the famous Sendie Division had been totally disrupted by one reinforced squad of the U.S. Marine Raiders, or jungle demons as the Japanese called them.

"Hey, Corp."

"Yeah?"

"How many we get last night?"

"Maybe fifty."

"No shit. You think so?"

"Maybe more."

"How 'bout back at the road? Twenty?"

"Yeah. Sounds about right."

"What happened to Georgio?"

"A 7.7 chopper got him. Hit three, maybe four times."

"Tough break, He was a good Joe."

"Never knew what hit him. Went out quick. That's the best way to go I guess."

"He was lucky. F..king monkeys. We should kill 'um all."

"Hey, Corp., look what Doc's got."

"Where you find them, Doc?"

"I caught 'um in that deep pool in the river."

"You gonna eat 'um?"

"Why not. We're short on rations. I'll make fish chowder."

"What kind are they?"

"Look like trout to me."

Doc made a small smokeless fire, filled his helmet with water and propped it over the fire with two rocks. While he cleaned the fish his comrades donated Japanese king crab, lobster, salmon and canned mackerel. Rations gleaned from the enemy. Some shallots and mushrooms were found and with Doc's salt, pepper and basil a fish chowder fit for a king was concocted and enjoyed by all.

"Doc. This is really good. I guess the Navy really does eat better than the Marines. Where you learn how to do this, Doc?"

"My old man showed me. He's the big outdoors type."

"You just got promoted, Doc. You're our new cook."

"Gee, thanks, Corp. That makes my day."

* * * * *

Ramirez' Team was evacuated the following night by submarine. They followed the river to a small lake and then headed south to the sea. A large rock formation hid them until the USS Cod picked them up at 0300 hours. Luckily there was no enemy contact since they were dangerously low on ammo. Many Raiders carried enemy weapons and ammo in addition to their own in case of attack.

The USS Cod dropped them off the next night at their bivouac on the north shore.

"Corp. Ramirez reporting, Sir. Mission accomplished, Sir."

"Let's hear it, Ramirez."

"Aye, Sir. Three tanks, ten trucks and other vehicles destroyed. Enemy battalion base camp disrupted. Seventy five to one hundred fifty enemy KIA, Sir."

"Casualties?"

"Two KIA, four wounded, one missing."

"Outstanding. Did you find those 155s?"

"All heavy weapons destroyed, Sir?"

"That's great, Corp. Well done. Congratulate your men with my compliments."

"Aye, Sir."

"Will the Major be writing to the families of the casualties, Sir?"

"Yes, of course. As soon as the island is secure."

"Please explain, Sir, that their sacrifice will save hundreds of lives in future actions against the Japanese."

"I'll do that, Ramirez. Thank you."
"Thank you, Sir."

* * * * *

As Rawlins headed for Guadalcanal compliments of the USS Halibut, the Japanese on Ruwawa were probing the defenses of the Marine strong point on the north shore.

"Sarge, I hear something."

Pop. A flare. In the eerie greenish white light thirty yards to their forward Japanese Soldiers stood in the stark light like evil demons from hell on Halloween night.

"Let 'um have it."

The Marine line exploded as the Paramarines opened fire. The Sgt. called for mortar illumination as the enemy was cut down with heavy fire. It was over in less than five minutes. A whole Japanese platoon gone, wiped out to the last man. Their mission was accomplished. But now the main force knew where the Marine line was and would attack in force. And there would be no quarter. There would be a classic banzai bayonet charge with no prisoners. The jungle demons would be pushed into the sea. The sons of Nippon would conquer the American gangsters once and for all.

"We really kicked their asses, Sarge."

"Yeah, dummy. One platoon. Now the whole battalion will come at us all at once. Just like Edson's Ridge on the Canal. I hope you're ready for one hell of a fight 'cause we're gonna have one."

As the night wore on sporadic gunfire erupted along the line as the Japanese probed the Marine defenses. The CP called for fire support to contain the enemy forces preparing an all out assault. Two PT boats were mustered from the night patrol list and re-routed to the area. Their assigned mission was to infiltrate the Ibu and Zimbu Rivers and fire on any infantry or special Naval Landing Force troops using the rivers to flank and infiltrate the Marine positions.

At 0400 hours the attack began in earnest. A 60 and a 90mm mortar barrage pounded the Marine positions for twenty minutes. Then they came, bayonets fixed, screaming like demon possessed banshees, the classic banzai charge. The same charge their Samurai

ancestors had used two hundred years previously to engage enemies
of the Shogun warlords. Only then they had employed spears, bows
and arrows and katana (swords).

"Sarge. There's hundreds of 'um."

"Pick a target and squeeze. And stay down. Fire and reload.
Fire and reload. Yer doin' fine."

The line exploded with firing. The Marines were taking
casualties now that the Japanese were breaching the main line. Men
were pulled from Headquarters Company and the Intelligence Section
and employed as riflemen, plugging the breaches in the line.

Both PT boats opened fire with their 50 cal. machine guns
with great effect. Designed for anti-aircraft use, these heavy caliber
guns were deadly against massed infantry. When suppressed to deck
level they cut huge swaths out of the advancing enemy.

"Hey, Sarge. We're getting help from the Navy."

The Sgt. didn't answer. A sniper in the tree line 600 meters
away had placed a 7.7mm slug in his brain, ending the war for him.

"Sarge. Sarge. Oh, shit no. You dirty bastards."

The young Paramarine picked up the Sgt.'s Thompson and
charged a group of Japanese Soldiers, pulling the trigger and
screaming like a man insane. He shot them all. As he found more
targets he felt the Tommy gun buck in his hands. The enemy fell
before him and he felt nothing. They had killed his Sergeant and they
would pay dearly for it.

Ramirez and Hays kept their men near the CP in case of a
breakthrough. They would protect their officers to the end.

Marines were fighting hand to hand in the lines. The enemy
was overrunning their positions. A big Marine Corporal was stabbed
and picked up his much smaller attacker and smashed in his head
against a tree. Another Marine used his empty M1 rifle for a club and
killed four enemy Soldiers. A Paramarine was bayoneted and shot
three Rikusentai with his 45 pistol before going down.

The enemy was closing on the CP and Hays and Ramirez
began directing fire against them.

* * * * *

"Lieut., the USS Essex and the USS Fordham are on station for fire support, Sir."

"Stand by, Joseph."

"Major, we have fire support. Two destroyers are on station off shore."

"Well, it's about time. They must be there to cover the invasion forces."

"Yes, Sir."

"Lt. Pruit. Order a fire mission and clear out these people knocking on our door."

"Aye, Sir. At 0500 hours two regiments of the First Marine Division and one regiment on loan from General MacArthur's 42nd U.S. Infantry Division will come ashore behind us and assault through our position. They will dispose of any remaining threat on this island once and for all. Joseph. Call the Essex and get some fire support."

"Aye, Sir."

"Plain language. We're being overrun."

"Aye, Sir."

"USS Essex. Fire mission. Over."

"USS Essex. Go ahead."

"Request fire mission, anti personnel. H.E. proximity fuse ten foot airburst. Also star shell illumination. Five inch main batteries. Give us all you got. We're being overrun. Repeat. We're being overrun. Fire fifty yards south of invasion beach. Will adjust. Over."

The first salvo landed on target, tearing a large hole in the enemy advance. The next rounds fell a bit closer to the beach with the same results.

"Right on, Essex. Fire for effect. Keep it coming."

Between the Naval barrage and the 50 cal. fire from the PT boats the assault was breaking up. Losing momentum because of the great gaps torn in the advance line.

A squad of Rikusentai broke into the Command Post perimeter.

"Joker. Your left."

Hays cut down three enemy Marines with his Thompson not ten feet away.

"Junior. Look out."

Darl Evans, alias Junior, the youngest Marine in the Second Raiders (17), an oversize Iowa farm boy, sidestepped a bayonet thrust. He punched the attacker in the side of his head so hard it broke the Jap's neck and killed him.

Ramirez, the temporary owner of the shortpecker, mowed down a gaggle of tightly packed infiltrators with a burst from the deadly weapon.

"Lieut. Look out."

Three sons of Nippon broke into the CP with mayhem in mind. The first was shot in the forehead by the Major with his ever present 45 auto pistol. The other two went for Lieut. Matsumo. One he shot with his carbine. The other rising sun hopeful disarmed the Lieut. and tried to bayonet him. As the two warriors struggled over the rifle, Joseph stood up from his radio, grabbed the enemy by the face, twisted his head around and stabbed him twice under the arm with his Ka-Bar. The seasoned killer looked shocked, grunted and died.

"Thanks, Joseph."

"Glad to help, Lieut. I was getting bored anyway."

* * * * *

The shelling had stopped. The Essex had exhausted her supply of five inch high explosive shells. Dawn was breaking and through the smoke and haze piles of Japanese dead were all around the Marines. The enemy's back was broken. The fight was over. The remaining Japanese troops headed for the other side of the island. They would dig in to the hills and make their final stand there. They would die for the emperor as was their tradition.

U.S. Navy LCVP Higgins Boats (landing craft, vehicle, personnel) and Marine Corps alligators (amphibious tractors) brought the assault waves ashore. These men advanced through the Marine lines in pursuit of the fleeing Japanese. The young men were shocked and horrified at the death and destruction they witnessed. Many were in combat for the first time.

Two LSTs (landing ship transport) beached themselves, their

gaping bow doors opening and personnel ramps dropping to load the Raiders and Paramarines who had fought so hard for this island. The men would be returned to Guadalcanal to refit and reorganize. Then liberty in either New Caledonia or New Zealand. They were more than ready for a well earned rest.

Chapter Seven

LIBERTY

Wellington, New Zealand. The chosen port of call for
Marines and Sailors fighting in the Solomon Islands. Lying south of
the equator, between Australia and New Caledonia, New Zealand has
an agreeable climate, English speaking population (being a British
colony), white sand beaches and snow capped mountains. Farming
and sheep raising is the main occupation. Americans were welcome
there because of the Japanese threat to the region. New Zealanders
were also our Allies, fighting the Japanese in the Solomons and the
Nazis in Italy and North Africa. Some American servicemen found
the country so agreeable after the hell of jungle combat that they
returned after the war and settled there.

"Lieut. Where we goin' this time?"

"New Zealand."

"Where's that?"

"Next to Australia."

"They got Japs there."

"Not yet."

"They got booze."

"Yeah."

"They got broads."

"Yeah."

"No shit."

"No shit."

"It ain't another stinkin' jungle, is it?"

"No jungle. It's like home."

"How long we there for?"

"Till the next operation."

"What do we do there?"

"Re-train, re-supply, re-arm and raise hell."

* * * * *

"Hot damn. I got the dope from the Lieut. They got broads
and booze and no jungle where we're goin'."

"Yer full a shit, slope head. There ain't such a place out here. Only jungle and more jungle. And the only booze is jungle juice and Aqua Velva and the only broads are fuzzys full a Jap clap. Yer dreamin."

"I'm tellin' you guys he's on the level."

"OK, Einstein, why would an officer tell a Pfc. anything?"

"'Cause he likes me, that's why."

"Oh yeah. Did he invite you to the next officer call so you can hold hands and sing songs together? Or maybe the Sergeant Major will come down here and tell you to report to Officer's Mess for dinner. Better put on your Class A uniform and shine your brass, Junior."

"Yeah. We'll see."

At that moment the klaxon rang out.

"Attention on deck. The Captain will address the crew and all Marine personnel."

"This is the Captain. Our destination is New Zealand. When we arrive in Wellington Harbour all Marine personnel will march to quarters and commence liberty thereafter. All off duty ship's crew will muster on deck in dress whites for inspection. Shore leave parties will rotate on three day schedule. That is all."

"I'll be a big hairy son of a bitch. The kid was right. Sorry, Junior. I thought you were bustin' my ass. Damn. It's been a long time. I'm gonna spend half my pay on booze and broads and the rest I'm gonna waste."

"I'm gonna find some princess to show me how to waste mine."

"Not me. I'm gonna buy a bottle, get loaded, and sleep for about five years. Wake me up when the war's over, boys. Just think. You can sleep without wonderin' if a Nip is gonna crawl up an' stick a knife in yer back."

* * * * *

Master Gunnery Sgt. Parker, promoted and back on duty, called order of march for the Raider column. As they marched through the sleepy town, heading for their bivouac two miles distant,

Master Sgt. called the cadence.

"Yer left, yer left, yer left right left."

"Yer momma don't want you no more."

And in answer from the platoon.

"Yer right. The Corps gave you a home. Yer right."

"Sound off. One, two. Sound off, three four."

"Sound off. One, two, three, four. One, two, three, four."

"Yer woman left you alone."

"Yer right. And jobys on the phone."

"Yer right. The Japs are waitin' for you."

"Yer right. What are you gonna do."

"Sound off. One, two. Sound off. Three, four."

And so it goes all the way to the bivouac.

* * * * *

The quarters were New Zealand Army field units on loan.

"Hey, Corp. How come they have wood floors in their tents and ours are mud?"

"They're smarter than us. But not as tough. Look at those racks. They're padded and have bug nets."

"Mail call."

The men picked up their mail, some of it two months old. It was discovered that there were two new fathers in the platoon and the usual number of "Dear Johns."

"That rotten son of a bitch."

"Joker, what's wrong?"

"My wife left me. That dirty whore left me for some 4F asshole. She says she's tired of waiting for me to finish playing war. She found a man that doesn't need a big title and a uniform. And he's always there for her. Wait till I get home. I'm gonna gut this bastard like a fish. He's gonna find out what happens when you take a Marine's woman. I'm gonna show him the war he missed all at once."

"Forget it, Joker. It ain't worth goin' to prison for. Just find another one. After the war there will be plenty to choose from. A lotta poor slobs ain't goin' home ever again. Which means lotsa unattached women around."

* * * * *

"The bus leaves in half an hour for town. The Lieut. says, 'put on your Class A's and shine yer brass.'"

THE KIWI BAR AND GRILL - WELLINGTON

As the squad burst through the door a lone Marine with a Raider patch on his shoulder caught their attention. He was sitting at the bar.

"I'll be a son of a bitch. It's him. Gunny Rawlins."

The squad gathered around their leader. They had a million questions.

"We hit a mine and I was thrown into the water with three swabbies. Twelve hours later we drifted to an island that had just a few Nip Sailors. We took care of them and than a Rikusentai patrol showed up with a barge. We waited till they were inland, killed the sentries and stole their boat. The next day we hid in a lava rock islet, but had to take out a Jap landing party and take their boat. The battle crusier they came from shelled us and we thought we were done for. Just then a sub picked us up and saved our asses. They dropped us off on the Canal."

"Wow, Gunny, somebody should write a book about you."

"All in a day's work, kid. Who would read it anyway. A lot of guys have been through worse. Like the crew of the PT I was on. All dead but three. They didn't have a chance. I hear you guys did well on Ruwawa."

"Aye, Gunny. We were lucky. We had a lot of support."

"What was the tally?"

"Over two hundred killed, one airstrip destroyed, one battalion bivouac destroyed."

"Outstanding. That should make the brass happy."

The party raged on and the Raiders got very drunk.

"You dirty whore. I'm gonna kick your ass."

"What's up with Joker?"

"He got a 'Dear John.' Wife's with a 4f joby."

"Poor bastard. Better get him outta here before the Shore Patrol shows up. He's lookin' for a fight. I can tell."

"OK, Gunny. See ya later."

"Gung ho, Junior."

"Hey, Rawlins. You old jarhead."

"Well, I'll be. Bill Lynch. I see you grew a couple stripes since China."

"I tried to hide but they caught up with me and sent me out here as Exec. on a sub chaser."

"Why you here?"

"We're on the convoy run from Numea to Brisbane. Stopped here to repair battle damage and take on fuel. How's the Corps treatin' you lately?"

"OK. Got some battle damage myself but not too serious."

"By the way, I ran into your wife in Washington."

"I don't have a wife."

"Well, she seems to think different."

"Was she with Romeo the Airdale?"

"He's dead, Ken. Went down over Truk. Unrecoverable."

"I heard he was MIA."

"Aussie Coast Watcher saw him go in. No chute."

"So what am I? The reserve unit?"

"She said she still loves you and she made a big mistake. She also says she will wait for you if you still want her. I told her I owe you from China and would find you and tell you. The rest is up to you. Now buy me a drink, you old devil dog. You owe me that much."

"Aye, Commander. I do."

* * * * *

Women. They're harder to understand than a General and tougher to deal with than a platoon of Rikusentai.

As Rawlins headed for his hotel room down the street from the bar the words echoed in his mind.

I will always love you. No matter what.

When Rawlins reached his room, he sensed there was something wrong. The scrap of a matchbook cover he had left in the doorjamb was on the floor. Someone was or had been in the room. The seasoned Marine pulled his 45 cal. 1911 pistol from it's holster under his Class A blouse. He racked the slide, stripping a 230 grain round from the seven round magazine, loading the chamber. Rawlins pushed open the door, back against the wall, revealing the dark interior. As the Gunny dove into the room and hit the floor two shots rang out. Rawlins fired twice. There was no return fire.

Turning on the light revealed a young blond haired man on the floor, blood pouring from his mouth. Two 45 cal. holes in his chest. Dying. Rawlins grabbed him and demanded:

"Who sent you, you son of a bitch? Tell me or I'll kill you."

Too late. The assassins eyes rolled up in his head and he was dead.

* * * * *

THE BRITISH CONSULATE, WELLINGTON BRANCH OFFICE OF M1 FIVE INTELLIGENCE

"Gunnery Sgt. Rawlins. Please be seated. According to the Wellington Constabulary and our own findings, your would be assassin was German Abvere. We believe he is responsible for the death of two M1 Five and one OSS operative. You were his next target."

"Why me?"

"You must pose a serious threat to the Axis in some way. They don't usually send their best field operatives this far out."

"Who was he?"

"Code name Adlar. Heard of him?"

"Yes. Back in England. The Eagle."

"Yes, quite right."

"Recruited by the SS, from the Hitler youth movement. Trained by the Feltschirmyaeger and Waffen SS. Also by the Gestapo and the Abvere as an assassin."

"I see you are well informed, Rawlins."

"Yes, Sir, thanks to M1 Five and British Commando."

"Why, thank you, Rawlins. I take that as a compliment."

"You're welcome, Sir."

"Tell me, Sgt., what happened. In your own words."

"Aye, Sir. I left the Kiwi Bar and Grill alone, 0200 hours. When I reached my room, I noticed a piece of paper on the deck that I had left in the doorjamb. I pushed open the door. The room was dark. I dove through the opening and hit the deck. Two shots were fired at me and I returned fire. I aimed where the muzzle flashes were and both rounds hit the target."

"Very good, Rawlins. Now one last question. Where is the assassin's weapon? It seems to be missing. We really need that weapon to pin this bloody sot to the Abvere."

"It's right here, Sir."

"You have it with you?"

"Yes, Sir."

"Outstanding. We knew we could count on you to do this right, Rawlins."

The OSS man slash U.S. Marine Raider produced a 9mm German Walther P38 pistol with suppressor and six 124 grain subsonic rounds in the eight round magazine.

"Ah, yes, Rawlins. That's the standard Nazi assassination weapon. We also found a Walther PPK 9mm Kurz in his waistband. May I keep this weapon, Sgt.? Our operatives have particular use for Nazi pistols."

"By all means, Sir. I have my 45 which serves me well."

"Yes, quite, Rawlins. The German pistol will prove very valuable to our people, Rawlins. I thank you."

"You're welcome, Sir."

"One last thing, Sgt."

"Yes, Sir."

"Don't go back to your room. These bloody bastards have been working in teams. I have arranged transportation to your unit's bivouac. Your kit has been picked up and delivered there. I don't think any Nazi is going to try to infiltrate a Marine Raider battalion. So I suggest you stay with your men."

"Aye, Sir, and thank you."

"Quite all right, Rawlins. We have to protect our people if possible. Now will you join me for a bit of Scotch and New Zealand beef?"

"Yes, Sir."

* * * * *

"Hey, Gunny. What happened in town last night?"

"Bad guy tried to rob me and I caught him in the act."

"Is he alive?"

"No."

"You kill him?"

"No, dummy. I petted him on the head and told him to be good. He shot at me and missed. I didn't. From now on we go everywhere as a group. Colonel's orders. There's a lot of low life around preying on lone service men."

THE KIWI BAR - ROUND TWO

Drunken Marines and drunken Sailors are the consequence of war in every bar in every town, in every theater of war.

"Rawlins. I'm glad yer back."

"Whatta ya want, Joker."

"Did you know my ollady left me for a 4F slob?"

"Yeah. I heard. Tuff break."

"I know, Gunny. Me and a million other poor slobs. I'm gonna kill that slob, Gunny. I'm goin' home and take the bastard out."

"Better wait till the war's over. It's a long swim from here."

"I ain't waitin. My war's at home now."

"Have another drink, Hays, and stand down."

"F..k you, Rawlins. I'm sick a your shit. As a matter of fact I'm gonna kick your ass."

"Don't try it, Hays. Go sit down and relax."

"Big tough guy. Givin' me orders off duty now. By the way, tough guy. Whose ass did you kiss to get your stripes back?"

The roundhouse punch came as expected. Rawlins blocked it and backfisted Hays between the eyes, knocking him senseless in his drunken state. He slid to the deck, leaned against the bar and began to cry.

"Russo. Ramirez. Take him to that coffee shop down the street and sober him up. I'll meet you there in an hour. And watch out for the Shore Patrol. He doesn't need any brig time in his state. He's liable to kill someone."

"OK, Gunny. See ya later."

Rawlins thought to himself as he drained another Johnny Walker:

This ain't good. One of my best men cracked up over a skirt. We go back in he's liable to mess up bad. Maybe get someone killed. Have to watch 'um close. Better shove off and get him back to camp.

"Gunny, I'm sorry. I was outta line."

"Forget it, Joker. I been there. I know how it is. Just remember you ain't alone. A lotta guys all over the world are getting 'Dear Johns.' How are you feeling?"

"Like shit."

"Good. That's better than feeling nothing. Forget the bus. Let's hike back to camp. It's only a couple of miles. It will help you feel better."

"OK, Gunny."

"I don't know how I'm gonna get through this, Gunny."

"You will. It hurts like hell but it'll pass. It just takes time. By the time we get home you will feel fine. And there will be a lot of women with no man by the time this shit is over."

* * * * *

"Hey, Doc."
"Yeah, Junior."
"I need a safe."
"here ya go. What you need it for."
"What you think?"
"Your rifle?"
"No."
"Your big toe?"
"No, Doc. A woman."

"No shit."

"No shit. I think I'm in love."

"Really?"

"Yeah, really. I met her in a coffee shop in town. I went there since I'm too young to drink. And tonight we're gonna do it."

"Do what?"

"You know. It."

"Oh, I see. That's why the safe. It's for it."

"That's right. She said I'd have to buy her dinner and a new dress with matching shoes and purse and then we can do it. As long as I have a safe."

"I see. What's she look like?"

"Oh, she's beautiful and she understands me."

"Wow. What a woman. Wish I could find one like that. Some guys get all the luck."

"I know, Doc. It's just something I got, she tells me, that no other guy's got. Animal attraction, she said."

"I see. Lucky you."

"Don't get mad, Doc. You'll find one some day."

"Gee, Junior. You think so?"

"Yeah, Doc. I'll teach you how."

* * * * *

"Hey, Ramirez."

"Yeah, Doc."

"You seen Junior's woman?"

"Yeah. I met her."

"Well?"

"She's old and married."

"Yer kidding."

"No, not kidding. She's at least thirty two and I heard her talking to another dame about hubby."

"What she say?"

"Hubby's in Italy with the Anzacs somewhere near Casino. And she's getting lonely and bored."

"Junior know?"

"No."

"You didn't tell him?"

"Are you nuts? I saw him kill a Jap with a punch to the side of the head and he wasn't even mad. I don't wanna see him when he is. Besides, I ain't his baby sitter."

* * * * *

"Form up on the road with rifle and field gear. On the double. Colonel's orders."

"Shit. So much for liberty."

"You had liberty. The Colonel's afraid you're getting soft. After all, you've been out of combat for two weeks. A little twenty mile hike is just what you sightseers need. You won't get into trouble that way."

"Form a column of twos. Right shoulder sling arms. Right face. Forward march. Yer left, yer left, yer left, right, left."

"As Rawlins called cadence, Ramirez bagan to sing."

"Gunny Rawlins is back in town. He will kick your ass and make you frown. Your right."

The Platoon replies:

"The booze is bad and the women worse. But the Japs will lay you in the dirt."

"Sound off. One, two. Sound off. Three, four."

"Gunny Rawlins is here to stay."

The Platoon:

"He's gonna make the Japs pay. Sound off. One, two. Sound off. Three, four."

"Sound off. One, two, three, four. One, two, three, four."

And so it went for the rest of the day. At dusk the Colonel called a halt. The men paired off and set up two man tents in a grassy field by a small stream and woodlot. The Colonel gave permission for a large fire since the enemy was at least two hundred miles away.

"Wow, this is great. What a place. Look at those stars. It's like we're in the middle of 'um. Hey, Lieut."

"Yeah, Junior."

"How come there's pine trees and woods, and grass like home

and no jungle? I heard there's even snow in the mountains on the South Island."

"We're below the equator far enough south for a climate change."

"Boy, I hope the Japs don't come here. They'll destroy the place."

"I don't think that will happen now. The Japs are trying to hold what they have. They didn't figure on all us Allies comin' out here fightin' together to kick their asses back to Japan."

"What happened to Lieut. Matsumo?"

"Left the Canal to return to his unit in Europe?"

"He was all right for a Jap."

"American Japanese. Big difference. I think he hated the Japs we tangled with more than we did."

"He sure had no problem killing them."

"He told me once that because they dishonored the homeland with their sneak attack on Pearl, Manila, Attu and Singapore, he considered them traitors. I have to agree with him. What I learned about the Samurai in college tells me this is something new for the Japanese. Normally, they would inform an enemy of pending attack to bring honor on themselves and the emperor. I think that for the first time in history, politics has played a major role in warfare. That's why Nipponese officers always kill themselves. To prevent capture. To maintain their personal and family honor."

The next day the Raiders stood down. They bathed and washed their dungarees in the stream, cleaned equipment, went fishing, and relaxed. They needed a break after weeks of brutal combat. This was the perfect quiet place for them to unwind.

"Gimme that, you son of a bitch or I'll kick your ass."

"Yeah, asshole. You and what army? You better bring a lunch. You got more shit than a flock of geese, you shitbird."

"You're a bigger pain in the ass than the Japs. Always stealin' stuff. Hey, Corp., Johnson stole my shit."

"So why you telling me?"

"Cause you're supposed to do something about it."

"Go kick his ass and leave me alone. I'm sleepin.'"

"Gunny, Johnson stole my stuff."

"What are you? Three years old? I ain't your mother. Go club him or something and leave me alone. I'm still recovering from my traumatic experience. I need solitude and tranquility."

"What the hell does that mean, Gunny?"

"You dummy. Didn't you go to school?"

"Only to the fourth grade. I had to go to work after that 'cause my old man went lookin' for work and never came back. So I don't know no big words."

"Johnson, give the kid his stuff before I slap the hell outta you. You're startin' to piss me off and I'm tired. You hear me?"

"Yeah, Gunny. I hear ya."

* * * * *

Rawlins sat down to write letters home for the first time in two months.

Dear Mom and Dad:

Last operation over. In New Zealand on liberty until they decide what to do with us. Doing fine. Feeling OK. No malaria or jungle rot thanks to our Corpsman (Doc) and his Atabrine.

Hopefully this will end soon. We have really been pounding the Japs hard out here and more troops, supplies and equipment are pouring in by the ton, day by day. It really helps. In the beginning we had nothing much to fight with. On the Canal we ate Jap rations half the time. The previous owners no longer needed them. We found their machine guns worked quite well against their previous owners too.

I hope everything is OK with you. I miss you all, even that damn old cat.

Gotta go take care of my children. Dad knows how that is. That old jarhead. Tell him to read this to the heroes at the center and God bless them all. They might enjoy hearing from another old jarhead.

Love, Ken

The Colonel bought a pig from a nearby farm and had it butchered. He also arranged for ten cases of beer to be delivered to the bivouac. There would be a pig roast tonight with the help of three Navy cooks borrowed from a Navy convoy lying at anchor in Wellington harbour. The Colonel just happened to know the convoy's Commodore.

* * * * *

The next morning the Marines packed up and prepared to move out.

"Where's Hays?"

"He's over in those trees, Gunny?"

Rawlins found him sitting under a tree reading the "Dear John."

"We're pullin' out, Hays. Time to go."

"I can't believe she left me. We were together since we were kids. I don't know how to handle this. It's killin' me. I can't eat, can't sleep, can't think."

"Why don't you talk to the Chaplain?"

"I did. He told me to get my shit wired right and act like a Marine instead of a high school kid. He told me that if I kept pining over a wife I shouldn't even have some Jap is gonna put me in a wooden kimono. He said that if the Marine Corps wanted me to have a wife they would have issued me one. If he was an enlisted man I woulda punched his lights out."

"Saddle up. We're moving out."

The march was long and hot. Not jungle hot but hot enough to make marching with a pack and rifle uncomfortable.

"Hey, Gunny. Where we goin'? This ain't the way back."

"Tokyo. Didn't the General tell you?"

"No. He slipped up somehow."

"I'll give him hell when I see him."

"Why we marching so much? We ain't boots, we're Amphibious Assault Specialists."

"Because you're a dummy, that's why. And you talk too much. Now stop whining and keep marching. Or you will wish you were a boot again."

"Gunny. I hear rifle fire. What the hell's going on?"

"We're going to the New Zealand Army rifle range so you dummies can sight in your new M1 Garand rifles."

"You mean a Garand for every man instead of one in five?"

"That's right, ladies. Time to turn in the turn bolts and get modern."

"Ready on the left, ready on the right. Fire at will."

The Raiders stacked arms and picked up their new rifles by platoon relay. After removing the Cosmoline (protective grease) from action and barrel, the rifles were test fired and sighted in. An armorer was on hand to make adjustments or repairs as necessary.

"Boy, these Garands really chew up ammo. Ya gotta be careful not to run dry. Not as accurate as a 903, but good enough for the jungle. It's got a grenade launcher attachment too. Be careful when you load it. The magazine releases the bolt carrier and tries to rip your thumb off."

"Clean your new toys and make camp. We stay here tonight."

"Officer and NCO call in the Range House in ten."

* * * * *

"Gentlemen. Your next target. The island of Bougainville."

The Raiders looked at the map hanging on the wall and were concerned.

"Heavy jungle and swamp, and frequent rain and humidity will be a worse problem than the enemy. Our goal, men, is to capture and hold this airfield. Whoever controls it controls the central Solomons and the supply route to Australia. This will be a large operation that we will share with the Army Infantry. The Third Raiders will hit the beach here in this bay near the Piva Trail and use it as their main advance route. The Second Raiders will land five miles south of the Third's position, cut through the jungle to the Piva Trail two miles inland. There they will form a blocking position and engage any enemy incursions either in patrol strength or attacking force, using the trail to eliminate the beachhead. Heavy patroling is expected to locate the enemy and gauge their strength in the area. In approximately three days the Third will join the Second on the trail and will attack the airfield as soon as possible. The Army will attack other areas to relieve some of the pressure and form a diversion. Prepare yourselves and your equipment for a long campaign. This is going to be a long, protracted engagement due to the nature of the terrain and the tenacity of the enemy. Write your letters home and have the new men make a will. God bless and good luck."

"All right. Listen up. We got a new op. More bad ass jungle and wet as hell. Waterproof your gear and keep a safe on your muzzle at all times. Clean you rifle as often as possible and keep it well oiled. We're gonna be in a swamp most of the time. Pack extra socks. Write your letters and make out a will. This will be your last chance."

That night there was no fire, no revelry, no getting drunk and womanizing. The men were quiet, subdued. They were busy making ready for war. They all knew some of their number would not return. But that is the price free men willing to fight and die for what they believed in might have to pay. And the Raiders were used to fighting and dying.

"Gunny. Where's your M1?"

"I'm sticking with a Tommy gun. The Brits gave me one from lend lease that they said they could live without. It's a 1928A1 with a Cutts comp and a fifty round drum. Takes regular mags too. It's even got a selector switch. And adjustable rear sight."

"Wow. Nice weapon. When you get killed I get first dibs."

"Gee. Thanks a lot."

Sleep was out as the Raiders wrote letters, re-checked and oiled equipment, sharpened knives and bayonets. Some played cards. Others talked and smoked quietly. Something was different. Ominous. Something just didn't feel right. Like they were being sucked into a jungle vortex capable of killing them in a thousand different ways. A great swamp where they would disappear never to be seen again. And jungle combat at its worst. A sniper in every tree. Banzai charges from ten yards away. Huge snakes waiting to crush the life out of you. Clouds of insects waiting to consume you and give you deadly malaria. No, there would be no relaxing tonight as each man wrestled with his own hidden fears.

"Johnson."

"Yo, Gunny."

"We got a new flame thrower. It's your baby."

"OK, Gunny."

Great. Now I get to be a bigger target for snipers. They just love to touch off a Zippo and watch the guy fry that's luggin' it. And instead of shootin' people; now I have to incinerate them. Great. This lash up is going from bad to worse.

* * * * *

"Gunny."

"Yeah, Joker."

"I ain't gonna get through this one."

"You don't know that. Nobody does."

"I know, Gunny."

"C'mon. Don't say that shit. You're just feelin' low right now."

"I've seen it before, Gunny. Guys get the feeling and sure enough they get it."

"Not everybody. I get that feeling every time we go in and I'm still here."

"I'm telling you I know. After it happens will you write my wife and tell her I'm sorry for being a foul up. And tell her I'll wait for her on the other side."

"Hays. Stow that morbid shit. You're gonna be fine. When you get home tell her yourself."

* * * * *

"Gunny. Junior's gone."

"Whatta ya mean gone?"

"Gone, not here. He jumped ship."

"Son of a bitch. We're leavin' here tomorrow. If he's not with us he will be AWOL. He can get twenty years or worse for that. I'll find him. Pack his trash and bring it along in the morning."

"Aye, Gunny."

Rawlins hitched a ride to Wellington and found Junior with his new woman. They were in the coffee shop where he had met her.

*Shit. There he is. How do I handle this one. If I piss him off
he'll break me in half. This one's gonna be tough.*

"Coffee and a crumpet, please."

*"*Gunny. What are you doin' here?"

"I saw you through the window. Thought I would say 'hi.'"

"You ain't allowed to be here tonight. Yer gonna lose your
stripes again. You better go back while you still can."

"Why bother. Nobody else follows the rules. Why should I?"

"Cause you're the platoon Gunnery Sgt."

"Yeah? So what? If you can be here so can I."

"I ain't goin' back, Gunny. I don't care what happens. I've had
enough of this war."

"Too bad. All your mates are shipping out tomorrow. They
will miss you. Oh, well. You will be OK as long as your woman here
hides you from the Shore Patrol. At least till her husband comes
home."

"He's dead, Gunny. Got killed crossing the Valturno River."

"Gee, that's too bad. You see the telegram."

"Well, no, but she wouldn't lie to me."

"Oh, no, never. Have you thought about your mates that are
gonna die because you're not by their side?"

"It don't matter. Someone will be there."

"Yeah, Junior. A bunch a boots that don't know shit.
Probably get half of us killed."

"Leave me alone, Gunny. I'm done with this war. Don't touch
that."

"Why, Junior. You're not a Raider any more."

"I earned it."

"Yeah, but it will look silly on your civilian clothes, probably
scare people. Maybe your whore can wear it on her brassiere. For
sweet memories."

Junior grabbed Rawlins by the throat, picked him up and
pinned him against the wall. The OSS trained specialist grabbed the
farm boys huge wrist with both hands, easing the pressure, grabbing
his thumb and wrenching it 180 degrees to break the choke hold.
Rawlins then pulled the arm wedging it under his own with the elbow
pointing up. Applying his weight to the giants elbow put him on his

knees, helpless.

"Don't move. Hold it right there. What the hell are you two jarheads doing?"

"Dancing the night away. I'm showin' Junior here some jujitsu. You Shore Patrol types could use it too instead of always beating people with clubs."

"Clubs work fine, Gunny, especially on bone headed Marines. You sure everything is OK? We would be happy to take twinkle toes to the brig. He can practice with the other brig rats."

"No, he's fine. He's going with me. You two are doing a good job. Now carry on."

"Aye, Gunny."

"You big son of a bitch. You ever try that again, I'll kill ya. You understand me? Well, do ya?"

"Aye, Gunny."

"You coulda got twenty years for that if I had told those swabbies the truth. You owe me, Junior. And you owe your mates that kept you alive this long. Now tell your princess we're leavin' and we will be back after this op."

"OK, Gunny."

The two Marines walked back to the bivouac discussing many things. They never had really talked before.

"Junior. You gotta realize women will come and go. There's good ones and bad ones. Come back here after the war and find out what really is happening. If it's a good deal, muster out and stay here. It's a great place. Especially for a farmer."

"Aye, Gunny. It's really nice here. A great place to farm and live. But I know I got responsibilities to my mates. I can't let them down."

"That's the spirit. Gung ho."

"Right, Gunny. Gung ho. You know, Gunny, when you were missing the whole platoon was real upset. Our three Corporals refused to believe you were dead. They all said you would show up. They said you wouldn't leave us like that. They said you weren't dead because you're the toughest son of a bitch in the Corps. And I believe 'um."

This made Rawlins proud to be a Marine. At least his men

respected him. Even if no one else did.

* * * * *

The Second and Third Raiders boarded ship in Wellington Harbour, all hands present and accounted for. Amen.
Next stop Bougainville.

Chapter Eight

BOUGAINVILLE

USCG Cutter Vanguard. Lying off the east coast of Bougainville Island, 0400 hours.

"All Marine personnel muster on deck and prepare to disembark in LCVP transports (Higgins boats)."

"You heard the man. Over the side and don't fall off the cargo net. If you fall you will drown or the sharks will get you."

A Naval barrage was pounding the shoreline five miles away. The Third Raider Regiments landing would be no secret. The Second Raider Regiments Second Battalion B Company First and Second Platoons would make the incursions to the Piva Trail. Third Platoon would be held in reserve and inserted where needed.

"Why the hell is it raining. We don't need this shit."

"What's a matter. The weather conflicting with your tanning schedule?"

"No, Gunny. My ass is soaked. And I hate a wet ass."

"I'm so sorry, Pfc. Next time we have an invasion I'll make sure to tell Admiral Halsey and General Smith to plan for better weather so we can protect your precious bum. Or maybe you can just stay home if the weather isn't suitable. If it was a starry, romantic evening so we could all hold hands and sing songs like good little Marines, the Jap 150s and 90s would have the range right now."

"They can't see us in this rain."

"Listen up. When we hit the beach get outta this boat and in the tree line fast. You will be less of a target that way. And stay with your squad. Don't go wandering around. Don't move inland till an NCO tells ya. And above all, be quiet. Sound carries over water and through the jungle. When we move in the jungle before light hold on to the man's web gear that's ahead of you. The Lieut. will set the course."

The jungle was black and ominous in the pre-dawn rain. You

couldn't see your hand in front of your face. The men were nervous. And the mud and insects were horrendous. The mud was so bad it sucked the boots off the men's feet when they tried to walk. The march turned into a confused nightmare. Men were separated from the main body and stragglers returned to the beach. Disaster was looming as the Lieut. conferred with the Gunnery Sgt. and the Master Gunnery Sgt.

"We gotta be close to the trail."

The luminous dial on the compass showed through the dark. The indicator arrow pointed dead ahead. According to the map the trail should be withiin 500 yards of their position.

"We're down to two thirds of our original strength. When it's light, Rawlins, egress our line of march and pick up as many men as you can find."

"OK. Lieut. Parker, you're with me."

There was the trail. In the early dawn the men saw a thin ribbon of open area running east to west. In the direction of the beach, down the trail, sporadic firing was heard. Gunny Rawlins slid through the wet misty jungle, avoiding mud holes and clouds of insects where he could. A half mile from the trail he began to see discarded equipment and ammunition. Soon he found men. Huddled together in twos and threes. Exhausted.

"C'mon, boys. You can't stay here. If the Japs find you they will skin you alive."

Rawlins found all but two of the lost men. He led them to the platoon position near the trail. There they dug in and waited for orders. The rain still fell in a monotonous cadence on their steel helmets and equipment. Their fighting holes filled with water as fast as they were dug. And leeches began to appear, clinging to any exposed skin they could find.

"Son of a bitch. This damn jungle shit hole. Why the hell did the Nips take this God forsaken mud hole. There's nothing here but shit and more shit."

"Rawlins. How many did you find?"

"All but two, Sir."

"We'll find them later. Right now I want Sgts. Ramirez and Russo to take First and Second squads up this trail five hundred yards and set up an ambush. According to intel there's a battalion bivouac between us and the airfield. You can bet the Japs will come down that trail in strength to reinforce their buddies near the beach. Tell your men to hit the main body hard and bail outta there fast before the enemy can recover and regroup. Have the squads fall back to this position."

"Aye, Sir."

"I want you and Master Gunny Parker to set up a defensive semi-circle. Leave the trail open so the enemy doesn't see you. Form two crescents, one on each side of the trail on an angle to the trail so you don't shoot each other and to guard against flankers. Got that, Gunny?"

"Right, Lieut. I'm on it."

Ramirez and Russo quietly led the squad through the jungle, near the trail, not wanting to expose themselves to the enemy. Ramirez took two grenades from his ammo bag and straightened the safety pins. The grenades were tied to bamboo stalks on both sides of the trail. A very thin piece of com wire was attached to the pin rings holding down the safety levers. The wire was stretched across the trail and would snag the boot of any unknowing passerby. This would pull the safety pins free and cause the safety levers to pop off, lighting the fuses that were cut to three seconds. With the detonation the Raiders would open fire and decimate any enemy fool enough to use the trail. The rest of the men found hidden positions fifteen to twenty yards off the trail. They would infiltrate the enemy and bug out quick before being overrun.

Parker and Rawlins set up a classic jungle defensive position like their Lieut. wanted. Thirty cal. Browning mg in an elevated position to rake the trail and the B.A.R. Team across the trail covering the 30 cal. position, riflemen and Tommy gunners forming the rest of the crescent. The CP was placed on the edge of the trail behind the mg pit.

"Looks pretty good, you old sea dog. Glad you decided to join us this trip."

"Yeah. I got tired of all those nurses craving my attention. I'm only one man you know. They were forever trying to get in bed with me. Gets tiring after a couple of weeks. I had to break their hearts and come back and win the war, I told 'um."

Sgt. Russo fed the short pecker a fresh belt of 6.5 Nambu, hoping to give the Japs back some of their own medicine. He would rake the forward element as soon as the grenades detonated.

"We ready, Ramirez?"

"Yeah, we're ready. All we need is a platoon of Nips."

"Here they come."

A platoon of enemy infantry came marching down the trail. They were in perfect step as if on parade for the emperor. A perfect column of two's. When the grenades exploded the line erupted with heavy fire. The forward element melted into the trail, shrapnel and bullet riddled. All down without firing a shot. The main body was shot up as well but reacted by vacating the trail of death and returning fire.

A new man, Pfc. Jackson from Bedford, Indiana was shot in the head and died soon afterward. Two more Raiders were slightly wounded. The Japanese were beginning to rally and organize a charge.

"Ramirez. There's too many of 'um. We gotta get the hell outta here. Tell your men to throw their grenades and bug out. And I'll do the same."

Amid multiple explosions which served to confuse the enemy, the Raiders abandoned their positions and disappeared into the jungle. They kept up a fast pace, knowing the Japanese were right behind them, mad as hell.

When the ambush patrol reached the dug in position around the CP, an artillery barrage was called in.

"Baker one. This is Baker six. Over. Do you copy? Over."

"Baker one. Go ahead. Over."

"Request fire mission. Over. Anti-personnel H.E. proximity fuse ten foot air burst. Over. Grid coordinates alfa, romeo, tango, 925er, east end of grid. Will adjust."

Finally the crackle and hum of static on the wet radio was broken.

"Fire mission approved. Firing five inch thirty eight cal. H.E."

In twenty seconds the rounds came in, crashing into the

jungle fifty yards to their left.

"Fire correction. Right fifty, raise fifty."

Now the 30 cal. mg and the B.A.R. Team was lying down suppression fires to hold the enemy in the kill zone. Another salvo crashed into the jungle.

"Right on the money. Walk 'um back and forth. Fire for effect, fire for effect."

The jungle was transformed into a seething cauldron of fiery death. Trees uprooted, foliage flattened, and dead and dismembered Japanese attackers lying everywhere.

"Ordnance expended. Fire mission over."

"Thanks, Navy. That took the fight out of them"

"Glad to be of service. Call any time."

* * * * *

The rain stopped and the jungle grew hot. Clouds of mist rose from the jungle floor. The stench of rotting vegetation and bodies permeated the air. Clouds of insects appeared when the mist burned off. Heat and humidity were intense.

"This is the worst shit hole we been in yet. Heat, mud and bugs. And my hole is full a water. Now I got jungle rot. My feet are comin' apart. Yesterday a rat walked by big enough to eat someone. What a shit hole."

"Stow it, crybaby. At least you ain't dead yet."

"Gunny. The Lieut. wants you."

"OK, Doc."

At the CP, Rawlins and the Lieut. conferred.

"I want you to take a recon patrol and try to get an idea of enemy strength in our zone for battalion. At the same time try to locate the MIAs."

"OK, Lieut."

"Good luck."

* * * * *

"All right. Listen up. We got a recon mission. Joker, Doc,

Johnson, Junior, Russo and you new guys. Saddle up. You just volunteered. Draw three days rations and two canteens. Two frags and an extra bandoleer. We're gonna be on our own. Johnson, leave the Zippo here and use Sgt. Russo's Thompson. He's got the short pecker. Get ready. We leave in ten."

Rawlins was entering his element now. This is what he was good at. Jungle combat. He slid through the jungle like some predatory jungle cat. His men behind him at ten yard intervals. Not making a sound, scanning the trees for snipers. Always at the ready. Five miles from the CP, moving inland, they made contact.

"Gunny. I hear voices."

Rawlins made the signal to drop and hold. He and Russo moved ahead until they found a stream. Following the stream to a small clearing, they melted back into the jungle and watched from heavy cover. The clearing was full of Japanese Soldiers. Bathing, washing clothes, cooking rations, relaxing. A patrol that stood down for the day. One Soldier wandered close to the Raider hide. Too close. He was cutting bamboo to build a shelter and was only three feet from Russo. Then two feet. Russo's Ka-Bar cut into the Japs ribcage, cleaving his heart. The enemy Soldier died without a sound and collapsed on his killer. The Sgt. dragged the body back into the underbrush.

Rawlins signaled Russo to move out and they vacated the area. Upon returning to the patrol he described the situation:

"There's a patrol up ahead, platoon strength. We had to take one of them out, so they're lookin' for us by now. We're movin' out in the other direction. Keep your intervals and keep quiet. After a mile or so we'll set up an ambush."

The squad found an intersection of trails in a clearing in the jungle. A perfect ambush site.

"This is it. Sooner or later those Nips tracking us are gonna come through here. We set up here. And remember, don't fire till an NCO tells ya. Russo, Joker. Rig the clearing and set up the Nambu. The rest of you guys form a semi circle around the Nambu and support it. When the grenades blow in the clearing, give 'um hell. Reload and bug out. We'll beat it down that farthest trail and re-group. Joker and Russo will bring up the rear and form a rearguard defense. Delay them as long as possible. I'll watch the flanks in case they're smart enough to try an end around."

The grenade traps were expertly prepared. The men found the best cover possible by piling rotten logs and vegetation in their front at the clearing edge. There was no time to dig in. Just as they were beginning to think the enemy had given up on them, the three man point element came into view. They pensively crept into the clearing, unaware of danger.

The three men who watched them lay prone on the ground and waited for the main body to catch up. Just what the Raiders hoped they would do. Soon the enemy platoon came walking into the clearing. Soldiers were milling about drinking water and talking. Trackers were trying to pick up the trail. Two grenades blew with a thunderous roar. A clumsy, tired Soldier had pulled the trip wire. Rawlins, up on one knee, yelled,

"Give 'um hell."

His Thompson grew hot from firing a long burst into the enemy before him. Enemy Soldiers crumpled and collapsed like dead trees in a hurricane. Russo's Nambu chopped them down like bamboo before a sharp machete, giving the empire some of its own ordnance back, on the hot end. Joker's and Johnson's Thompsons finished the job with 230 grain 45 cal. autofire death. The other riflemen didn't even fire. There was no point. Better to conserve ammo.

"Cease fire. They're all down. Let's get the hell outta here."

The squad dropped back into the jungle and disappeared. After an hour or so they came across a trail with the evidence of heavy use.

"Russo, Joker. Let's follow this trail for a couple of miles and see what gives."

"OK, Gunny."

"Stay in the jungle. We don't want to stumble into any Tojo look-alikes."

The going was tough, even for these combat hardened Raiders. Ravines, gullies, jungle vines, and creepers. Huge cedar trees with exposed roots, bougainvillea. All trying to trip and capture the exhausted Marines. Oppressive heat and humidity took its toll.

"Pass the word. Take five. Drink some water. No smoking.

The Nips will smell it. Take off your steel pots and strap them to your ruck. Wet down your soft cover and wear that. Make sure your boots are tied tight. If your feet swell you will need the support. Check your weapons bolt body for rust. They can rust solid in this humidity in a couple of days. Break out a C rat and try to eat something. And take a couple of salt tablets. You will feel better. It will be night soon. It will cool down some. Let's move out. Joker, take point."

"OK, Gunny."

"Take two men with you."

A half mile down the trail the point element found a gruesome spectacle. Two men. US Marines, tied between two trees. Stripped, raped, tortured, and used for bayonet practice. The point men returned to report.

"We found the missing guys."

"How bad?"

"Both dead, raped and tortured. Just like the Canal."

"Son of a bitch. Dirty little bastards. I swear they ain't human. They leave any sign?"

"Lots. Five or six of 'um."

"OK then. We find them and kill 'um all. No quarter. The wanna be animals we'll treat 'um that way."

"Sounds good to me, Gunny."

The squad buried the dead Marines and marked the spot on the map for Graves Registration and later exhumation after the war.

"Get their dog tags, Doc?"\

"No tags, Gunny. They keep them for souvenirs. No weapons, either. No ammo. They took everything."

This made Rawlins even more furious.

"The evil bastards are gonna get theirs when we catch 'um, Doc. I gotta ask you to turn a blind eye. It ain't gonna be pretty."

"No problem, Gunny. These bastards deserve to die. What happens in the field stays in the field."

"That's the spirit, Doc. Those two men are the last Marines they're gonna murder."

"All right, you guys. It's getting dark. Dig in on that ridge and keep quiet. There may be activity on this trail tonight. Two man holes. Two hour shifts. Try to sleep when you're off. And no talking.

If it rains catch water for your canteens."

And rain it did. Torrents. Foxholes filled with water. Everything was soaked. And leeches were everywhere. In the men's dungarees, in their hair, on any exposed skin. Sleep was impossible. But at least they were safe for the moment. The enemy fared no better.

Dawn broke, a lighter shade of gray. No sun was visible. No birds, no lizards or snakes, nothing. Just endless jungle and humidity. Clothes and equipment were beginning to mildew and rust. Jungle rot was rampant causing sores that would not heal. Malaria was draining the strength of the infected men. Doc gave them quinine but that's the best he could do for them.

"Saddle up. We're movin' out. Russo. See if you can track those bastards we're after."

"OK, Gunny."

A part of a Japanese split toe tabi track here, a broken twig there was all that remained of the murderer's trail. The heavy rain had taken its toll. Finally, after six hours of tracking, the squad caught up with the enemy patrol.

"Fix bayonets. We're gonna take them hard and fast. There's six of them. Make sure we got them all."

The Raiders low crawled to an attack position near the enemy. The Japanese were unaware of their presence.

"Let 'um have it."

The underbrush erupted with fire. Everyone fired until their weapon was empty.

"Finish the bastards."

Every man walked into the clearing with revenge on his mind. One wounded Jap yelled something at a Raider and held up his hand. He got a bayonet in the stomach for a reply. Another tried to charge Rawlins with a bayonet. Five rounds from his Thompson changed the Jap's plans. Seeing Doc's aid bag with the Red Cross on it prompted one rising sun hero to grab the corpsman's leg, hoping for sympathy. Not this time. Doc pulled out his forty five and shot the killer twice in the face. Junior butt stroked a would be attacker as he tried to stand. The big farm boy put a size twelve boot on the son of Nippon's throat, shutting off his air, choking him to death. Russo drowned a wounded imperial rapist in a mud puddle. The rest were already dead.

"Good job, men. Their murdering days are over. Take any of our stuff they have and let's bug outta here."

For an hour they marched through uncharted jungle.

"Dig in and form a night defense perimeter. The Nips may be tracking us. Get some sleep now. Be prepared for action tonight."\

The Raiders dug their fighting holes, made gun pits for the Nambu and B.A.R. Then they ate if they weren't too sick, smoked, and cleaned and oiled their equipment.

Sunset. The jungle grew quiet. Birds and reptiles went to sleep. A large snake slithered by, on the hunt. A light rain began to fall and lulled the men on watch to sleep. They were all exhausted. The temperature began to drop with the sinking of the sun. The torrid heat was replaced by a cool breeze. The men were beginning to feel better, with the heat lifting.

"Hey, Sarge."

"Yeah, Wallace."

"You think they will come tonight?"

"Yeah."

"How come?"

"We pissed 'um off plenty. They gotta come. Their honor is at stake."

"Oh. In the rain?"

"Yeah."

"Bastards."

"You shouldn't swear like that."

"Why not?"

"You're too young."

"You do it all the time."

"I'm supposed to."

"Why?"

"'Cause I'm the Sergeant. We're supposed to swear. Marine Corps tradition. If ya don't swear you can't ever be a Sergeant."

"No shit?"

"No shit."

"How old you gotta be"

"Twenty five."

"That's old. I may not live that long."

"Don't sweat it. If you don't make it you'll be in Marine Corps heaven where nobody's allowed to swear."

"How do you know, Sarge?"

"'Cause I'm a Sergeant and we know secret stuff."

* * * * *

Maline you die. Joe me gonna get you. Me gonna cut you deep."

"Son of a bitch. They're here. No sleep tonight. They're beginning to piss me off. Hold your fire. Pass the word. They're gonna probe us and try to find our positions. Put your pig stickers on your rifles. And keep your Ka-Bar handy. Take 'um out quietly."

Enemy Soldiers began to infiltrate the perimeter. One jumped in Rawlin's hole and was promptly stabbed in the chest twice, the English stiletto saving the Raider once again. Three Japs with bayonets jumped into the machine gun pit and tried to kill the crew. Russo grabbed one attacker's rifle and deflected the bayonet thrust. With his free hand, he pulled his Chicago switchblade and drove it into the Jap's neck, killing him quickly. Grabbing the Arisaka rifle from the dead owner, he plunged the bayonet into the back of an enemy Soldier on top of the B.A.R. gunner, trying to stab him with a dagger. The Jap looked shocked, looked down at the blade protruding from his chest, grunted something in Japanese, and fell over dead.

"Thanks, Sarge. That was close. I owe ya one."

The last attacker was clubbed to death with the B.A.R. loader's M1. The loader became enraged when the would be killer stabbed him in the shoulder.

"Everybody OK? All right. Listen up. We gotta get outta here now that they found us. Every man throw one grenade on my mark. If a bigger force shows up here we're in deep shit. After you throw, make for that high ground to the south, pronto. We'll re-group there on the back side of that hill. Ready. Throw."

As the grenades exploded the Raiders withdrew. When all were gone Rawlins stood in his hole and fired a full fifty round drum magazine into the Jap area of advance, trying to slow them down. He then rolled out of the hole, got behind a large tree and ran like hell. When he could run no more, he re-loaded his Thompson and straightened the safety pins on two M2 frags. He figured a rear guard action couldn't hurt.

Now the diversion. He would throw the frags at the enemy and charge them as they detonated. Hopefully this would throw them off kilter. Then he would run through them, firing his Tommy gun as he ran. Hopefully they would follow him. In the dark he would appear to be more than one man. It was high risk but necessary. If they found the squad they would pin them down and wipe them out.

In the distance a point of light was coming through the jungle. Up, down, back and forth.

What the hell is that, he wondered. Then he realized. *A cigarette. Some dumb bastard is smoking. I don't believe it. It's gotta be a Jap. Our guys know better.* Then he heard sticks breaking. Then talking. *These guys must be boots. The ones we're used to fighting are real pros. These guys act like they own the jungle and nobody else is here.*

Rawlins threw his frags and charged. They detonated so close to him that shrapnel tore through his ruck and his upper arm.

Shit. I'm hit.

He raised his Tommy to hip level, blood running down his arm, and squeezed off a burst. He was in the Jap position now, blasting enemy Soldiers to the right and left. They were totally confused and surprised. Gunny Rawlins tripped and fell into a deep ravine and lay at the bottom stunned and bleeding. The Japanese fired into the ravine but no shots came close to his position. Soldiers ran into the ravine past his position and kept going. He was hiding under the exposed roots of a huge banyan tree. They never saw him. The ruse had worked. The Japs were going in the other direction, following the phantom enemy.

Rawlins pulled his First Aid Kit from his belt, tore open the sulfa powder packet with his teeth and dumped it on his wound. Then he wrapped the battle dressing around his arm, leaving the O.D. wrapper attached for camouflage. He decided not to use the morphine syrette yet. It would put him to sleep and he didn't want to wake up with a Jap staring him in the face. He would use it later when the pain was worse and he had a better hide. He had to move now in another direction. The Japs would be back and pick up his trail. He had to lead them away from the squad.

The wounded Marine set a course the length of the ravine. It broke into a flat plain of kunai grass. He followed the edge for a mile or so. Then he came to a stream. He entered the water and traveled down stream as far as he could. It was breaking light and he was exhausted. Rawlins found a large cedar growing half in the water. There was a deep pool under the tree. The bank was undercut at this point and held the tree's root system. Gunny Rawlins crawled under the bank, tied his pistol belt around a large root and around his chest under his arms. This would keep his head above water. His ruck was used for a pillow and he fell fast asleep.

* * * * *

Gunny Rawlins awoke with a start. Disoriented at first, he then realized where he was. The pain in his arm and shoulder reminded him. Undoing the pistol belt, he slid out of the tree roots that held him and sat on the creek bank. He checked his Thompson and replaced the almost empty drum magazine with his last thirty round stick. His two 45 cal. pistols were unfired and held full seven round magazines. And there were four reserve mags in canvas pouches on his pistol belt. His Ka-Bar was strapped to his ankle and his stiletto to his web gear. Breaking out a C ration, he ate the canned dog food and smoked a Chesterfield, which made him dizzy. Not enough sleep and stale tobacco, he reckoned. After filling his canteens and burying his trash he was ready to move out.

The hard core Marine followed the stream looking for enemy sign. Maybe three miles further along he sat down against a mahogany tree and began to doze in the midday heat. Insects buzzed and clicked around his head.

I'll love you forever. I'll never leave you.
Son of a bitch.

In his dream state the familiar words came to him in Susan's voice, being spoken by a big Jap standing over him, pushing a bayonet through his chest.

I never get any peace. If it ain't the Japs, it's her.

Rawlins stood up, walked a few feet and hit the deck. Four Japanese Soldiers walked by his position not twenty feet from him. He heard their footfalls in the dry leaves on the trail they were using. Lucky. He had almost walked into them. He watched as they walked by. They were close enough to see their collar insignia. Looked like Twenty Third Infantry Regiment, Imperial Army. He decided to follow the Soldiers. The trail was wide with a hard surface.

Hard enough for trucks, he thought. *This must be the other end of the Piva Trail.*

The veteran Raider kept following for about a mile, always keeping his distance and staying in the jungle. He watched as the enemies stopped for a break. One Soldier walked off the trail and into the jungle. Rawlins cut a parallel course to intercept the wanderer. And there he was. Ten yards away, urinating. The jungle fighter laid his Tommy gun on the deck, pulled his stiletto and quietly walked up behind the Nippon hero, long Arisaka rifle slung over his back. A large hand grabbed the Jap's face and shut off his air. As the enemy began to struggle the stiletto found it's mark. Rawlins pushed it to the hilt in the Jap's neck, under his left ear. The Nippon conqueror grunted, kicked twice, and died. The Marine dragged him into some underbrush, went through his pockets and found his identification booklet. Just what he was hoping for. Intel like this was very valuable.

The wounded warrior headed around the dead man's comrades in a wide arc. Then back to the Piva Trail. After a half mile or so he had to stop and rest. His wound, the heat, and fatigue were wearing him out. Rawlins headed deeper into the jungle and found a gully in which to hide. Lying under the rain drenched bank and covering himself with leaves, he fell asleep.

Rawlins woke up after dark. He ate his final C ration, checked his gear and returned to the Piva Trail. His arm and shoulder were throbbing with pain.

No morphine yet. Mission first, he told himself.

Traffic was heavy on the trail. It appeared as though an infantry unit down the trail was being relieved. Lots of troops

heading both ways. Also, trucks and equipment. The Raider decided
to follow the trail to see what was happening. After two miles of
carefully paralleling the trail his answer came into view. A large
marshalling area cut out of the jungle. Trucks, guns, motor pool,
outbuildings, barracks. A battalion bivouac at least. Most likely the
marshalling area for forward elements of the Japanese 23rd Infantry
Regiment. And a mile down the trail was his platoon, completely
unaware. If these troops came down the trail in force his platoon
would be overrun. The thought of it reminded Rawlins of his dreams
back in D.C. when he saw his men screaming and dying as the Japs
overran them, killing them all.

        The Raider had to do something to warn them. In his ammo
bag he found two fireflies. Small charges designed to be placed in the
fuel tank of a vehicle. The fuel would eat the outer wax coating and
allow the acid fuse to detonate the composition B charge, causing a
large, hot fire and explosion. They had been given to him a year ago
on an experimental basis. He was to test them in combat if possible.

                    * * * * *

        The Motor Pool was largely unguarded. Two roving guards,
no dogs, no gun towers. This would be easy. Rawlins covered his
face and hands with the ever-present mud, covering any white that
might show. Leaving his Thompson by a large tree, he pulled his
forty five from it's shoulder holster and chambered a round. Pushing
the thumb safety up to engage, he drew his stiletto with the other
hand. Low crawling through the underbrush put him in position next
to the parked trucks. He lunged across an opening to the first one
without being seen. Reaching under the driver's seat he tripped the
hold down lever on the spring loaded seat and it tilted ahead. The fuel
tank filler neck was now exposed. The tank was under the driver's
seat on the Mitsubishi 1.5 ton truck. Rawlins removed the waterproof
wrapper and dropped the mini bomb in the tank. Replacing the filler
cap on the neck and returning the seat to it's former position, he
moved on to the next truck. At the same time a sentry rounded the
corner and walked into him. Rawlins plunged the heavy 45 pistol into
his right eye, dropping him. The dazed enemy lay on the ground long

enough for Rawlins to jump on his chest and cut his throat. The Raider dragged the body under a truck and finished his work. A thermite grenade was rigged to a nearby remote fuel tank with a trip wire. This would burn through the sheet metal skin of the tank and cause a fire that would be seen for miles. Rawlins crawled back to his Tommy gun and headed away into the jungle to watch the show.

The squad returned to the CP just before dark. They were surprised to see that two companies of the Third Marine Division had landed and moved up the trail. The Third Raiders had been pulled out to make an assault on nearby Puruata Island.

"Where the hell you boys been?"

"To hell, mud Marine, while you were sunning yourselves on the beach."

Damn Raiders. Always smart asses.

* * * * *

"Sgt. Russo reporting, Sir."

"Come in, Russo. Have a seat. Like some coffee?"

"Yes, Sir."

"You may smoke if you like."

"Thank you, Sir."

Russo took the coffee from the young Marine on radio watch, lit up a Camel, and began his report.

"Penetrated five miles, Lieut. Lots of patrols. Regular Infantry. Lots of activity. We were dogged by a platoon strength force from the first day. Lots of skirmishing."

"Any losses?"

"Just Gunny Rawlins."

"Rawlins. What happened?"

"He's missing, Sir. We were in a night defense position about to be overrun. Gunny told us to throw grenades and bug out. He set up a rear guard action to give us some breathing room. We heard two frags blow, his Thompson firing. Then lots of Arisaka firing. But coming from another direction. And then fading away. We waited all night in a pre-determined position for him but he didn't show. At dawn Hays and I made the decision to move out before we were found by that reinforced platoon. We were all low on ammo and too far out for support, Sir."

"I see. Do you think Rawlins is dead?"

"No, Sir. I've seen him do this before. He will lead the Japs all over the jungle, giving his men time to move out. And he will recon the area at the same time. And give the Japs just enough attention to keep them interested."

"Is that it, Sgt.?"

"Yes, Sir."

"Disperse your squad among those Third Division people that moved up yesterday. They're pretty green."

"Aye, Sir."

* * * * *

0300 Hours -

Two explosions up the trail aroused the attention of the men at the road block.

"What the hell is that? There's nobody that far out except Japs."

Then a larger explosion and fire a hundred feet in the air, lighting the dark tropic sky like a huge meteor slamming into the earth.

"There's your answer, Lieut. Gunny Rawlins."

"You think he caused that explosion?"

"Yes, Sir. He's telling us there's Japs up the trail. Lots of 'um. We're probably gonna get hit with a large force soon."

* * * * *

"There's our Gunny."

"Are you for real?"

"Yeah. That's him. He likes to go out alone and mess with the Japs."

"Is he nuts? Bad enough being a mud Marine, but the shit you guys do is insane."

"Yeah, I guess. But we're never bored."

"Yeah. You don't live long enough to get bored."

* * * * *

"Joker."

"Yes, Sir."

"Do you think that's Rawlins out there?"

"Yes, Sir. That's him all right. Something big is in the wind and he's letting us know, Sir."

"By the way, Sgt. Any sign of those missing men out there?"

"Yes, Sir. We found them. Dead, Sir."

"How."

"Raped, tortured and bayoneted, Sir. We buried them and marked it on the map for Graves, Sir."

"Those rotten little bastards. Can't even kill a man decent. OK, Joker. Dismissed."

"Aye, Sir."

* * * * *

Rawlins was reveling in the devastation. He loved to destroy enemy equipment. And he held a ring side seat, watching the carnage before him. From a good hundred yards away he felt the heat from the burning fuel tank, roasting everything and everybody near it when the thermite grenade set fire to it. Dead Soldiers charred black lay around the tank. Killed while fighting the lesser truck fires. One of them pulled the trip wire on the thermite charge, sending them all to hell. The destroyer of Japanese confidence left the area. Mission accomplished.

* * * * *

Gunny Rawlins avoided the trail and took a circuitous route back to the CP, fearing enemy patrols would be searching close to the trail for him. He was just as afraid of entering the Marine zone of the trail at night because nervous, trigger happy boots might gun him down by mistake. It had happened to recon patrols at night in the past. He found a large banyan tree with exposed roots and dug an opening with his E-tool. Removing his ruck he pushed it under the roots first. Then he crawled under himself with just enough room to lay on his side. He pulled out his forty five pistol and held it in his hand. Just in case. And fell asleep.

* * * * *

The jungle around the CP was quiet. Too quiet. No birds chirping or screeching. Just the low tones of men talking in their two man holes. And the soft patter of rain on their helmets. Then all hell broke loose as 60mm mortars hit the line with a terrible crash.

"Hit it. Incoming."

Men dove to the bottom of their holes. The earth shook around them. Men were shredded with shrapnel. Some disappeared outright from direct hits in their holes. Maybe a foot or hand left to bury. When the barrage lifted the mournful cries of the wounded were heard.

"Corpsman. I'm hit."

"Corpsman. Help me."

Then they came. A great wave of humanity in company strength. Screaming and yelling,

"Maline, you die. Tenneco banzai, imperialist gangster."

Marines fired their rifles with great effect at this short range. Fifty yards or less. Guardians of the empire died like flies. Massed thirty cal. fire at point blank range annihilated the attackers. Very few made it to the Marine line. Those that did went no further.

As dawn broke the scene was terrible. Dead Marines in their holes. Some still holding rifles, staring at an unseen enemy with dead eyes. The Japanese lay in piles. Over one hundred dead. A whole infantry company as dead as the emperor's dreams. Men felt ashamed they had killed so many. But what choice had they been given? If the enemy had lived then they would most certainly be dead. There is no mercy in the Code of Bushido, which is what the Imperial Army follows.

* * * * *

"Who the hell is that?"

"That's Gunny Rawlins. The guy who set off the fire works last night."

As soon as the squad spotted him they ran out to meet him.

"Gunny. You all right. You're wounded. Here, gimme your ruck and Tommy. I'll clean it for you. You want a litter, Gunny? We'll carry you."

"Naw. I'm all right. Just a little tired."

"Damn, it's good to see you, Gunny. You really scared us."

"Good to see you guys too. Tired of hangin' out with Japs all the time. They just don't understand me."

This brought a round of laughs from the squad.

"Thanks for tippin' us off last night with the fire works. We figured it was you."

"Yeah, it was. Just wanted you guys to know I wasn't gold brickin' out there."

"That would be the day."

* * * * *

"Gunnery Sgt. Rawlins reporting, Sir."

"Gunny Rawlins. Damn, it's good to see you. You're wounded and you look like shit."

"Thank you, Sir."

"Doc. Get in here. Our Gunny is wounded. Orderly. Get coffee and cigarettes for this hero."

"Aye, Sir."

Rawlins lit a Camel and drank some coffee.

"Oh, that's good, Lieut. It's been a while."

"Have all you want. You earned it. How is he, Doc?"

"He's dehydrated and he needs surgery. There's shrapnel in his arm. I'm tagging him."

"I'm all right, Doc. Gimme a shot and I'll be fine. I ain't leavin' the line. I ain't leavin' till this fight is over."

"Shut up, Gunny. It's my decision, not yours. You're going to sick bay and that's that."

"Why, you swabbie s.o.b. If I felt better I'd slug you."

"You will have to wait till you're released from the hospital ship, Gunny. Then you can slug me."

"I agree with Doc, Rawlins. You're a mess. And if that wound gets infected they will take your arm."

While the Lieut. had Rawlins attention Doc stuck a morphine syrette in the warrior's shoulder.

"Hey, what was that?"

"Morphine, Gunny. You need it."

"Doc, I'm gonna kick your Navy ass, you shit bird."

"Yeah, Gunny, I know. That should hold him, Lieut., until we evack him."

"Thanks, Doc. Sorry for the insults."

"I'm used to it. Every wounded Marine I ever worked on was like that. Fight me right up to the end. Never quit. Real pain in the ass, Sir."

"Semper fi, Doc."

"Yes, Sir. By the way, what's the count from last night?"

"Six dead, eighteen wounded."

"And the enemy?"

"One hundred thirty two killed, Sir."

"A whole company?"

"Yes, Sir."

"OK, Doc. Dismissed."

* * * * *

Rawlins felt hot all over and sick to his stomach. But the pain was gone. Two Third Division Marines laid him on a litter. His three squad leaders were there.

"Gunny. What do you need?"

"Ramirez. Take my forty fives and keep 'um clean till I get back. Russo. My Ka-Bar and dagger. And don't leave 'um stuck in some Jap. Joker, stop thinking about that broad. Remember what I told you before. Stay focused. It's a jungle out there. If you get killed 'cause a that broad I'm gonna kick your ass. You hear me?"

"Aye, Gunny. I hear ya."

"Lieut."

"Yes, Rawlins."

"Watch my children, Sir. Keep 'um outta trouble."

"Aye, Gunny. Will do."

Rawlins was carried down the trail to the beach with the other wounded, then transported by Higgins boat to the hospital ship. The last thing he remembered was being placed on a table, a respirator being placed over his face and the smell of ether. Then the big Jap was back, standing over him in the jungle with his rifle and bayonet.

I'll love you forever, in that unmistakable feminine voice he knew so well and missed so much.

"Doc. What do you think? Will he make it?"

"Are you kiddin'? That tough old gyrene. He's been through worse that this. And besides the devil's afraid of him and God don't want him messin' up heaven. So he can't die."

"Pack your trash, boys. I just got word. We're goin' to the beach for some R and R. The 145th Infantry is movin' up to take our position. We're goin' into a reserve position by the beach. Let the Army tangle with these monkeys. Good practice for 'um. We gotta find some booze. Pick up all the Jap stuff layin' around. We can trade it for booze (swords, pistols and battle flags commanded a high price from rear echelon troops)."

The green Army troops were shocked at the condition of the Raiders they relieved. Sick, unshaven, covered with mud and blood, they were a deplorable sight. The Soldiers, normally ready with insults for their rivals, felt sorry for them. They even helped them get to the beach.

"Gimme that ruck, gyrene. And your ammo. You look like hell. We're gonna kick ass for you guys. We shoulda moved up sooner. Damn officers takin' their time."

The Second Raiders moved into the Army's 37 Div. bivouac.

"Wow. This is the life. Don't have to dig in. Everything is done. Hey, Johnson. Those doggies over there have a still."

"No shit."

"They said that if we got the stuff we can make booze with it."

"Hey, Eyes."

"Yeah."

"You got the Jap stuff."

"Yeah. Right here."

"See those swabbies down the beach loading supplies?"

"Yeah. I see 'um."

"Let's see if they wanna trade."

"Hey, Navy."

"Yeah. What do ya want?"

"We got good Jap stuff. Wanta do some business?"

"Let's see. Wow. Lotsa good shit. The Aussies will pay good for that stuff. Hey, Chief, c'mere and get a load a this stuff."

Chief Boatswain Mate Stewart, also known as Scavenger, surveyed the Raider goodies.

"Let's see what you boys have. Three Type 94 Nambu pistols, one German P08 Luger, two battle flags, two officer swords, Nikon binocs, two Yashika cameras, one dagger. Nice catch. What do you want for it?"

"The doggies have a still and we wanna make some Jungle Juice. Can you get the stuff?"

"I dunno."

"C'mon, Chief. You're the Scavenger. You can get anything."

"Yeah, but this is a tall order. I gotta raid Ships Stores for this. If I get caught it's a month in the brig, bread and water and I'll lose my stripes."

"You gotta have someone in your pocket in Stores."

"Yeah, but it's the principal, you know. I would be responsible for influencing your young minds on the wages of sin. And breaking Naval regs too."

"C'mon, Eyes. Forget this clown. We'll find someone else."

"Wait a minute. Stand fast, boys. I suppose I could help you out, being heroes and all. But you're going to have to sweeten the deal a bit."

"Like how, Chief?"

"Like I get pick of all the enemy trinkets for the remainder of the campaign."

"Done."

"Okay. Meet me here in four hours and I'll have your stuff. Gimme two pistols to seal the deal."

"OK, Chief."

* * * * *

"Ten pounds of sugar, two cases raisins, one case dried apples, one gallon wood alcohol, one case Aqua Velva. This will get you started. See you later. The Army chipped in a bale of cut sugar cane they found in a village in their zone. And two liters of sake the villagers stole from the Japanese."

All ingredients were poured into the big copper vat that once had been a boiler on a small Dutch coastal frigate the Japanese had destroyed. The vat was found in the village, reason unknown. Rumors claim the local cannibals used it to shrink heads. The water outlet valve was piped into a condenser taken from a 30 cal. water cooled Browning mg. A small fire was built under the vat, and after an hour or so the water tube began to drip juice into the condenser. In six hours the condenser was full.

"Here, Marine, you get the first drink."

Eyes dumped some into his tin mess cup and drank.

"Damn. That tastes like hell but what a kick. Burns all the way down like Daddy's moonshine."

"All right. It's ready. Everybody grab some."

This was one of those rare times when branch of service was forgotten. Even Sailors working on the beach were invited. Soldiers, Sailors, Marines all came together and got drunk. Jungle Juice was a great stress reliever. The officers allowed it. Some even took part.

* * * * *

Itsociro Tashi, Senior Sergeant, leading Scout, Tracker for the Japanese 23rd Infantry Regiment, watched the revelry from a tree positioned fifty yards away. Tashi seethed with hatred.

They kill my brothers, these jungle demons. And disappear like the wind. Now I have them. These foolish Americans. They dance and cheer like idiots. They drink until they cannot stand. Have they forgotten us? Their sworn enemy who watches from scant meters away. These fools will learn what happens on this island when they ignore their enemy. Their foolish acts will be well rewarded tonight. When I make my report and the Imperial Commandos are unleashed, they will be sorry indeed.

* * * * *

"Where the hell am I?"

"In the surgery recovery room of the hospital ship, Guardian."

"Who are you? You ain't no swabby."

"No, Sergeant. I'm Nurse Trumbolt. Eleanor Trumbolt."

"You the President's wife?"

"No, Sergeant. That's Eleanor Roosevelt."

"Yeah, I know. I know their kid."

"You do?"

"Yes, Nurse Turnbolt. He's a Marine Raider."

"Really, Sgt."

"Yes, Turnbolt. Really. By the way, it's Gunnery Sgt. Rawlins."

"That's different. Gunnery is the strangest first name I've ever heard. And my name is Trumbolt, Gunnery."

"Just call me Gunny."

"Can I call you Ken?"

"Who's that?"

"You, according to your chart."

"Must be some mistake."

"What did your mother call you?"

"Gunny."

"Oh, my. And your father?"

"He was the Sergeant Major."

"You Marines are all alike. Full of the devil. Good thing we love you all."

As she moved on to the next man, Rawlins was thinking, *I should get hit more often.*

* * * * *

The enemy Commandos slid through the wet slimy mud of the jungle floor like large snakes on the hunt. The rain was falling again and visibility was near zero. Perfect time for a raid. The Army sentry stood leaning on his rifle, half asleep.

No Japs tonight, he thought.

The dagger that cut his throat was the biggest and last shock of his life.

The enemy infiltrators were in the perimeter fanning out to attack their targets. They reached the Raider position without incident. The newly promoted Corporal Johnson died in his sleep as a Commando slid into his hole and slit his throat. The three squad leaders (Sgts.) had the good sense to stay awake and not get too drunk. Joker saw them first.

"Up and at 'um, Raiders. Gung ho."

He cut down two with a burst from his Thompson.

Eyes, right next to him, was firing his 45 Colt pistol with one hand and his 38 cal. Smith and Wesson revolver with the other. Two dead Japs lay on the edge of his hole. Baby, with its turnbolt design and telescopic sight, was useless in a close fight like this.

Ramirez was moving along the line shredding enemies as he went. One determined killer charged him with a bayonet. Ramirez turned his chopper loose on the attacker at four feet. The 45 rounds nearly sawed him in half. The dead Jap fell at his feet.

Russo was in a machine gun pit directing rifle fire because the enemy was mixing with the Marines. Four Japs jumped in the gun pit and a vicious hand to hand fight ensued. The Sgt. was cut across the ribs as he deflected a bayonet plunge. He shot the attacker in the face with his forty five.

Junior disarmed another commando, picked up his small body and smashed in his head on the Browning Machine Gun receiver.

A new man was killed when two Japs bayoneted him from behind. They both died in a hail of 45 cal. bullets from Russo's pistol.

Master Gunny Parker's shotgun took it's toll as he helped out his platoon, killing two at the CP door.

Joseph disposed of two with his M1 Carbine, by his radio. Lieut. Pruit was in the corner beating a Jap's head in with his empty 45 pistol, as the intruder tried to stab him.

The attack ended as dawn broke with the surviving Commandos retreating into the jungle.

"Sneaky bastards. Why can't they fight like normal men. Always trying to knife you in the middle of the night. Hey, Sarge. Look at this."

Wallace pried a small submachine gun from the dead hands of a Commando.

"What is it?"

"Type 100 8mm Nambu smg. I saw a couple in Ruwawa. They only give 'um to Commandos. Weird lookin' piece. Bet it will bring a good buck."

"What's the count, Doc?"

"Eight of our guys dead including Corp. Johnson. Twelve wounded, including Sgt. Russo. Twenty seven dead of the enemy. The wounded killed themselves."

"OK, Doc. Take care of 'um."

"Aye, Sir."

* * * * *

"Sgt. Gunny."

"Yes, dear."

"Time for your meds. I have a nice big shot for you. Roll over."

"Where you from Turnbolt?"

"Niagara Falls."

"New York?"

"That's right."

"No shit."

"No swearing, Gunny. Have you been there?"

"I grew up in Buffalo. Really, Turnbolt."

"Where do you live now?"

"In the jungle."

"You know what I mean."

"Wherever the Corps sends me."

"Lifer?"

"Yeah, I guess."

"Single?"

"Yeah."

"You sure?"

"Yeah."

"You sound married."

"Not any more."

"She left me for a swabbie."

That's too bad. A nice guy like you. Hard to believe. They married?"

"He's dead. Killed raiding Truk Lagoon. Her, I don't know about."

"What a shame."

"How about you, Turnbolt?"

"My boyfriend was killed at Kassarine Pass in North Africa a year ago."

"Sorry to hear that. This lousy war is messing up a lot of lives. It ain't fair."

"Nothing is, Ken. But we survive somehow. If we're lucky. Now you get some sleep. We'll talk later."

"OK, Turnbolt."

For the first time in many years Rawlins was becoming interested in a woman.

* * * * *

"Ramirez. Take a patrol up the trail as far as the blocking position. Two squads as skirmishers out to two hundred yards on either side of the trail. One squad on the trail. You and Joker take fhe flankers. Master Gunny Parker will take center and be in command."

"Aye, Sir."

* * * * *

"Second Platoon. We're movin' out."

The Sgt. briefed the men and they took their positions and struck into the jungle. Blood trails were found and discarded equipment was strewn about. At the edge of a small clearing five hundred yards out a shot rang out. The Raiders hit the deck. Another shot. A wounded enemy Commando had been left behind to slow any followers and to die with honor. Eyes spotted the muzzle flash 150 yards away, at the other side of the clearing. The enemy had his rifle laying across a dead tree on the ground. Eyes put baby's crosshairs on the killer's forehead and squeezed the trigger. At the report of the shot the Jap's head snapped back and came to rest on top of the rifle, now pointing at the sky. A cheer went up for baby. Rack up another one.

"All right. Let's move out."

Another wounded Jap was found trying to crawl under some brush and hide. Junior grabbed the jungle warrior by the ankles and picked him up amid a storm of curses.

"Sarge. You want him?"

"Put him down ya damn monster. He'll choke to death. We need him for intel."

"OK, Sarge."

"Doc."

"Yeah, Sarge."

"Fix the Nip."

"OK, Sarge."

The terrified Commando expected a quick end. Instead he was given water and morphine.

Two dead Commandos were found that had succumbed to their wounds and had been left behind by their comrades. The rest of the patrol was uneventful. The Raiders spent the night with Soldiers of the U.S. 145th Infantry Regiment after checking their position on the Piva Trail.

"Master Gunnery Sergeant Parker reporting, Sir,"

"Captain Jacobs, Master Gunny."

"Pleased to meet you."

"Thank you, Sir."

"Did your position get hit last night? We heard the firing."

"Yes, Sir. Jap Commandos infiltrating the supply dump, Sir."

"Little bastards won't fight like normal men."

"No, Sir."

"I trust you Marines disposed of them properly."

"Yes, Sir."

"Did your patrol reveal anything?"

"We have a prisoner, Sir."

"Really? Alive?"

"Yes, Sir."

"That's great, Master Gunny. May we have him?"

"Yes, Sir. My pleasure, Sir."

"Is there anything we can do for you and your men, Master Gunny?"

"My men have been awake for at least twenty hours, Sir. Request permission to spend the night, Sir."

"Yes, of course, Parker. Have your men double up with mine so they won't have to dig in."

"Thank you, Sir."

This was one of those rare times when Soldiers and Marines could be together without fighting. Fighting with the enemy and the terrible conditions they had endured was enough. Fighting holes that were half full of water. Leeches everywhere. The only way to rid your body of them was to touch them with a lit cigarette or match. Swarms of insects hanging in clouds, waiting to eat whoever they could. Malaria and jungle rot rampant. Some men could no longer walk. On top of all this, Japanese snipers and infiltrators harassing the men night and day.

"Master Sgt. Reese, this is Master Gunnery Sgt. Parker."

"How are ya, Parker?"

"OK, Reese. Good to know ya. How's it been for your boys up here?"

"Pain in the ass, really. Snipers and infiltrators. Just enough to keep you on edge. Send out a patrol to clear 'um and they're back two hours later."

"Yeah, I know the feeling. My platoon set up this position on D Day. Kinda spooky way out here. Scuttlebutt says some Third Division people and my outfit are gonna move up in a couple days to support you fellas in a push 1500 yards up the trail. Then the 43rd Infantry Division is gonna widen the perimeter and build an airfield.

Then we'll have real support. These smartass Nips are gonna get a taste of napalm. Hope they enjoy it."

"Sounds good to me, gyrene."

* * * * *

"How's the wound, Russo?"

"Not too bad, Lieut. Doc left me some morphine in case it really starts to bother me."

"You sure you don't want to be evacked to the hospital ship?"

"No, Sir. I'm the only NCO you have since Johnson got it, and the platoon is out on patrol."

"I can get a replacement from battalion."

"He might piss you off, Sir, and Leavenworth, Kansas is a cold son of a bitch."

"Aye, Sgt. You're right."

"And besides Gunny Rawlins is on that ship. By now I'm sure he's a miserable son of a bitch. If he saw me with no body parts missing on that ship, he'd drop me for fifty for being a slacker."

* * * * *

"HI, Ken."

"Hi, Needle."

"I'm not a needle."

"Then why are you always stabbing me?"

"You're bad and needles make you better."

"How old are you, Turnbolt?"

"Thirty two. Don't you know you should never ask a woman that?"

"I musta missed that chapter when I read the manual."

"How about you?"

"Eighty five."

"You're thirty six. I checked."

"Why?"

"Oh, you know."

"I do?"

"Of course you do."

"What would happen if I showed up in Niagara Falls after the war and looked you up, Turnbolt?"

"I might try to mother you or nurse you. Take your pick."

"None of the above. How about something more exciting?"

"We'll see. Sgt. When the war's over."

* * * * *

"We're moving out, Sir, with your permission."

"Master Gunny Parker. We hate to see you go."

"Sorry, Sir. We gotta get back before our C.O. gets nervous."

"Stop back again, Parker. We could use the company."

"Aye, Sir. I'm sure you will see us again."

"Carry on, Parker, and good luck."

"Thank you, Sir."

The return patrol was uneventful. No enemy to be found. Only discarded enemy equipment. And two wounded Jap Commandos that had killed themselves to avoid capture. The sucking, sticking mud was the biggest problem as it drained men's strength. Basic infantry loads had to be divided among the healthy men to help the sick navigate the mud. After eight frustrating hours the Marines broke through to the trail head and their position.

"Master Gunny Parker reporting, Sir."

"Find anything, Parker?"

"Equipment, blood trails, bodies, one prisoner, and the Army, Sir."

"Casualties?"

"One wounded, Sir. We left him with the Army medics."

"What's their status?"

"Two companies of the 145th Infantry Regiment, Sir. Night infiltrations, patrol actions, probes."

"Do they have enough men, Parker?"

"In my opinion, no, Sir."

"The prisoner?"

"We left him with the Army, Sir. He was pretty beat up."

"I'm surprised he didn't commit seppuku (suicide)."

"Junior grabbed him before he could, Sir."

"OK, Master Gunny. Good job. Carry on."

"Aye, Sir."

The Lieut. left for an officer call. At battalion H.Q. the officers were briefed by the Lieut. Colonel on their next operation.

"Gentlemen. In two days at 0600 hours we will begin a push 1500 yards past the blocking position on the Piva Trail. Companies A and B, Second Battalion, 3rd Division will be reinforced by two companies of the Army's Thirty Seventh Infantry Division. Lt. Pruit's platoon of the Second Raiders will be the point element since they are familiar with the area. Good luck, gentlemen."

* * * * *

"Ken. I have good news. You're being released for duty."

"That's good news?"

"Well, it could be worse. At least your arm is OK."

"Yeah. Too bad."

"I thought you were the big tough Marine Raider; invincible."

"I'm tired of being invincible."

"Well, here's my address. Write to me and I'll write back. And remember we have a date after you win the war."

"OK, Turnbolt. You're on."

* * * * *

"Gunny Rawlins, you're back."

"Yes, Sir."

"How are you?"

"Fine, Sir."

"Ready for action?"

"Yes, Sir."

"We need a patrol 1500 yards up the trail. We make a push tomorrow and we need intel on what's up there. You're the best man to lead this if you're ready."

"I'm fine, Sir."

"Good. Shove off when you're ready. Take Second and Third

squads since they know the area."

"Aye, Sir."

* * * * *

"Us again. We just got back. Why do we always get the shitty details?"

"Cause you're always bitchin' and whining. Now shut the hell up and saddle up. We're movin' out."

Rawlins was having difficulty concentrating, between the pain in his arm and the two women on his mind. This was something new for him. Something he couldn't afford right now. It could get him killed. The jungle grew hot and mist rose from the jungle floor like a white burial shroud. The men were exhausted when they reached the blocking position. Rawlins called a halt. The Army fed the two Raider squads and let them fill their canteens at their water purification station. Captain Jacobs conversed with Rawlins while they ate.

"I hear you're the guy that lit up the Jap position a week ago."

"Yes, Sir."

"Were you alone, Gunny?"

"Yes, Sir."

"Why didn't you get the intel and bug out?"

"I wanted to let our people know what was ahead in case I didn't make it back, Sir."

"I see. Well, your plan worked. My Soldiers are still talking about one crazy Marine tipping off the whole regiment."

"Yes, Sir."

"You Raiders really are nuts, Gunny, but God love ya."

"Thank you, Sir."

After chow the Raiders said thanks and goodbye and headed up the trail. Strangely, there was no contact. Not even a sniper. The Japanese were gone. A thousand yards down the trail they found a bunker complex abandoned. On the other side of the complex the trail was much wider. More like a two lane road. The Raiders were on the road instead of in the jungle when it happened.

Wham. A Bouncing Betty land mine detonated when Sgt.

Hays stepped on it.

"Doc. I'm hit. Doc. You hear me. I'm hit."

"Easy, Sarge."

Doc gave him two morphine syrettes and tried to stop the bleeding. The rest of the men formed a security perimeter. Finally Doc found Rawlins.

"Who got it, Doc?"

"Sgt. Hays, Gunny."

"How bad?"

"He's all busted up inside, Gunny."

"Son of a bitch. He knows better than to walk on a trail like that. Shit. I told the dummy to get squared away."

"Joker. What the hell did you do now?"

"I'm finished, Gunny. I can't see and I'm cold all over. Tell my wife I'm sorry. I dan't feel anything, Doc. Doc, you there?"

"I'm right here, Sarge."

"Gunny. Don't leave me like this. If the Japs get me they'll skin me alive."

"Don't worry, Joker. We ain't leavin' you. Junior, c'mere and watch Joker. We'll be right back."

"Gunny, we can't move him. It will kill him for sure if we do."

"If the Japs find him you know what they will do to him. How much morphine you give him?"

"Two syrettes, the most he can have at one time. Any more and his blood pressure will drop too low."

"Give him two more."

"Gunny, I can't. It will kill him."

"He's already dead. It's a better way to go."

"I can't do it, Gunny. That's murder."

"Don't you understand you'd be doing him a favor?"

"No. I can't do it."

"Give me the morphine."

"Gunny, this ain't right."

"Shut up and give it to me."

"Hays. I got morphine. It's your choice. You're all busted up. We can't move you. And we can't stay here. What's it gonna be."

"Give it to me, Gunny. Better to end it here."

Rawlins gave his friend the morphine and held his hand while he slipped away.

"Sorry I was such a pain in the ass, Gunny."

"Forget it. You're a good Marine. Always got the job done."

"Write the letter for me, Gunny. Tell my family I went out like a Marine."

"Will do, Joker."

"See you on the other side, Gunny."

Sgt. Hays (Joker) was gone. Another good friend of Rawlins killed by this lousy war. It hit him hard. They had been together all the way back to Guadalcanal, where they had met in the First Raider battalion with Colonel Red Mike Edson (Edson's Raiders).

Son of a bitch. I should know better than to make friends. They always get killed. First Johnson and now Joker. Wonder when it's gonna be my turn. By the time this war ends we'll all be dead.

"Wrap him in a poncho. We'll pick him up on the way out. We ain't leavin' him here."

The rest of the patrol was uneventful. The Raiders advanced five hundred yards further down the trail with no contact. The enemy had pulled back. Joker's body was placed on a litter and carried back to the CP.

"Gunny Rawlins reporting, Sir."

"Find anything, Gunny?"

"No, Sir. We penetrated two thousand yards. No contact. The enemy has pulled back, Sir."

"Casualties?"

"One, Sir."

"Who?"

"Sgt. Hays. He's dead, Sir."

"Son of a bitch. Shit. We can't afford to lose squad leaders. We're short now with Johnson gone and Russo wounded."

"Yes, Sir."

"How did it happen?"

"He stepped on a mine, Sir."

"On the trail?"

"Yes, Sir."

"Damn it, Gunny, he knew better than to walk on a trail like that. Where were you/'

"In the rear, Sir."

"You leading from the rear now, Rawlins? That little vacation of yours make you soft?"

"No, Sir. Semper phi, Sir."

"You getting smart with me, Gunnery Sgt."

"No, Sir."

"I can't hear you."

"NO, SIR."

"Lieut. Pruit, Sir."

"Get the hell out of my CP, Rawlins."

"Aye, Sir."

Rawlins was infuriated.

That lousy punk, ninety day wonder shave tail. Giving him a cigar like he was a boot was just too much. What the hell does he know about anything? He's a baby. How the hell did he become a Raider anyway. Much less a Marine officer. Shitbird pantywaist son of a bitch. He's gonna pay for that mistake. No one talks to a Gunnery Sergeant like that. I ever see him on liberty he'll be sorry. I was leading combat patrols when he was in grade school. Son of a bitch.

The night passed without incident. The Raiders prepared for the push the next day. They cleaned their weapons, loaded extra magazines for the B.A.R.s and carbines, link belted 30 cal. ammo for the Browning L1A6 machine gun which was cleaned and oiled. Bayonets were sharpened. Equipment checked and re-checked.

"Hey, Gunny. How many Japs you think are out there?"

"Millions. Don't matter how many we kill. There's always more. There's no end of 'um."

"How far we going tomorrow?"

"Till we make contact and the infantry catches up with us. Junior. You got the Zippo tomorrow since you're the biggest guy here."

"OK, Gunny."

Rawlins decided to write a letter. Who knew when he would get another chance.

Dear Turnbolt,

Lost a good friend today on patrol. One of my squad leaders. Good Marine. He will be missed. This war is killing all my friends. Hope you're OK. Just wanted to say "hello" and thanks for taking care of me on the love boat. Gotta go now. My children need me. Don't forget our date back in the world. After I win the war.
Love, Ken.

* * * * *

Rawlins was feeling strange. Whenever he thought of the little nurse on the ship he felt a strange gnawing excitement in his gut. And he thought of her often. More than he wanted to. Thinking like this could make you dead. Thoughts of Susan and all the pain that was associated with her were fading. Slipping away into the past.

* * * * *

"All right. Saddle up. We're moving out."

Three platoons of Raiders jumped off. They were leading elements of the Third Marine Division and the U.S. Army's 37th Infantry Division. They would lead the way. All was quiet for the first hour. Then the Raiders began taking sniper fire on the flanks. One nineteen year old Raider was shot through the head and died instantly. A B.A.R. gunner spotted the muzzle blast in a tree a hundred yards away in a small clearing. The gunner expended a full twenty round magazine of 30 cal. M2 ball into the tree branches, blowing the sniper out of the tree. Three men were dispatched to find the body. When found the corpse's torso had five holes in it, making the enemy very dead. The dead Raider was placed in a poncho. His bayonet fixed rifle was shoved into the muddy earth, helmet placed on the butt. The rear element would find him this way and transport the remains to Graves Registration.

As the point element neared the abandoned bunker complex they began taking heavy fire.

Son of a bitch. The Japs have moved back in. They must have been rotating units when we were here.

As the Raiders moved up, leap frogging by team and squad, the unmistakable noise of a woodpecker (Nambu mg) opening up was heard. Then another. The Raiders were caught in a cross fire. And too close to the enemy to call in fire support.

"Junior. Get up here."

Junior crawled to Gunny Rawlin's forward position.

"Ya see the muzzle blast from that Nambu?"

"Yeah, Gunny."

"We're gonna fry 'um. C'mon, Junior."

The two men crawled through the mud and rotten vegetation until they were within twenty five yards of the bunker, as yet unseen by the occupants. Consisting of logs with earth on top, the bunker was impregnable to rifle fire or grenades.

"When I tell ya to, light 'um up. You hear me?"

"Yeah, Gunny. I hear ya."

Junior was sick at the thought of burning people alive. But there was no other way. Besides, Japs weren't people. Or so he had been told.

Rawlins got up on a knee and fired half a magazine into the gun port with his Tommy gun.

"Now, Junior. Give it to 'um."

The flaming liquid arched through the air and into the gun ports. Screaming, burning Japanese Soldiers ran from the bunker hatch and Rawlins cut them down. Now on to the next bunker with the same results. Junior vomited from the stench and destruction of their handiwork.

"Them or us, boy. You better get used to it. It's gonna be a long war."

How does a man get used to mass killing, Junior wondered.

* * * * *

After the bunkers were neutralized, the platoon moved into

assault formation. The Raiders attacked the trench complex supporting the bunkers. Close fighting broke out and the Raiders fought hand to hand in the trenches.

Ramirez threw a grenade into a trench and jumped in behind it. Four men joined him. They rounded a corner and ran into a squad of Japanese infantry. The Sgt. mowed down three with his Thompson. Then a bayonet fight ensued as his comrades charged the enemy. The Japanese were quickly dispatched by the stronger, bigger, more experienced Raiders. Small groups of Raiders and Japanese clashed, until the main assault force arrived.

Junior dropped the flame thrower with its empty tanks and used his inherited Tommy gun. He and Rawlins and Eyes found a Jap command post.

"Listen up, Eyes. You and Junior get behind this bunker. I'm gonna frag it. Take out any that get out the back door. You got two minutes to get into position."

Rawlins could hear talking in the bunker not ten yards away. And radio traffic. At the two minute mark, the Raider popped the fuse on an M2 frag, and dropped it in the bunker. At the detonation half the log roof blew off and much of the earth covering it. Two Japanese officers staggered out the rear door and were cut down.

Another door, unseen by the Raiders, opened and out stepped a Jap officer, unhurt and very pissed off. Holding a Nambu Type 94 8mm pistol in one hand, and a sword in the other, he came face to face with Rawlins, and fired first.

The Gunnery Sgt. felt a sledge hammer blow to his left shoulder. Stunned, he was spun around and knocked to the ground by the bullet's impact. The Jap Captain holstered his pistol and stood over Rawlins, raising his sword, preparing to administer the death blow as was the custom according to Bushido. He never got the chance. Eyes placed a thirty cal. bullet in the back of the Captain's head, sending him off to the land of the rising sun. His dead body fell on Rawlins in a heap, staring at Rawlins with dead eyes.

"You all right, Gunny?"

"Yeah, I'll live. But Tojo here with half a head, won't. Why did you have to drop the stinkin' Nip on top of me like that?"

"Sorry, Gunny. Next time I'll wait till he cuts your head off.

Then I'll shoot."

"All right, smart ass. Thanks. I owe you one. Junior. Get Doc up here and get me outta here."

"Gunny. What happened?"

"No mind over there shot me."

"You're lucky. Went right through. No broken bones."

"O joy. I'll hafta celebrate. Son of a bitch. I hate getting shot. Such a pain in the ass."

"Could be worse, Gunny. That Jap layin' in the bunker doesn't have an ass or a head either."

Doc poured sulfa powder on the wound and gave Rawlins a shot of morphine. Then applied a battle dressing. A litter was made and the Raider was carried off the field and placed with the other wounded.

The main body of infantry troops, both Army and Marine, were surging past the Raiders in full attack. Second platoon fell back to the rear, their job completed.

* * * * *

"Ken. What happened."

"I asked a Jap to shoot me so I could come and see you again."

"Does it hurt much?"

"No. It feels great. I like to get shot now and then just for fun."

"You're being nasty, Sgt."

"Sorry. I'm just overwhelmed with your loveliness."

"That's better. You should always be nice to your nurse."

"Yes, dear."

"What's going on, Ken? Wounded have been pouring in all morning."

"Big push by the infantry."

"Where were you?"

"Point element. Out front."

"How did this happen?"

"Jap officer walked out of a bunker and shot me. Never saw

him. Then he tried to cut my head off."

"Why."

"They like to do that. Makes 'um feel important. Eyes took care of him."

"Is he dead?"

"Very."

"Who is Eyes?"

"Platoon sniper."

"Oh."

* * * * *

The Second Raiders were held in reserve and used to haul supplies to the front until the new perimeter was formed by the Infantry.

"This is bull shit. We're elite Commandos, not mules."

"Stow it, dummy. At least we ain't getting shot at."

"Yeah, but it ain't right."

"What the hell is? You should be happy you're still in one piece. A lotta guys ain't."

"Yeah, I know. It just pisses me off."

"Everything pisses you off."

"Where's the fuzzies that are supposed to do this?"

"They quit 'cause the officers took their shrunken Jap heads."

"So we're the next best thing."

"You got it."

* * * * *

"Ken. You have visitors."

"Rawlins. You on vacation again?"

"Master Gunny and Lieut. Parker."

"How do you feel, Gunny?"

"Like shit."

"That's the spirit. We got good news. We're pulling out tomorrow. Going back to the Canal. We're done here."

"That's great. Wish I was going with you."

"You will be in a couple of weeks."

"You guys find the graves?"

"Johnson and Hays are buried next to each other on the edge of Third Division's area, with the Third Raider's dead."

"That's good. Maybe after the war they can go home."

"The Colonel recommended you for the Navy Cross. For valor above and beyond the call of duty in the face of the enemy. Congratulations, Gunnery Sgt."

"Thank you, Sir."

After his friends left, Gunny Rawlins began to think of all the men that had been killed in this terrible war and wondered why he was still alive.

"Penny for your thoughts, Ken. Friends gone?"

"Yeah. They had to shove off."

"Well, I'm still here."

"I see that."

"You know I was kidding when I said to win the war by yourself."

"I thought you were serious. Silly me."

"The word is that you won the Navy Cross."

"All because of you."

"You damn fool. You almost got killed."

"Are you crying?"

"No, you big dumb jarhead. My eyes are watering from no sleep from worrying about you."

"Sorry."

"Stop taking chances like you do. You know there are other people to consider."

"OK, Turnbolt."

"And don't call me Turnbolt. You know my name."

The little nurse sped away.

Crying, Rawlins thought to himself. *This is getting interesting. There may be something happening here.*

* * * * *

Rawlins' war was over for now. He would recover from his

shrapnel and bullet wounds in time. The emotional wounds from losing friends and killing his fellow man in close combat would take longer. The nightmares from places like Bougainville and Guadalcanal would haunt him for the rest of his days.

He would receive his Navy Cross and two Purple Hearts for the Bougainville campaign. These would be sent home to his father and added to the rest of the emblems of honor on the parlor wall around his picture. And the citation would be read to the heroes at the VA Hospital residence where his father donated his time. The father and son, both combat Marines, were well liked and respected there. Each man there knowing the hell of combat first hand. Regardless of service branch, they were all brothers and American heroes. Never asking their beloved America to pay a debt that it never could. They gave their bodies and souls to keep their country free without question or a second thought. The finest men America will ever know. Veterans from World War 1, World War 2, Korea, the Cold War, Vietnam, Panama, Iraq, Afghanistan and all the small actions in between. They all deserve to be honored and held in high esteem for their sacrifices.

* * * * *

Now Rawlins was fighting another battle; this one in his mind. The warrior of many battles was in combat again. This time emotional combat. The Raider NCO had never faced anything quite like this before. He was growing closer to Nurse Turnbolt every day. She fussed over him like an old mother hen, always worrying about his comfort. And spending more and more time with him every day, something Rawlins was not used to. His relations with women had been hard and fast and over in a hurry. Including his ex-wife. Susan was haunting him too. He felt loyal to her still, after all that had happened. Would he be able to trust her again? Could he forget the past and the other men? Would she leave him again down the road?

Master Gunny Parker had told him once,

"If you go back with her, every time she goes out the door you will wonder where she may really be going. And if she comes home late it will torment you. If you see her with another man for whatever reason, in the back of your mind you will always wonder. You will be quick to judge and quicker to accuse. Going back after a split is a rough deal no matter what the reason. And remember, a Marine ain't home much to take care of things. Probably shouldn't get lashed up at all."

Sound advice from the old gyrene, thought Rawlins. *He was always good for that. Even officers asked him personal questions. Oh well, what the hell. It's gonna be a long war. This bullshit will take care of itself. All I gotta do is stay alive long enough to see the outcome. Semper phi.*

EPILOGUE

The Raiders that fought on Bougainville Island returned to Guadalcanal. They were relieved by the Army's Thirty Seventh Infantry Division and Third Marine Division. Wounded Raiders followed a short time later. Most were diverted to Australia or Pearl Harbour. The less serious cases rejoined their units at Guadalcanal.

The Marine Corps High Command finally prevailed in 1944 and the Raiders were disbanded. The Corps contention was that there was no need for an elite unit within an elite unit. And the Corps needed experienced men for their infantry units. Particularly NCOs. And most surviving Raiders by this time were NCOs.

Small unit combat was overwith by now also. All future operations were large scale multi-division size invasions. The Fourth Marine Division and newly formed Sixth Marine Division needed men desperately. The men of the Raider regiments were given to these combat infantry divisions.

Large battles in the Pacific campaign were yet to come. Guam, Saipan, Tinian, Kwajalein, Eniwetok, Iwo Jima and Chi Chi Jima and the final and largest Pacific battle of the war, Okinawa, were fought by ex-Raiders and veteran Fleet Marines and US Army Soldiers. The flag raising on Mt. Suribachi, Iwo-Jima, the bloodiest battle in Marine Corps history, had two ex-Raiders in its party.

The Raiders fought from the Makin Island raid to Bougainville and a hundred recon and Commando raids in between. They terrified the enemy with their lightning raids through the Solomon Islands from submarines, PT boats and SBD destroyers. Swift, silent, deadly. They gave American back the pride that was lost at Pearl Harbour. They gained victories, when victories were needed most. While the Army suffered through Kasserine Pass in North Africa, Anzio and Monte Casino in Italy, Marine Raiders were terrorizing America's enemies in the South Pacific. They also helped to keep the life line open to Australia and New Zealand.

"Gung ho," or "work together" was their motto. Never quit, never surrender, never leave a man behind. Death before dishonor. Many paid the ultimate price to keep America free. No man can ever say that they didn't do their duty, and well beyond.

ABOUT THE AUTHOR

Paul Nickerson is a military and firearms historian. He is also a wildlife photographer.

His family has been involved in every conflict in American history since the Civil War. They have served in all brances of the military and in all theaters of operation. Like the U.S. Marine Raiders, they have done their part in protecting their country and families.

Paul Nickerson feels that the story of the Marine Raiders should be told.

The Navy U.D.T. units (underwater demolition teams) were the forerunners of the Navy S.E.A.L.s. This first special service force combined Canadian and American troops to form "the devil's brigade." The U.S. Army Rangers and the British Commando and M15 Intelligence also were among the first special forces and the model for many units to come. They preceded the German (Luftwaffe Felschirmyager "paratroopers") and the German Abvere (Intelligence). All of these special units did their missions with distinction, suffering high casualties but always getting the job done regardless. Military hierarchy at the time disliked them but could not deny their effectiveness in combat.

The Raiders are the least known of these units. Sadly, Raider vets are slipping away, to be united with their brothers, lost so long ago. Historically, these men answered the call, without question, to defend their nation and the people they loved.

Paul Nickerson has created this story to bring honor to these fine American heroes.